Taylor Gray grew up watching too much TV and reading far too much romance. Now she's a writer, she calls it research. She spends her days scribbling illegible notes in a notebook and wishing she could type as fast as her characters thought. She lives in a house overtaken by plants and pictures with her husband, son and cat.

facebook.com/TaylorGrayAuthor
instagram.com/taylorgrayauthor

Also by Taylor Gray

The Autumn Falls series
Autumn Falls
Silver Sky
Redemption River
Starlight Mountain
Midnight Promise

SILVER SKY

TAYLOR GRAY

One More Chapter
a division of HarperCollins*Publishers* Ltd
1 London Bridge Street
London SE1 9GF
www.harpercollins.co.uk
HarperCollins*Publishers*
Macken House, 39/40 Mayor Street Upper,
Dublin 1, D01 C9W8, Ireland

This paperback edition 2025

1

First published in Great Britain in ebook format
by HarperCollins*Publishers* 2025

Copyright © Taylor Gray 2025

Taylor Gray asserts the moral right to be identified
as the author of this work

A catalogue record of this book is available from the British Library

ISBN: 978-0-00-879757-7

This novel is entirely a work of fiction. The names, characters and incidents portrayed in it are the work of the author's imagination. Any resemblance to actual persons, living or dead, events or localities is entirely coincidental.

Printed and bound in the UK using 100% Renewable Electricity
by CPI Group (UK) Ltd

All rights reserved. No part of this publication may be reproduced, stored in a retrieval system, or transmitted, in any form or by any means, electronic, mechanical, photocopying, recording or otherwise, without the prior permission of the publishers.

Without limiting the exclusive rights of any author, contributor or the publisher of this publication, any unauthorised use of this publication to train generative artificial intelligence (AI) technologies is expressly prohibited. HarperCollins also exercise their rights under Article 4(3) of the Digital Single Market Directive 2019/790 and expressly reserve this publication from the text and data mining exception.

For my son,
because when I asked who I should dedicate this book to,
he said, "Me."

Playlist

Too Sweet - Hozier ♥
Golden - Harry Styles ♥
The Giver - Chappell Roan ♥
Tornado Warnings - Sabrina Carpenter ♥
Slow Burn - Kacey Musgraves ♥
we can't be friends - Ariana Grande ♥
Can't Help Falling in Love - Lick The Tins ♥
Look After You - The Fray ♥
Stick Season - Noah Kahan ♥
The Swimming Song - Loudon Wainwright III ♥
July - Noah Cyrus ♥
They Don't Know About Us - One Direction ♥
Perfect - Fairground Attraction ♥
Bags - Clairo ♥
Out Of The Woods - Taylor Swift ♥
Need You Now - Lady A ♥
Close To You - Gracie Abrams ♥
She Calls Me Back - Noah Kahan ♥
Landslide - Fleetwood Mac ♥
Ophelia - The Lumineers ♥
Say Don't Go - Taylor Swift ♥
Tennessee Mountain Home - Dolly Parton ♥
Daylight - Taylor Swift ♥

Chapter One

It was a beautiful spring day in Autumn Falls, the trees were bursting with lush green leaves, the birds were singing and the sun was bouncing off car windshields.

Noah Carter sat in a booth at Joe's Diner in a foul mood. In less than three days he had to move five hundred cattle and their calves to the summer pasture and three of his top ranch hands were sick. He'd called about every person he knew to see if they could help but so far, no such luck.

"What can I get you?"

He glanced up from his phone to see a waitress—blonde, small, teeth overlapping a touch at the front when she smiled. "Where's Loriana?" he asked with a frown. He always got his coffee from Loriana. Everyone got their coffee from Loriana. It should be called Loriana's Diner, but Loriana didn't want the hassle of a new sign.

"She's out the back." The waitress stood with her pad and pencil. Her uniform was too big so she'd tied the apron really tight and wore it with the collar unbuttoned so all her necklaces hung on her pale bare skin.

Noah wasn't keen on change. "Are you new?"

The girl's lips twitched. "Yes, sir, I'm new. What can I get you?"

Loriana knew his order. "Just a coffee."

"Black?"

"White."

She wrote it down on her pad. He noticed her name tag, Ren. What kind of name was that?

"You want anything else?"

Noah had been up since five and realized he was not only exhausted but actually starving. "Yeah, I'll have a slice of pie."

His phone lit up with a message from one of his ranch hopefuls and Noah immediately grabbed it to see whether the guy could help. It was another no.

The waitress brushed her over-long bangs out of her eyes and said, "What kind of pie? We've got blueberry, peach, raspberry, apple. We got a new lime and—"

"Apple," said Noah, cutting her off, annoyed with the message, distractedly trying to work out who else he could ask. Everything in his life was going wrong at the moment.

"Okay." She wrote down apple in her big, looping handwriting, her bright pink nails wrapped tightly around the pen. "You want cream or ice cream with that?"

Noah had to stifle a sigh as he said, "Just the pie."

She paused, glanced up, pen still poised on the paper. "Well, aren't you a joy to serve."

Startled by the comment, Noah flinched. "Excuse me?"

"You heard," the waitress replied, tucking her pen behind her ear and walking back to the counter.

Noah huffed in surprise at the comment and took a moment to play back the interaction realizing that he certainly hadn't been at his best. But then he had other things on his mind. It wasn't just the cattle drive, it was everything—from his mom badgering him to move out of his trailer on the ranch to huge, engulfing things like the anniversary of his brother Jack's death, that always put a cloud over everything—a reminder of what they'd lost in both a brother and the fracturing of their family—and made Noah struggle for breath if he thought about it too much.

But still, he felt he should probably apologize. Glancing back to the diner counter he tried to catch her eye but couldn't see her.

As he was looking, his older brother Logan strolled into the diner. There was another problem in his life. His return had sparked a turning point, not least in their mom who saw him now, happily settled with his girlfriend, Bella, and decided they could all learn a lesson or two from the changes he'd made.

Logan slipped into the booth seat opposite, hands flat on the table, eyes curious at Noah's expression. "What's wrong?"

"I upset the new waitress." Noah made a face like it was the last thing he needed right now. "Where's Loriana when you need her?"

From the look on Logan's face as he said it, Noah realized, without having to turn around, that the waitress—Ren—was standing behind him. He glanced and there she was with the coffee pot. She didn't do anything to hide the awkwardness, just let it hang in the air while Noah actually felt his cheeks get hot. He didn't know when the last time he blushed was.

Ignoring him completely, she turned the full wattage of her smile on Logan and said, "Coffee?"

"Thank you, ma'am," Logan said, all gentlemanly and polite, overcompensating for Noah, and moved his cup over to make it easier for her to pour.

She then poured Noah's cup without looking at him or asking him.

"Thank you," he half mumbled.

"You're more than welcome," she replied, throwing him a faux butter-wouldn't-melt smile before leaving them again.

Logan raised a brow. "How did you upset her?" he asked, picking up the laminated menu and absently perusing it.

"By ordering pie."

Logan looked at him bemused but didn't push it. Instead, he tucked the menu back in between the condiment bottles and said, "So have you managed to get hold of anyone?"

Noah shook his head. As if on cue, his phone buzzed again with another no and he chucked it frustratedly down on the red linoleum table. "There's no one. They're either sick or they're already working."

"Can you postpone the drive?"

Noah made a noise like he couldn't even believe Logan would ask.

Logan nodded, "Sorry, yeah, stupid question."

"You've been in the city too long."

Raising his cup, Logan said, "Hey, you've gotta be nice to me, I've said I'll help you." He took a sip of his coffee then smiled as Noah had to apologize, although Noah couldn't understand why anyone would need persuading to go on a cattle drive. Sometimes he would be out on horseback, sun just rising over the mountain, dew still on the grass, silence except for the rustle of the pines, and wonder what his brothers were doing not being there, think what they were missing out on.

What he hadn't counted on, however, with Logan coming back, were the memories it would stir up, like muddy water that had lain settled for so long.

"You may not like her," Logan said, nodding toward the waitress, "but she makes a good coffee."

Noah took a slug of his own drink and had to admit it was good, maybe even better than how Loriana made it.

When Ren came and slid the slice of apple pie in front of him, he said, "Good coffee, thanks."

She didn't bat an eyelid, just said, "Your pie. No cream, no ice cream, just the pie."

Logan, clearly amused by her blanking of Noah, said, "It really is great coffee."

She beamed at him. "Thanks."

Noah rolled his eyes.

Logan said, "Are you new around here?"

She shrugged, "Just here for the season."

Logan nodded. "It's a nice place to be for the summer."

"Yeah, everyone seems really friendly. Well, almost everyone."

She gave Noah a look and he sat back with a sigh. "Sorry for earlier, I was distracted. No excuse, but you know … sorry."

Seemingly surprised that he'd apologized, she said, "I accept, thank you very much," and smiled a smile so wide it took up her whole face. Like she could flick a switch and turn off any hint of animosity. She glanced around the diner, checked there were no customers who needed anything and said, "So, what's eating you guys?"

Noah was about to say, "Nothing," but Logan got in there first, and nodding in Noah's direction said, "My brother's got a cattle drive in three days and all his ranch hands have got the flu."

Ren made a face. "That's too bad."

Noah huffed like that was an understatement and turned his attention to the sugar-dusted pie wondering why anyone would ever have it any other way than plain.

Just then Loriana appeared from out the back carrying plates piled high with pancakes and bacon for one of the tables in the far corner. She paused at Noah's table.

Always an enjoyable character to have around, Loriana was the same age as Noah's mom but dressed like she was twenty years younger: silver-blonde hair always piled on top of her head in a messy beehive and lips painted as pink as bubblegum.

"I hear Emmett's trying to rope Hank into your drive at the weekend?" she said.

Hank was Loriana's husband and Noah's dad,

Emmett's, oldest friend. He was pretty creaky nowadays, but in Noah's current situation beggars couldn't be choosers. "I've got my fingers crossed," Noah replied through a mouthful of pie, covering his mouth with his hand as he spoke.

Loriana laughed, her big gold heart earrings swinging at the movement. "You must be desperate if you're relying on Hank!"

"It'd be an honor to have someone as experienced as Hank," Noah countered.

"You're a charmer, Noah Carter." Loriana smiled fondly at him while Ren raised a brow clearly in surprise at the change in him. "I warn you, though, he's learning the banjo."

Logan snorted at the comment. "Lucky us."

"Well, if he does come," Loriana added, moving away to deliver her pancakes to the waiting customers. "I am more than happy to drive out with your mother and bring you supplies. Anything you need."

"Never say no to your chili, Loriana," Noah called after her.

"Done," she replied over his shoulder.

As Noah went back to his pie, the new waitress, Ren, took her biro out of her hair, put it between her teeth and retied her short blonde ponytail garbling something incoherent as she did so.

Noah could feel his patience once again waning, he was tired out by the idea of what a motley crew he was relying on. "I'm sorry, what?"

She took the biro out of her mouth and stuck it back in

her ponytail. "I said, I'm not working this weekend, I could help you."

Caught off-guard, Noah scoffed a laugh. That was the last thing he'd imagined she was going to say. He assumed she was joking, but her expression was deadly serious.

It was then that it dawned on him she must be a fan. Since Logan had sat down, she'd perked up, and was now all sweetness and light.

When they were in their teens, Noah and his four brothers had been in the band Silver Sky—named after the ranch. A spur of the moment audition—originally intended to cheer up their mom as she underwent a course of chemo—turned into them winning the TV talent competition they had entered. Five platinum albums and three sell-out global tours later, everyone recognized Logan. Noah, not so much. While he'd had his legion of fans at the time, he was pretty unrecognizable nowadays, he made sure of it. His hair was longer, almost jaw length, rather than the clean-cut short back and sides he had while in the band. And he always had at least three days of stubble. His skin was tanned the color of treacle from being out in the sun all day and he'd bulked up from all the ranch work, no longer the sinewy teenager.

On the rare occasion he looked at photos of himself from the band days, he barely recognized the wide, open fresh-faced fifteen-year-old looking back. He wondered, though, if he could glimpse the sadness and fear behind his eyes or whether he just saw it there with hindsight. Either way, they were days he'd rather forget. But with Logan back, and since Jack's death, they seemed to be cropping up more and more.

Logan on the other hand didn't look too different to his time in Silver Sky; just more chiseled with age and an air of wealth and maturity that was only made more apparent by the navy-blue polo shirt he had on with the Silver H Polo Club logo emblazoned on the front. He'd bought the club after selling his hugely successful record label, Carter Media, and was coaching the junior squad. He'd never looked more relaxed and happy, which was good for Logan but not so great for Noah because it made his mom more intent on trying to get them all to shake up their lives. Hence why she'd gone and served him notice on the trailer, a request he was currently intent on ignoring.

Noah watched the waitress, skeptically thinking of course that was why she was trying to get on the cattle trail. So stupid of him not to realize. He said, a little more curtly than he might normally, "Thanks for the offer but we're good."

Ren's eyes widened at being so obviously knocked back.

Logan, ever the diplomatic businessman, stepped in and said, "You have experience herding cattle?"

Noah doubted it.

But Ren said, "I spent a bunch of time on a ranch as a kid. I know what to do."

"And you'd want to help?" Logan confirmed.

She shrugged a shoulder. "I'm new here, I've got nothing else to do."

Logan glanced at Noah with a look that Noah knew meant he should take her up on the offer. Noah felt himself bristle and gave an almost imperceptible swipe of his head to decline.

To Ren, Logan said, "Maybe you could write down your number and we could get back to you?"

Ren looked at Noah, he felt his jaw tense, and she laughed—a sound much huskier than he'd have expected—then turning to go, she said with a grin, "He knows where to find me if he needs me."

Chapter Two

The Carter family were gathered around the huge wooden table in the ranch house kitchen. Martha, Noah's mom, was making dinner along with Logan who was meant to be helping but kept stopping to turn around and get involved in the conversation at the table, eating the carrot he was meant to be chopping. Rocky, the family's border collie who usually favored Noah but was still in rapture over Logan's return, was leaning possessively against his legs.

Noah—refusing to be jealous of the dog's affection but wishing at times like this that it was back to just him and his mom and dad living in Autumn Falls, a quiet, hardworking life where everyone just got on with whatever it was they had to do—had laid the table, one hand absently on his phone as he'd gone a level deeper into his contacts to try and round up help.

His dad, Emmett, had just come in from the barn and

was pouring himself a glass of water. "No luck?" he said, once he'd taken a large gulp.

Noah shook his head.

Logan's girlfriend, Bella, sat at one of the chairs cradling a cup of tea, having been repeatedly assured there was nothing she could do to help with dinner. Noah's sister, Willow—the youngest in the family—had come home for a couple of days on a break from her dance schedule, and sat opposite Bella, legs crossed underneath her, dreamily catching up on all the gossip about her and Logan getting together. Noah had been trying for most of the evening so far to block them out.

In answer to their dad, however, Logan said, "There was someone," throwing Noah a wry smile as he popped a slice of carrot in his mouth.

Noah narrowed his eyes back.

Emmett lifted a brow. "Who?"

Noah muttered, "No one."

Bella and Willow stopped chatting to listen as Logan told them about the waitress at the diner.

"She sounds great," Bella said, blowing on her tea before she took a sip.

Noah could kill Logan. "She wasn't that great."

"Why, because she's a girl?" Willow asked, brow raised in challenge.

Martha glanced around as she checked on the roast chicken in the oven. "Surely not. I've done it most years and so have you, Willow." His mom was out of action this year because she'd hurt her back, and Willow because her dance insurance forbade horse riding.

"No, not because she's a girl," Noah sighed, trying to deflect attention by checking his phone.

Willow made a face like she didn't believe him for a second and, piling all her red curls on top of her head, said, "What is it, then?"

Noah realized they were all looking at him. He didn't like so many pairs of eyes fixed in his direction and wanted the subject closed. "It's because she's small, talks a lot and doesn't look like she knows what she's doing. And she clearly only offered because she recognized us from the band."

Logan frowned. "I didn't get that impression at all."

"You only think it's because of the band because she's a girl." Willow let her hair tumble back to her shoulders. "What if she was a man, would you take her then?"

"Not if he was small, talked a lot and didn't know what he was doing."

Bella laughed. He silently thanked her for it and pulled out the chair next to her to sit down. "Do you want to come?" he asked her a touch desperately.

Logan snorted, "Have you seen Bella on a horse?"

Bella threw him a look, to which Logan smirked apologetically. To Noah she said, "I'll drive out with the sandwiches," and gave his hand a squeeze in solidarity.

By the stove, Martha slapped Logan's hand away from where he was picking at the roast chicken, and said, "Noah, honey, I don't know if you're in a position to be this choosy."

Emmett took a seat at the head of the table. He rolled down the sleeves of his shirt and did up the buttons at the cuffs as he said, "What about Rudy Myers?" Noah shook his head. "The Sanderson twins?"

"No."

As if sensing his desperation, Rocky left Logan and came and lay down over Noah's feet.

Bella sipped her tea and said, "What about Brodie?"

They all laughed, even Noah, at the idea of his twin coming on the drive.

Logan said, "On Instagram yesterday he was on a yacht in St-Tropez."

Emmett tutted, and the rest of them shifted uncomfortably at their dad's obvious disapproval.

Willow moved so she was sitting with her knee up, arm wrapped around it, and, beckoning to Rocky under the table, said, "I think your girl sounds like the best option."

Noah narrowed his eyes, felt the comforting weight of the dog leave his feet as it padded over to his sister. "Let's get one thing straight, she's *not* my girl."

They all laughed again. All except Noah.

Chapter Three

When Noah Carter walked into the diner two days later, Ren sent up a silent prayer of thanks. Since the mention of the cattle drive, all she'd hoped for was that he'd come back and ask her to join them.

She was in desperate need of some space to clear her head and get her thoughts in order—or maybe just some time to build up her courage—and a few days in wide open country sounded perfect.

When she'd sheepishly told Loriana that she'd offered to help Noah, even though she didn't technically have the weekend off, Loriana had immediately thrown her hands wide and said, "Don't be silly. If Noah says he needs you, then you have to go. That's what we do around here, we help each other out." Then she'd added with a cheeky wink, "And who could turn down Noah Carter. He's definitely the most underrated of those brothers. If I had to choose, I'd pick him any day."

"Loriana, you're old enough to be his mom."

"I can appreciate a fine-looking man as much as the next gal," she said, stacking the plates from the dishwasher.

Ren laughed, "I'll let Hank know."

Lorianna cackled as she flipped the dishwasher door closed, "Please do! Bit of jealousy might do Hank the world of good."

Every time Ren spoke to Loriana she wondered if mid-sentence the woman would stop talking and suddenly realize who Ren was. But it never happened. Instead, Loriana's glossy, coral-painted lips split into a mischievous smile and she said, "Oh, to be young again."

Ren was by nature a drifter, but she had come to Autumn Falls with a purpose. When the private investigator she'd hired had circled the small town on the map and said, "That's where your mom lives," Ren had packed her bag and driven across the country. She'd walked into the diner intending to tell Loriana who she was but had found herself asking for a job instead, too afraid suddenly for the words to come out of her mouth. She hadn't been in town long, but observing all the friendships and the families while waiting on them at the diner, she thought, *imagine growing up a part of this?*

And yet she couldn't bring herself to confront Loriana with what she'd found out. She had tried, more than once, but she froze each time. With the truth, she realized, there came the paralyzing prospect of rejection. She'd never thought of herself as lacking courage before, but she'd never needed as much of it as she needed now. Looking at Loriana, currently shouting at Maurice the chef with her hands on her hips and a biro behind her ear, all she saw was everything she'd ever wanted her whole life.

It was too big. Came with too much hope, but also the very real possibility of utter heartbreak. And it made Ren scurry back every time she psyched herself up to speak.

That was why she'd kept her fingers crossed ever since meeting him that Noah would be forced to take her up on the offer.

She'd found herself gazing longingly at the wild, rugged landscape in the distance as she walked home after work. A couple of years ago she'd worked as a guide on horseback tours in California, it'd been condors flying above her as she rode through giant redwoods as high as the eye could see, here it would be eagles and pines towering like arrows to the sky. She needed that space, that calm, to feel as free as the birds circling above her, and then, she was certain, she'd find her courage.

So, it had felt like fate when she'd overheard the brothers trying to recruit people for the cattle drive, and Ren never turned away from fate. Possibility, she knew, lived around the corner.

Now, she watched as Noah pushed open the diner door and swaggered to the counter. She had to keep her heart at a steady beat, try not to show how desperately she wanted him to have changed his mind.

"Hey," he said, sliding onto one of the high stools. Taking his hat off, he raked a hand through his hair, tucked it behind his ear.

"Hey, yourself," she replied, trying to play it cool by focusing her attention on the coffee machine.

Even out the corner of her eye she could see he was uncomfortable, nervous even. He tapped the counter with the fingers of one hand, bit the corner of his lip.

"Coffee and a slice of apple pie, just pie?" she asked, still not wanting to get her hopes up.

Noah shook his head. "I'm all good. I didn't come for coffee, I er—" He ran a hand through his hair again.

She stopped what she was doing, raised a brow as she waited for him to find his words. Her heart beating the word *please* in her ears.

"I wanted to take you up on your offer." The tips of his cheekbones pinked. "If you're still available."

Ren had to stop her mouth from stretching into a grin. "Oh, you did, did you?" she said, as nonchalantly as she could. The fact that he was very easy on the eye was certainly an added bonus.

He swallowed, nodded, pulled at the neck of his threadbare white T-shirt with his finger. "If you're still willing. I mean if you're not, then that's—"

"I'm still willing," she intercepted, the corner of her mouth tipping up against her will, her palms a little sweaty with excitement.

A flash of relief crossed Noah's face but quickly disappeared. "Okay, good," he said. "Thanks. I er—I appreciate it." He pushed up from his seat and held a hand outstretched. "I'm Noah Carter, by the way."

She wiped her hands on her white, frilly apron then took his cool, calloused hand in hers. "Ren."

Noah said, "Nice to meet you, Ren." But almost as soon

as their palms touched, he let go of her hand. Put his in his pocket and proceeded to give her the lowdown on details.

When he'd covered timings and logistics, he said, "We can lend you a tent and a sleeping bag. Other than that you'll need—"

Ren said, "I know what I need. This isn't my first rodeo, Noah."

Noah put his hat on. "It's not a rodeo. Don't come expecting a rodeo."

She laughed at the frown on his face, "Are you always this serious?"

"Yes," he replied, pulling his hat low as he stood up. "You better get used to it." Then he turned and walked back out the way he'd come.

Chapter Four

Noah had been too busy organizing logistics of the cattle drive to think too much about his newest recruit. But when he did think about her, he thought she talked too much and had too much attitude. He couldn't deny it however when Ren's battered old car pulled up in the yard and, when she got out, Willow laughed out loud and said, "Well, you missed the bit about how pretty she was."

Noah was so focused on all her former negative points, that he had actually glossed over what Ren looked like. As she stood behind the car door in the dusky morning light, surveying the ranch for a moment, Noah tried to see Ren the way his sister, standing next to him, was seeing her for the first time—the breeze whipping her short blonde hair across her face before she tucked it back behind her ear, the collar of her bright blue shirt framing her face and, even from this distance, making her eyes glimmer pale as a wolf's. He hated to admit it but when he stood back now and looked objectively at her, he could see that some people might easily describe Ren as incredibly pretty.

Then she slammed the car door and he saw that she was dressed in well-worn cowboy boots the color of ripe cherries, perfectly fitted pale blue jeans, a million gold necklaces around her neck and her cobalt western shirt with white piping was tied at her midriff as if she was gearing up for a hoedown.

"I knew this was a terrible idea," he muttered as she grabbed her hat, slung her bag over her shoulder and sauntered over, looking smaller than ever, a big wide smile on her face, lips painted as red as her boots.

Willow frowned. "What are you talking about? She's fantastic."

As Ren came closer, she said, "Hi, there," to both Noah and Willow.

Willow stepped forward, hand outstretched. "Hi, I'm Willow, Noah's sister. I was just saying that no one said how pretty you are."

Ren shook Willow's hand at the same time as throwing Noah a wry glance. "I imagine your brother didn't appreciate that comment too much."

Willow laughed in surprise. "How well you know him already."

Noah didn't have time for this nonsense. It was painfully early. They needed to get going—all the horses were already in their trailers, everyone was gearing up ready to leave. "We gotta go," he said. "You ready?"

"Absolutely. Can't wait," Ren replied, a touch too bright and breezy for that time in the morning for Noah's liking.

Then she looked around again in wonder and said, "This is a really awesome place you got here." He could almost feel her drinking it all in—the giant red-roofed barns, the vast green pastures that swept out to meet the military rows of pines, and beside them the main ranch house with its wraparound veranda and trailing pink roses around the door.

Again, for a second, Noah was forced to see what he saw every day with different eyes. What he took for granted as home and work, seen with Ren's enthusiasm suddenly seemed better than average. But then Willow said, "The eyesore over there is Noah's place," pointing to where the corner of his trailer was just in view.

Unexpectedly embarrassed to have it pointed out in such a fashion in front of Ren, Noah found himself trying to gloss over the subject. "Like I said, we need to get going." Then glancing at what Ren had on and, internally rolling his eyes again, he added, "It's cold up there this time of the morning."

Ren looked back from where Willow was still lamenting the state of the trailer, and said, "I've got a coat, don't worry, Noah." A little smile played on her lips. "As I said, it's not my—"

"I know, I know, it's not your first rodeo, whatever." He waved a hand and turned and walked in the direction of the waiting vehicles, ignoring his sister who was biting down on a grin as Ren followed along behind him, still smiling, enthusiasm unquenchable.

They left the ranch in a procession of horse trailers. He left Ren in the care of Willow who was driving Noah's Jeep filled with all the equipment. They could joke about him all they liked as long as he wasn't there. Or of course they might not talk about him at all. He didn't care either way.

Noah loved the drive out to the winter grazing pastures. Bringing the cattle back to spend the warmer months on the ranch marked the beginning of spring for him, had done since he was a little kid champing at the bit to go along with his dad. He'd been the one at the door eagerly ready and waiting for instruction in his hand-me-down boots and brand-new hat, while Logan would have been cursing at his dad under his breath, Jack hiding by the barns doing as little as possible. Brodie would still have been asleep and Ethan most likely banned from going because he was in trouble for something or other. But for Noah, it was the best time of the year.

The route up the mountains was particularly scenic, filled with wildflowers and an epic view back over Autumn Falls, Main Street, and the Redemption River snaking alongside. For a moment, Noah imagined Ren seeing it for the first time and felt stupidly proud, like it was his view and he was letting her in on a secret. He caught his own eye in the rear-view mirror and raised a brow in disbelief at his thoughts.

When they got to the point where the trail began and they parked up, it was the same organized chaos as it was every year. Willow had an early-morning dance training session so dropped Ren, then shot off in a screech of Noah's beloved Jeep's gears. Noah tried to divvy up the tasks, but already things weren't going to plan as he heard Logan and Emmett conferring about whether Noah had picked the best route. Distracted by what they were saying, he put Ren with Hank Murphy to unload the horses while Bella and his mom sorted out equipment. Normally he'd be with his dad, cross-checking the route and the weather, but had to step away. There was something about Logan being there that made him feel like a teenager, afraid he'd lose the autonomy of choice, go along with things as he had before whether he wanted to or not. It put his dad on edge, too, he could tell; like they were all in their corners wary of what was to come.

Instead, Noah went over to help Hank and Ren, whistling for Rocky, who was weaving excitedly in and out of the trees.

Walking around the trailer, distracted by the fact his dad and brother were picking his route apart, he stopped short when he saw Ren whispering softly to Star, a sweet but skittish chestnut mare with a white star between her eyes who wasn't fond of the trailer.

Since he'd seen her at the ranch, Ren had put on a thick fleece jacket printed with camouflage the color of eggplant, and brown leather chaps, she'd tied her hair in a low ponytail, had a gray scarf tucked into her collar, and a well-loved black gaucho hat hung on a string around her neck. She suddenly looked every bit the serious cowgirl.

Noah ignored how calming he found the scene and went over to run a soothing hand down Star's neck. "Everything okay?"

Ren's head shot up in surprise to find Noah there, then

she smiled and said, "Yeah, she just wanted to be out of that trailer—" she turned to speak directly to the horse, eyes adoring "—didn't you?"

He wished for a second that he was just here for the horses. That there were no underlying family machinations to contend with. "Star's never liked to travel. She's Willow's," he said, tightening the saddle, "I brought her for you, thought she'd probably be a good fit."

"Really?" Ren's eyes lit up, he hadn't thought it was possible for them to grow any wider.

She went around and put her foot in the stirrup. "It's been way too long since I've ridden."

The statement didn't fill Noah with much hope, but then he watched her hoist herself up with the effortless ease of a seasoned rider.

"Ahh," she grinned as she relaxed into the saddle and he found himself smiling a tiny bit inside, mainly with relief that she clearly knew what she was doing.

When he walked over to check his own horse, Blue—named because his black coat shone cobalt when it hit the light—he heard Ren say, "Best place to be in the world."

He paused momentarily because he felt the exact same way, and was about to agree when he looked back and realized she was talking to the horse, completely lost in her own world, blonde hair fallen forward over her eyes as she leaned down close to Star's ear, red lips talking softly.

As if aware he was watching, she glanced up and their eyes met. He felt himself momentarily freeze, unnerved by both the fact he'd been watching and that she had caught him. A small smile of, perhaps, victory flickered in her eyes.

Then his dad's voice called, "Noah, get over here!" And to his relief, he could turn and stalk away.

They set off soon after that. Rocky bounding ahead. Sun low in the misty blue sky. Supplies packed. And while the route was agreed on, there was now a low-level friction in the air between the three men. Hank was very wisely staying out of it.

Martha, Loriana and Bella would drive out and meet them at various points over the next couple of days with more food and refreshments. The air was cool and crisp. Noah turned the collar up on his old shearling-lined leather flying jacket and pulled his hat lower. His dad was wearing his slicker to keep off the cold. Logan had none of the right clothing anymore for ranching because he'd only recently moved back from New York, so wore a flash new black technical fleece and baseball cap and kept complaining that his ears were cold.

"You going to grouch all day?" Noah called back to his brother.

"I'm not grouching," Logan replied with affront, "I'm merely stating that it's absolutely one hundred percent ridiculously freezing."

Noah rolled his eyes. "You're such a baby."

From the back, Ren laughed, then she called, "I'm with Logan. It is colder than I thought it would be."

"Thank you!" Logan replied, as if vindicated. "So you're cold, too?"

Ren said, "Oh, no. I'm toasty. I prepared."

That made Hank bellow a laugh and Noah's lips twitch but he didn't turn around to show it.

Chapter Five

They spent the first day rounding up the cattle from where they'd grazed over the winter months, getting used to working together. Hank and Emmett, seasoned experts, just fell into their roles. Logan had to get back into the habit of not only keeping the cows in check but being told what to do. Noah could see the same tensing of his brother's shoulders as when they were kids, when their dad issued an order. Now Logan was having to deal with Noah telling him what to do as well. He had to admit that Logan was doing well not to show his frustration. Noah wasn't sure he'd be the same if the roles were reversed. He tried not to do anything he didn't want to nowadays.

To Noah's surprise, Ren knew exactly what she was doing, nimbly darting off into the thicket to retrieve stray cattle and urging them back into the herd.

Rocky was loving it, as usual, dancing about the place barking as he corralled disinterested cows and chasing after the last remaining ones that Noah had missed as they started to move the herd forward.

Emmett took the lead as the point man, as he always did and always would until he could no longer ride. As they came out of the trees onto the rolling plains, Logan, Ren, and Hank were on the flanks. Noah hung back with Rocky, pushing the slower cows forward, keeping everything moving, all the while watching and assessing the team in front of him. Hank was tall and solid in the saddle, like an old General. Logan looked happy enough, but Noah knew he'd struggle to ride all day, not that he'd ever show it. Ren, he wasn't sure about. She looked pretty agile, almost like she was more comfortable on Star's back than she was day-to-day, but he put her in the same camp as Logan—too stubborn to even admit if she was in agony.

The weather got warmer after lunch. Ren pulled off her sweater and rode in her shirt and gaucho hat. To Noah's relief, she'd untied the shirt at the front and tucked it in, looking less like she was at a fashion show. As they fell into a steady rhythm, Logan rode next to her, chatting amiably. Occasionally, when the breeze was right, Noah heard her laugh above the noise of the cattle and wondered briefly what was so funny, but then he focused back on what he was doing, pleased he was alone at the back, more than happy not to have to chat.

By evening, tiredness had kicked in and no one was talking much.

As Ren put the last peg in her tent, she stood up and stretched her arms above her head and said, "I don't know about you boys, but I am exhausted. I'd forgotten what it feels like to be in the saddle all day."

Hank agreed. "I think I might be too old for this," he said, unfurling his sleeping bag in his tent.

Emmett, whose tent was already up and ready, stoked a crackling fire and frowned. "Never too old for this."

"Too old is the day you die," Noah said, because that was what his grandfather used to say.

Emmett nodded. "Exactly."

Beside him, Logan rolled his eyes that they were still going through that same routine.

Noah didn't care, just gazed out at the evening light over the mountains, the sounds of the cattle shuffling around, the fire popping and spitting, and the stars a blanket of silver overhead, and hoped he never would get too old for this.

"Bet you didn't get this when you were in New York, did you?" Hank said to Logan, gesturing toward the landscape and, in the shadows, what looked like an everlasting horizon.

"No, sir." Logan shook his head, sitting as close to the fire as he could get, his jacket done up to the chin, a bottle of beer in his hand, but when he turned to look at the view he added, "I haven't seen this view since..." He paused, as if wishing he hadn't brought it up. "Well, I guess since before we left with the band."

Noah's insides tightened at the reference.

Ren walked over to the fire, taking a swig from her water bottle before saying, "What band is that?"

Noah looked up sharply. He wanted to see if she was joking but her expression was innocently nonplussed.

Hank spread his arms wide, graying brows raised under his battered cream hat, as he said, "These boys were famous. Didn't you know?"

Noah saw his dad frown.

Logan clarified, "We were part of a boy band a few years back. Silver Sky?" he offered.

Ren's eyes widened. "You were not?"

Logan laughed. "We were."

Ren stood looking in disbelief around the group.

Hank and Logan grinning at how dumbfounded she was, but his dad, like Noah, seemed to want to move on to another subject. To Emmett, all Silver Sky had been good for was scattering his sons far and wide, shattering his family and playing an inevitable part in Jack's death, and while he was better at having the past raised than he used to be, he still didn't like it much. But Ren's big, unconcealed emotions seemed to have an effect on people, even an old curmudgeon like Emmett Carter. And when it became apparent she was looking to him for absolute verification, he finally nodded and said, "They were."

Then suddenly Noah felt her bash him on the arm and say, "Why didn't you tell me?"

He rubbed his arm in surprise. "I thought you knew," he replied, confused as to why he should have been the one to tell her, her question making it seem like he was her closest ally there.

"I just—" She opened and closed her mouth. Frowned.

Held her hair back with her hands as she stared at him with her wide owlish eyes. "Silver Sky? Like *the* Silver Sky?"

Now even Noah found himself cracking a resigned smile. "Yeah," he said, cheeks reddening—although thankfully no one could tell in the darkness—at the attention.

Ren plonked down on the fallen pine log next to him. "I just can't believe it."

Hank cracked open a beer, and holding it between his knees so he could zip up his big fluffy coat, said, "You didn't recognize them?"

Ren looked up at Logan, narrowing her eyes. "You, maybe. But you—" she turned her attention to Noah who tried to remain impassive as she scrutinized him but got increasingly awkward as the inspection continued "—not at all." She shook her head. "I just remember a cute guy with messy blonde hair and dimples."

"Brodie," said Logan and Noah at the same time.

Ren was still shaking her head. "I'm stunned."

Noah unscrewed his water and took a long gulp, surprised how pleased, or rather relieved, he was that she wasn't here as a fan. In his experience, anonymity didn't feature that often in the outside world.

"You have to tell me all about it!" she said, sitting forward, eyes glinting in the firelight, and rubbing her hands together. "I want to know everything!"

But too aware of his dad's—and his own—discomfort with the subject, Noah said, "No, you don't. Believe me."

"I do!" Ren countered, swept up with the excitement.

Noah saw his dad's jaw clench and wanted to say to Ren, "Please, not now."

But she was almost giddy. "I can't quite get my head around it. You must have *so many* stories to tell."

Emmett took his hat off, swept his hair back and as he replaced it, stood up and said, "I'm going to check on the horses."

Noah watched Logan's eyes follow Emmett, then glance back to Noah to see if he, too, was watching their dad's reaction. They shared a look of wary concern. Noah would have changed the subject, but Logan shrugged a smile and said to Ren, "Go on, then, what do you want to know?"

"Anything," Ren said, eyes alight. "What was the wildest thing you got up to?"

Logan made a face. "We were working too hard to be wild."

Ren scoffed. "Oh, please, you never smashed up any hotel rooms?"

Logan shook his head. "No, no hotel rooms were destroyed by us, we were very well behaved."

Ren wasn't convinced and turned to Noah on her hunt for gossip. "What about you? What crazy stuff did you get up to?"

"Nothing." Noah shook his head.

Ren frowned, incredulous. "Oh, come on!"

But Noah stood up and, brushing his pants down, said more abruptly than he'd intended, "There's really nothing to tell." Then, when it looked like another question might be on Ren's lips, added, "It's a long day tomorrow, we should get to bed."

Ren looked from Noah to Logan and back again, narrowing her eyes at him uncertainly before she nodded. "Of course. Yeah, I'm pretty tired, too."

Chapter Six

As soon as Ren got into her tent she googled Silver Sky. The signal was pretty bad, so it took ages for the page to load but the first thing that came up was the recent death of their brother Jack Carter. She put her hand to her mouth. Of course, Jack Carter, movie star. How could she have been so stupid and not put the names together. She considered all the scandal that used to be splashed about Jack Carter's life in the newspapers and online. Ren didn't pay much attention to things like that, but it was hard to miss stories about Jack Carter—a good-looking guy with a devilish twinkle in his eye—he'd sold newspapers.

She scrolled through pictures of the Carter family at the funeral. The brothers with their eyes downcast. Then there was a publicity photo of them when they were younger in the band, goofing around, doing stupid poses. And then there was Noah at the back, standing slightly apart with a shy smile. She tried to zoom in, but her phone wouldn't let her, the signal was still too weak.

Ren drifted off to sleep wondering what it was they weren't saying around the fire. What it was really like being part of a world-famous band, but also she realized how utterly different their life was from hers. It felt like she'd only just stopped thinking about it when the warm morning sun woke her and she heard the lowing of the herd and had to remind herself where she was. She unzipped the tent and popped her head out, feeling the fresh chill on her skin as she wriggled her sleeping bag around and sat in it, arms wrapped around her knees, watching the dawn start to lighten the sky.

She'd always woken early, it was a childhood habit she'd never been able to break, but to her it was the best part of the day—it belonged just to her, everyone else asleep.

Or so she thought, until a movement caught her eye and she saw Noah walking back from where he'd been checking the horses. Hair all mussed from sleep, his old leather jacket slung on over a T-shirt, boots untied. Rocky bounded alongside him, waiting eagerly for the stick Noah was carrying to be thrown then shooting off to retrieve it. When he came back, Noah would pause to ruffle his fur, trying not to let the dog lick him on the chin, wincing a laugh as he did.

Ren tipped her head as she observed. It was like seeing a different person from the evening before, a version of Noah that was unencumbered and at ease—she would have said happy—but realized that was a word she would never have aligned with Noah.

"Morning," she said when he got closer and

immediately his smile vanished. So suddenly, in fact, she'd have been hard pushed to believe it ever existed.

"Morning," he replied with his usual reticence and then turned to change course, deciding to go and sort out the camp rather than head back to his tent next to hers.

Before she could say another word, he put two fingers in his mouth and whistled then shouted, "Let's get moving."

A few minutes later, Logan stuck his head out the tent yawning, his hair sticking up at crazy angles. "If you're going to whistle at me, you'd better have coffee ready."

Noah pointed toward the pot boiling on the camp stove.

Logan narrowed his eyes. "Good."

Ren smiled. There was a calming sense of safety to being around the brothers and their friendly bickering. She wriggled back into her tent to get dressed. Noah had said the night before that they could wash in the river when they had a break later in the day and it was warmer. She pulled on her jeans and a clean T-shirt, her favorite yellow one that was soft as a cloud from having been washed so many times and then all her jumpers and finally her fleece.

It was cold again as they saddled up. They changed out the horses to give them a rest. Ren was on a sleek black mare, with sad cinnamon eyes, called Titania. Their breath billowed in clouds as they rode out.

At one point, Emmett looked up at the sky and said, "It's going to rain."

Noah snorted in disbelief and said, "It's not going to rain."

Emmett just shrugged, clearly sticking to his stance.

Ren didn't think it looked like it was going to rain either, but Emmett was wearing his heavy black slicker in preparation, and his craggy, lined face didn't truck with any argument. She wondered what it was like to have grown up with him as a dad—was he harsh but fair or aloof and bullish, it was hard to tell. She was always scrutinizing different family dynamics, wondering if hers might have been like that if she'd had one.

As they went on, the route narrowed into a gulley between the pine trees and they had to funnel the herd in. It was slow going because the cows kept bunching up like freeway traffic. Rocky was loving it, Ren watched him nipping from one side to the other keeping the cattle in check. Every so often, one of the cows would veer off into the forest and Ren made it her job to go in after it, ducking under the low-hanging branches, urging Star up alongside so she could usher the errant cows back into the pack. By the time they were all safely through, trundling on in a narrower line through the trees, Ren popped out of the pines to find herself at the back with Noah, the space too narrow for her to go further up ahead.

"Hey," she said.

He nodded. He had his hat tipped low at the front so she couldn't see his eyes. His jacket hung open, scarf looped lazily around his neck.

They rode on in silence. The cattle pressed close together like a blanket in front of them.

Ren was terrible at silence, more so than ever at the moment. Silence would lead her brain to thinking about why she'd actually come to Autumn Falls and what she was building up to when she got back there. Silence was all the months and years of searching and the nerve-wracking terror of finally finding it.

She looked around a bit, mouth twisting this way and that as she tried to pass the time without saying anything. When she looked back, Noah was in the same position, head, shoulders, hands, unmoving.

"You know," Ren started, "we've got three days of this. If you're not going to say anything it's going to get real boring."

For a second, she wondered if he was going to speak, but instead he just glanced her way then back at the metronomic amble of the herd.

She rolled her lips together, annoyed that he'd ignored her. It was common courtesy to converse. "You might not be aware, but it's called a conversation," she went on. "You might start with a question. Something like, 'So you grew up on a ranch?'"

He glanced across again then away, his body rolling gently under the rhythm of his horse's gait.

"And I might say," she kept her eyes steady on his profile, "yeah it was a big old ranch in Texas. I was a foster kid there for many years."

Attention caught, Noah's head swung around in surprise at the information, expression like he was seeing her properly for the first time.

She smiled widely back at him, aware that it was a cheap trick to use her past to shock him into finally acknowledging her, but it was worth it for that look, as if what he thought about her might be different to what she was. "See, that's how you get to know each other."

Now he didn't seem to know what to say, rather than refusing to say anything, so Ren said, "Then I might add something like, 'How about you, did you always want to be a rancher?' And you might tell me. That's how we might pass the time, get to know each other, maybe even become friends."

Before he could give her one of his brow-raised, sardonic looks, she clicked for Titania to pick up the pace and, smiling to herself, rode away to join Hank on the far side of the herd now that the space had opened up again.

Chapter Seven

By lunchtime the sun was beating down and Ren was rolling up the sleeves of her shirt. Her muscles were starting to ache, but she wasn't going to complain, not to Noah anyway, Logan, maybe, because he'd been moaning about the cold all morning. When they got to a point where the river broke through the trees, Emmett called for them to stop. They would have lunch there and the herd and horses could drink and they could wash.

Ren walked up the riverbank and found a bit of privacy in the shade of the trees where glimpses of sun broke through the branches and glistened on the river like silverfish.

The cold water was a shock to the system but quite a relief for her aching muscles. As she scrubbed her face clean, she remembered all the times she'd washed in rivers, moving cattle in Texas, or run through a freezing shower when she was last in a long line of kids. What she relished about this time—and so many experiences that mimicked times in her childhood—was that now she was doing it of her own free will. It was completely up to her if she wanted to stand in the water and soothe her sore feet, take her time staring up at the sun flickering through the pines, dip down and let the water cascade through her fingertips. What she loved was the freedom to control her own destiny. That was why the news about her mother came as such a shock—she'd been searching for the truth, but now she had it, it meant handing her emotions over to someone else. And that was something she'd learned not to do.

When she'd got dressed, tied up her hair and pulled her boots back on, she wandered back to where she'd left the others. The cattle were grazing happily, the horses stood in the shade of the trees, but a Jeep had pulled up and parked on the grass. When Ren got closer, she saw it was Loriana and Martha, handing out freshly made sandwiches and cold bottles of water for lunch. The sight made her heart clench with a strange mix of longing and envy that she tamped down as soon as it arose.

"What a treat," she said brightly, "thank you." She took a huge cheese and salad sandwich from Loriana, who was wearing a tangerine cowboy shirt for the occasion and huge hooped earrings in a matching enamel. She let her hand linger a touch too long as she took it but not long enough that Loriana would think it was strange.

Bella had come with them, too, and was standing with Logan by the back of the Jeep, his arm draped around her shoulders. Ren thought they looked great together. Noah had his back to them, talking logistics with his dad. Hank leaned against the truck eating Cheetos, the tips of his white mustache covered in orange Cheeto dust, while Rocky lapped water from a bowl in the shade of the truck.

Loriana called over, "Hank, wipe your mouth, your mustache is orange!"

Hank wiped it on his sleeve making Loriana roll her eyes and stride over with some paper towel, tenderness softening her face as she got close.

Ren knew from gentle probing in the diner that Hank and Loriana had only been together fifteen years, so he was no possible relation to Ren, but seeing them together it fascinated her to see those quiet gestures of care from Loriana who was usually so no-nonsense. It added another possible scenario to Ren's fantasy of telling Loriana who she was, one where Loriana's face would soften with the exact same tender affection it wore right now.

As Ren bit into her sandwich, lost in her daydream, Loriana turned her way and said, "You doing okay, Ren? These boys not giving you a hard time?"

Ren almost choked, afraid suddenly that Loriana had read her mind. She had to compose herself and finish chewing before saying with a smile, "Oh, sure, I'm fine. Always fine."

Noah sauntered over then and, pushing his river-damp hair back, said, "She's doing better than Logan."

Which made Bella laugh, Logan scoff, and Ren try not to feel anything akin to pride, because she knew it was more a dig at Logan than praise for her.

But then Noah glanced her way with a look that could almost be taken as them being in cahoots—maybe his way of making up for hardly speaking to her before, if she chose to read into it, which, when it came to Noah Carter, she was aware would be a mistake.

"That reminds me," Bella said, extricating herself from Logan and going around to the back seat of the Jeep, "I brought you this." She hauled out a massive black Puffa jacket and an army-green trapper hat with fur-lined ear flaps and handed it to him.

Logan's eyes widened as he took the jacket from her and held it out like it was priceless treasure, and said simply, "I love you."

"I know how much you hate the cold." Bella laughed, her eyes crinkling as she pulled the furry hat down on his head.

Like families, Ren always found herself watching relationships with awe—Hank and Loriana, Bella and Logan—wondering what it would be like to feel like that about somebody, or have somebody feel that about her. For somebody to know her so well that they could predict her discomforts and try, without asking, to make them better.

She glanced at Noah and saw a look of pitying disbelief on his face at the fact Logan needed such home comforts, but there was a fondness there behind his eyes, too. She noticed that when it was something to do with his brother and Bella—or the dog—Noah's face softened. It had been there with Willow, as well, just tempered by the resignation of her winding him up. That was what family meant, and Ren found it almost unbearably addictive, knew that immersing herself in it wasn't healthy, but couldn't look away. She wondered for a second what it would be like to have Noah look at her like that, not romantically or anything, just not with, at worst, irritation and at best detached politeness. She imagined it was quite special to have made it onto the inside with Noah.

After lunch, Loriana ran through instructions for the chili then hopped in the Jeep with Bella and Martha and they all headed back. They'd brought warmer clothes for everyone, if they wanted them. Ren borrowed a thick, paisley wool scarf simply because it was Loriana's. Emmett took an extra fleece vest. Hank, a sweater and a pair of gloves. Noah took nothing.

The afternoon ride was an easy one, they followed a wide track in a relaxed rhythm. The weather cooled quicker than it had the day before, clouds drifting in over the sun, and Emmett once again muttered about rain.

Ren wrapped the scarf around her neck and buried her chin in it up to her nose, breathing in Loriana's perfume, knowing that was what it would be like to have had a mother, recognizing the scent of fragrance on clothing loaned with care.

It made such a lump form in her throat that she turned to Noah and said, "You want to try a conversation?" Her voice was slightly muffled by the big scarf so she tried to push the material down with her chin.

He shook his head. "Not really." But there was a slightly different tone to his voice, a wry reluctance, as if he'd resigned himself to the fact that it was going to happen, whether he liked it or not.

Ren waited, let the silence roll along with them.

Noah glanced over to see if she was looking at him,

which she was. He sighed. "What do you want to talk about?"

She had to hold in a smile. "I don't know."

He shook his head like, *why did you even ask, then*.

She tucked the scarf further into her fleece so she could talk and said, "You married?"

The idea clearly amused him because he said, "No," with the hint of a laugh.

"Ever been?"

"Nope."

There was a pause. The cattle trundled on ahead, Rocky trotting along in step beside them.

Then as if Noah were learning the rules, after a while, he said, "You?"

It was Ren's turn to be amused. "No."

"Ever been?"

She laughed. "I've never even really kissed anyone."

Noah almost choked in surprise. "You're kidding."

Ren grinned broadly at his reaction—he was so easy to catch off-guard that she found it fun to try. "It's true."

He pulled his horse up short. She'd actually stopped him in his tracks. "You've never kissed a man?"

"I mean like a peck from Jordan O'Hara in high school, but otherwise…" She shook her head.

Still obviously a little stunned, Noah started up again, clicking for his horse—a palomino named Dove—to continue at a slow walk. "It must have been some bad peck if it put you off doing it again."

"Stop it," Ren laughed. "He was sweet."

Noah raised a disbelieving brow. Then to her absolute

surprise, his mouth tilted up into a half-smile. Not a full one, but enough to show that she'd maybe cracked the surface. And he said with slow bewilderment, "You've really never kissed anyone?"

Now she felt a little too exposed. Like she'd tried to shock him and in doing so revealed a bit too much about herself. She knew her cheeks reddened when she tried to explain it. "I just—I haven't ever found anyone that—I don't know." She felt suddenly silly, especially as he'd probably had a legion of fans at his beck and call. "I guess I'm careful of my feelings. Don't want to go giving them away."

Noah tipped his head, and she couldn't decide if it meant he understood or he thought she was crazy.

"I wanted to find someone special, you know,' she added, "and the more I didn't do it, the more the person didn't seem special enough. And well—" she shrugged, even more embarrassed now that she was over-explaining to justify "—special became like super important."

As if reading her mind, he said, "You don't have to justify it to me."

"I'm not justifying it," she replied, too quickly, and it seemed defensive.

"Sounds like you are," he replied, looking straight ahead, but there was that little tip up of the mouth that this time made her blow out a breath, half annoyed with him, half with herself.

One of the cows dropped its pace and she took the opportunity to cajole it back into position. When she came back up alongside Noah, she'd got her composure back.

"I am justifying it. I know it's stupid," she said. "I mean, I should probably just kiss anyone and get it over with. Get over the hurdle, don't you think?" She looked back at Noah to get his reaction and as she did and their eyes met, she realized that it might sound like she was talking about kissing him. She felt her face get hot. "I didn't mean you, by the way."

"I know you didn't mean me."

"No offense," she added.

"None taken," he replied, looking straight ahead, but again, there was that little tip up of the mouth that made her have to hold in her own grin. Why did it feel so good to make him smile?

Riding on over the undulating plains, patches of scrubby brown and lush green under clouds that swept thick like marshmallow as far as she could see, it felt like maybe she'd prized open a tiny crack in Noah's façade. Enough for her to ask, "You date lots of famous people in your band?"

"No," he replied simply.

"Really?" She narrowed her eyes at him not sure whether to believe it or not. "Is that a lie so I don't ask you who?"

"No, it's not a lie." He looked over at her and, expression neutral, said, "I had a girlfriend back here the whole time."

"The whole time? Wow. That must have taken a lot of commitment, especially with all those fans throwing themselves at you." She looked out ahead at the blanket of cloud, thinking again of her stupid admittance that she'd never kissed anyone. He must think her some fool. "And you're not with her now?"

"No."

"What happened?"

Noah rolled his shoulders like he was uncomfortable in the saddle, then said, "She died."

"Oh!" Ren put her hand over her stupid big mouth. "Oh, Noah, I'm really sorry."

She thought of Mrs. Robertson her liaison officer looking across at her in the silver Ford as she drove her back to the foster home from a failed meeting with a family, saying with a sad sigh, "Ren, honey, I've told you time and time again, you have to learn to speak only when you're spoken to."

Noah just shrugged. "It was a long time ago." Then he looked up at the horizon and seemingly assessing the route they were taking, said, "You okay here on your own? I'm gonna check in with Dad."

Ren nodded. The conversation clearly over.

Chapter Eight

Noah kept himself busy when they set up camp that night, collecting wood for the fire, helping Hank put up his tent because his back was aching after the day's ride, checking on the horses. He had surprised himself by mentioning Livvy to Ren, he hadn't talked about her in years. Her memory had stayed firmly wrapped up along with his time in the band, carefully stored away. But Ren was so free with her memories and her vulnerabilities that it was like he'd been lulled into admitting one of his—it was a trick he'd have to be more watchful of.

They were all sitting around the fire eating the chili and tacos that Loriana had dropped off. The hot food was welcome in the cool evening, he could feel it warming his insides. Not that he'd admit it, but he was definitely colder than he'd anticipated. He should have taken an extra sweater off his mom, but he tended to avoid her at the moment in case she badgered him about his life choices, or was it Logan being there that made him more stubborn, retreat further into his own way of being? Noah glanced at his brother in his giant Puffa jacket on the other side of the fire chatting amiably with Ren.

There was something about Logan's presence that kept bringing Noah back to the days in the band, when everyone else's voices were loud and the laughter, the almost mania of it all, while Noah had watched, detached, unable to understand how they could be the way they were. Where all the fun and energy came from, how the others could handle the barrage of questions, the intrusive interviews with the mic thrust in their faces, the packs of photographers outside their hotels, the giggling girls who wanted pictures, who wanted to press their hot, tear-stained cheeks against theirs.

Now, as he looked at Logan entertaining Ren with some story, Noah felt himself retreating further, just watching the familiar way his brother's mouth moved when he spoke. Noah had always seen him as the peacekeeper, the negotiator, the diplomat, the one who kept them together as a whole. He was brilliant at it. So good that it allowed Noah to slip away, back into his familiar spot, watching from the sidelines.

He finished his food and put his empty bowl down on the ground at his feet, then stroked the dog lying at his feet as close to the fire as physically possible, his fur hot as toast.

Ren was talking now. "We did all the normal jobs, but I loved the horses." Noah found himself petting Rocky for longer than he normally might, wanting to hear what it was she was saying. "That was my thing. I didn't care if I got to ride, I just wanted to be there taking care of them, mucking out, grooming, anything that was needed. I was the horse girl." She laughed. "I'd be out there all day, if I could. If I was really tired, sometimes I'd just sleep in the stables."

"Noah used to sleep in the stables, didn't you?" Logan called over. "Anytime anything went wrong he'd grab a blanket and go off in a sulk," he laughed.

Noah, refusing to rise to the childhood ribbing, raised a brow and said dryly, "It was the only place I could get any peace."

"Yes!" Ren agreed.

"Total madness." Logan shook his head at the pair of them.

Noah glanced over at his dad. Emmett wasn't watching them, but Noah knew he was listening and wondered what he was thinking. Whether he remembered the time he'd found Noah out there one morning after they'd won the talent show that put the band on the map, when Noah had woken up bleary-eyed and, seeing him there, said, "How are you going to manage when we're gone?" In retrospect, he wished he'd said, "Please tell me not to go."

But Emmett had barely looked up from what he was doing and just said, "Same as I ever did."

How different Noah's life might have been if his dad had stopped him. Or perhaps if he'd been brave enough to stop himself. But when they'd found out they'd won, Noah'd been excited as the rest of them, swept up in the euphoria.

He heard Ren laugh at another of Logan's anecdotes, wondered why he wasn't as free with the storytelling as his brother. He was out of practice, he thought, getting up to chuck another log onto the fire. He spent his days working all hours on the ranch, there wasn't time for idle chitchat. Not that he wanted to chitchat.

He sat back down. This was a place you could be silent and be alone with your own thoughts. Like his dad, who was sitting happily alone, hands clasped in his lap, face contemplative as he gazed at the fire.

That was the way they did things. Silent, meditative. One man and his dog. It was Ren and Logan who were the anomalies.

Reaching forward, Noah picked up one of the thinner branches they'd collected for the fire and getting his penknife out his pocket started whittling it down.

He heard Logan say, "Where were you before this?"

There was a pause, like Ren had to think for a moment—as if she'd been too many places to remember. "I spent last summer in Long Island staying with my friend from the ranch, Liane. She runs a motel in Montauk, so I worked for her for the season. Then in the winter I went up to Banff in Canada because the skiing's so good." Noah saw Logan nod in agreement. "Then a bit of time in Vancouver just because I'd never been there before, and then here."

Noah tried to stay focused on the carving but couldn't help being distracted by her answers.

Logan said, "Why did you come to Autumn Falls?"

Ren shrugged. "I liked the name."

Noah frowned, hand stilling on his knife.

Logan scoffed in surprise. "That's it?"

Ren nodded. "Yes."

Noah shook his head at the ridiculousness of the answer.

But then to his astonishment, across the campfire, he saw his dad lean forward and say, "You make a decision about where to live on a name?"

Ren laughed at the incredulity in his voice, "Not just a name. I guess I want to go to as many places as possible and I hadn't been anywhere around here yet."

To Noah's surprise, Emmett tipped his head and replied something that made her laugh again. Noah watched his dad then settle back into solitude, but was that a vague smile on his face? Noah couldn't believe it. Ren had somehow bewitched his father.

The evening continued in a similar vein. Noah reminding himself that solitude was the desired state while over the divide of the fire the conversation ebbed and flowed. Hank, who'd been doing his physiotherapy back stretches in his tent, came to join them. Emmett pitching in occasionally.

Noah stuck resolutely to his whittling, at first annoyed with Ren for managing to alter the status quo and get even his dad talking, annoyed with Logan for being his usual charming self, annoyed with himself for retreating further and further away. Then not annoyed with them, at all. Envious. And annoyed with himself for the envy.

As it got darker and the clouds hung thick and heavy above the mountains, Hank got out his banjo and started strumming.

Ren said, "Is someone going to sing?"

When no one obliged, she said, "I thought you boys were in a band? Noah, why don't you sing."

Noah snorted, head bent as he shaved slices of the wood. "No, thank you."

But Logan couldn't resist. "Yeah, Noah, why don't you sing?"

Noah threw him a look, would have happily got up and shoved him off the log he was sitting on. "Because I don't sing. Why don't *you* sing, Logan?"

Logan grinned. "You always had a much better voice than me."

Noah rolled his eyes. "That's the first time you've ever said that."

"It's just singing?" Ren made a face like they were being ridiculous. But Logan and Noah were in a brotherly standoff. "I'll sing if no one else will," she said.

And she sang, just like that. Completely unselfconscious. A soft sweet voice like a hummingbird with a little wobble on the top note.

Noah paused, knife stilling on the wood as he couldn't not listen. It wasn't the best voice in the world, but there was a haunting innocence to it that made it one of the most beautiful. Like listening to his mom sing. How music should be, not what it had become to the boys.

Noah felt a lump in his throat. Had to look away. He felt suddenly all sorts of memories flutter to the surface of his mind like they were drawn there by the music, snapshots of a time.

He saw the overwhelming blur of twenty thousand faces and the deafening roar of the stadium crowd, felt the crippling nerves that had him retching before every appearance, the out-of-body experience of stepping foot on stage, hands shaking, panic racing his heart, vision tunneled, and then suddenly it being over and having no memory of what happened—whole chunks of his life simply vanished into thin air.

Then suddenly he could viscerally recall the phone call to tell him Livvy was much sicker than they'd first thought. Like memories of the band didn't exist without that final heart-pounding, slow-motion flight home. The press photographer he shoved at the airport, Livvy's soft smiling eyes in her hospital bed, the angry horror of wasted months on a tour he didn't want to be on, the coolness of her hand, the beep of the machines, the suffocating rage of regret.

Noah screwed his eyes shut tight trying to rid his brain of the pictures. He kept his head down and tried to focus on the wood but found his hands were trembling and he could carve nothing.

As Ren's voice lilted in the cool air, Noah felt a familiar tightening in his chest, like the confusion of memories was pressing down on him, stopping his breath from entering his lungs. There was no escape. No barn to stalk off to, no work to consume him, he couldn't get up and leave midsong. He had to ride it out, endure the melancholy of her voice as it shivered up his spine like ghosts tapping for attention.

But then when she stopped, he felt the emptiness in the air. Found himself back exactly where he was, alone on his side of the campfire, Logan clapping enthusiastically, Emmett giving a nod of approval, even Rocky barked. Ren gestured to Hank who took a mock bow. All Noah could do was try to take a breath to calm his fast-beating heart while focusing solely on the useless bit of carving in his hand.

He heard Ren say, "That's enough excitement for me. I'm going to bed, gentlemen."

And Logan say, "Yep, me too."

Noah pretended to be deeply entrenched in whittling the piece of wood, eyes lowered, till they were gone and he could tip his head up to the wide black sky and exhale. Then he stood up, chucked the bit of wood in the fire, and went to bed.

Chapter Nine

Ren couldn't sleep. Her entire body was exhausted, but her mind was wide awake. She kept thinking about Noah sitting across from them around the campfire, head bowed, even more distant than he had been before. She thought about him telling her about his girlfriend, hearing how he would sleep in the horse barn to find peace. She should leave him to it, she knew, but there was something in the way he looked sitting around the fire that she couldn't ignore.

It reminded her of the newbies when they first arrived on the Texan ranch, young and vulnerable, before they found their tribe. Sometimes when she looked at Noah, she saw that same lost aloneness, a wary self-sufficiency that kept him apart from the world.

She knew she wasn't going to get to sleep staring up at the ceiling of her tent, so pulling on her thick purple, camo fleece, she wriggled out of her sleeping bag and, unzipping her tent, climbed outside to go and sit under the stars for a while.

It was only when she'd straightened up and started walking to the campfire that she realized Noah was already sitting there. He raised a hand—not entirely enthusiastically—when he saw her.

They had rolled some logs over earlier as seating and she went and sat at the one closest to him. "Can't sleep," she said.

He shook his head, eyes focused on the dying embers of the fire.

"No, me neither."

Silence settled in the air. She could feel the chill through her leggings and pulled her thick socks up. "I like this time of night. Sometimes I get up and go outside on my balcony at night just to look at the stars and the sky. Be reminded that it's just you and the massive wide world."

Noah sat forward, elbows braced against his knees, head hung slightly. He turned to look at her as she spoke.

She paused. He had a way of looking at her, gray eyes hooded, so she couldn't tell what he was thinking—yet at the same time, she seemed to know completely. Right then, it didn't take a genius to know he most likely thought she was talking too much. "I appreciate that might be what you're trying to do, and I'm here babbling on, ruining it."

He shook his head politely.

She didn't say anything else just looked up instead. "I haven't seen stars like that for the longest time." There wasn't a cloud in the sky just the endless milky way. Hands on the log behind her, neck cricked back she stared, trying to take it all in.

Noah looked up, too, and said, "It's pretty hard to get tired of it."

Ren gazed and gazed at the glistening blanket of stars. "Hey, that's the Big Dipper!" she pointed up to the saucepan constellation.

Noah snorted. "That's not the Big Dipper."

"Yes, it is!"

Pointing up to a completely different bit of the sky, he said, *"That's* the Big Dipper."

"Oh," she said, scrunching up her face when she saw where he was pointing. His most definitely *was* the Big Dipper. Hers in comparison looked like a shallow frying pan of stars. When she looked back at Noah, she felt a small thread of camaraderie at the mistake, which he maybe felt, too, because when he looked down at where the fingertips of his hands touched together, she wondered if she saw the hint of a smile. "Maybe I'll have better luck with Orion's Belt."

Noah raised a brow. "They the only two you know?"

"How could you tell?" Ren laughed.

"They're the only two anyone knows," he replied, and looking up again at the inky sky and pointed it out for her, along with a whole bunch of others ending with the W shape of what he was pretty certain was Cassiopeia.

Ren couldn't make out the W, but she didn't care. The fact he was talking to her was enough.

Into the silence that followed, she said, "I'm sorry about earlier, when I said you were lying about not dating famous people. I didn't know what had happened to your girlfriend." She tried to picture her. She imagined her as ethereal, with long blonde flowing hair, rosebud lips and translucent skin. Angelic and untouchable.

He shook his head. "It's okay." The embers of the fire glinted in the breeze. He sat up straighter, pushed his hair behind his ear. "I don't talk about that time much."

Ren watched him in the shadowy darkness. "I can understand that."

He glanced her way for a second, hair falling back over his eye, then almost as quickly turned away, examined the callouses on his hands.

She picked up a stick from the ground and chucked it on the fire making a cloud of sooty dust.

Noah got up off the log and kneeling in front of the fire, blew on it to get little flames to lick up around the stick she'd thrown on. She watched him, a thousand questions running around in her mind that she knew better than to ask.

She was about to ask him something innocuous about the day's ride instead, when there was a sudden commotion over by the horses, like something had startled them in the darkness.

Ren felt all the hairs on her body stand on end.

Noah jumped up from where he knelt by the fire. "I'll go check."

"I'll come." Ren stood up, too, alert now with adrenaline.

Noah went to grab a torch from his tent while Ren

pulled on her boots, then they walked over to the far side of the camp together.

The horses weren't happy. Snorting and unsettled. As Ren and Noah approached, she could hear the animals jostling, the torch light picking out the movement and the horses' wide shining eyes in the otherwise pitch black.

"It's spooky." Ren could feel a nervous pulse in her head.

"You want to wait here?" Noah asked.

"Why?" She frowned.

"Because you just said it was spooky."

"But I want to know what's going on."

That made Noah half smile in the darkness.

"Why is that funny?" she asked, wary of the utter blackness around them.

"I guess I wouldn't expect anything less."

Ren wasn't sure if it was a compliment or not, but him saying it lightened the atmosphere a fraction.

The horses seemed to have settled when they got there. Noah checked each one, swept the ground with the flashlight.

"Can you see anything?" she asked in a whisper.

"No."

Ren used the flashlight on her phone, shining it up in the trees and all around her. Then suddenly she felt the weight of Noah's arm across her body, pushing her back behind him as his voice said very softly, "Don't move."

The seriousness of his tone made her go instantly statue-still, but she let her eyes move in the direction of his flashlight and saw the rattlesnake watching. She blinked.

Noah's arm still blocked her body, his hand firm on her waist, locking her there. She wondered if he could feel her heart thumping like a drum. "What do we do?" she said, lips unmoving like a ventriloquist.

"Stand still," he replied in an equally rigid whisper, lowering the flashlight so it didn't antagonize the creature, leaving them with just the snake's outline.

One of the horses snorted. The snake seemed to flinch.

Ren inhaled sharply. Her palms were sweating.

"Try and stay calm," he murmured.

Ren's eyes adjusted to the dark and she could make the snake out clearer, watching them as they watched it. Noah had slowed his breathing, she slowed hers to match, their chests rising and falling together. She felt the pressure of his arm against her body, thought how he'd automatically stood in front of her. No one had ever done anything like that for her before. Not that she needed protecting, but the thought, the instinct, made her want to say thank you.

The minutes ticked by. The only movement seemed to be the rise and fall of their breath.

Ren had learned to be good at waiting, growing up always hoping for a miracle. She could stand there all night if she had to.

Without moving her head, she glanced at Noah, wiled away the time looking at his jaw, the dark shadow of stubble, the sharp length of his nose and the serious line of his lips. She looked at the way his hair curled behind his ear and tucked in behind the collar of his jacket. He smelled of soap and worn leather.

Above them, the clouds moved and a shaft of moonlight

shone through, picking out the pattern on the rattlesnake's back.

Noah muttered, "I hate snakes."

Ren pulled her lips tight so she didn't smile.

The snake did a lazy sway of its head.

Noah's grip tightened on her waist.

Ren's breath caught.

They stood unmoving.

A couple of minutes later, Noah said, "You okay?"

"Yes," Ren replied out the corner of her mouth.

"Wish you'd stayed in your tent?" he whispered.

"No."

She glanced across and saw him smile. Wondered how that simple thing could make her feel so good when they were facing down a rattlesnake.

Next minute, there was a movement over at the campsite, an unzipping of canvas and some heavy-footed clattering about and the snake shot away like it, too, was waiting for something to break the stalemate.

Noah dropped his hand from her waist. She felt the cool loss of it.

He swept the area with his flashlight but the snake was long gone and he tipped his head back in relief.

From the camp, a voice—Logan's—shouted, "What's that? Who's there?"

"It's us," Noah shouted.

Logan strode over, squinting in the darkness. "What's going on?"

Noah said, "Rattlesnake."

"You're kidding?" Logan's eyes widened. "Are you

okay?" he asked them both but predominantly Ren.

She nodded and said, "We were pretty lucky you came along."

Logan cocked his head and looking smugly at his brother, said, "So technically, I just saved your life?"

Noah scoffed. "We had it under control."

But his stubbornness just made Logan laugh and say with a touch of delight, "Yeah, right. I think you two are very lucky that I needed to take a leak."

Ren could feel the adrenaline of the encounter slipping away, making her shiver. Whereas Noah just shook his head, loping back to camp, chucking a casual, "Watch your step out there," to his brother, which made Logan immediately less cocky.

Wrapping her arms around herself as she followed Noah back to camp, Ren couldn't decide if she was relieved or sad that the moment had ended.

Noah paused in front of her tent, hands in the back pockets of his jeans. "You going to be okay on your own?"

There was a beat of awkward silence where the question could have been misconstrued. Ren's lips twitched while Noah rolled his eyes at the idea he was being anything other than gentlemanly.

"I'll be fine, thank you," she replied.

He gave a small nod of his head. "Well, if you need anything—"

He pointed toward his own tent and again looked a touch despairing as she held in a smile and said, "I'll be okay, but thanks."

But once inside her tent, Ren felt weirdly alone. She

wasn't someone to rely on others, but she could still feel the comfort of the protective pressure of his arm across her body and the synchronicity of their breath. Like now she'd felt it, she was sad it was gone, whereas before she hadn't even known it existed. She lay on her back thinking that was probably how she felt about Loriana. If you'd never had something, it was harder to miss it. That was why it was easier to stay closed off. Open her heart just a crack, and Ren's fear was that everything she'd ever hoped for would come tumbling out.

Chapter Ten

The next morning, Ren woke up to Noah shouting, "Get up. Let's get out of here!"

The weather was atrocious. Sheet rain hammered on her tent and she poked her head out to see rivulets of water snaking through the camp soaking anything that had been left out.

Noah, wearing a long dark green slicker, was emptying out pots and bowls, chucking everything into bags.

Ren dressed as fast as she could. It was cold as well as wet. She kept her leggings on under her jeans, piled on every layer she'd brought with her and wrapped Loriana's scarf around her neck. Then she rummaged through her bag and pulled out her rain jacket. It was a vibrant vermilion and hard to miss. She yanked it on and zipped up before stepping out. The color made Noah pause for a fraction of a second when she climbed out her tent, but he made no comment.

Logan however appeared from his tent, dark hair all

over the place, and when he saw her said, "You look like a giant strawberry."

Ren laughed. "That was the look I was going for." As she got to work dismantling her tent, Logan screwed up his face against the downpour and muttered, "No one said anything about rain."

Emmett appeared at the same time, clad in his long black jacket, gray hair neatly swept to the side. "I've said a fair bit about rain, but everyone chose not to listen."

Logan stifled a groan. Ren looked over and caught Noah's eye and to her surprise he winked, as if apologizing for his dad and bringing her in on the brotherhood at the same time.

The rain got harder. The landscape all around was shrouded in thick mist, the clouds low like rolling gray smoke.

Ren's fingers, cold and soaking, struggled with the fiddlier bits of taking down her tent and annoyingly her hood kept slipping back making rainwater trickle down her spine.

Noah came by on his way to the horses, Rocky sloping along at his heels. "You need a hand?"

"No, I got it, thanks," she replied, jerking back as a particularly stubborn peg came loose.

Noah put down what he was carrying and came over to help her anyway. He had his leather jacket on under his slicker, both zipped up almost to his nose, his dripping wet hair refusing to stay tucked behind his ears. "Quicker with two," he said, matter-of-factly.

She didn't say anything, but felt herself smile inside, wondering if he would have helped her the day before.

Two tents over from Ren's, Logan pulled his hood down low over his hat and muttered, "This is a nightmare."

Hank, whose bad back had clearly slowed him down when getting dressed, came creaking out of his tent and looking up at the sky said, "I like a bit of rain. Makes me feel alive."

"I feel pretty alive when the sun's shining," Logan replied humorlessly.

Striding over to the horses, Noah called, "Stop gassing and get moving!"

Logan grumbled as he packed up the last of his soaked belongings.

With her tent dismantled and packed away, Ren went over to help Hank.

"You are a sweetheart," he said, wincing as he bent over to pack up his belongings.

"Are you sure you should ride?" she asked.

"Riding's the only time it feels better," Hank replied, eyes crinkling when he smiled.

They set off under a thunderous sky. A shaft of morning sunlight lit the grass like emeralds, while above them, huge slate clouds churned with the foreboding of an angry god.

Ren was back on Star who did not enjoy the rain. "She doesn't seem to like getting her feet wet," Ren said to Noah as they saddled up.

"Introduce her to Logan," he quipped, tying his pack down and hoisting himself up on Blue in a movement as smooth as breathing.

"Hilarious," Logan muttered, his furry hat so low on his head that Ren could barely see his eyes.

"Let's keep this moving!" Emmett called from up ahead, which made Noah's eyes widen because that was what he'd been saying all morning.

The herd had bunched together but weren't particularly bothered by the downpour, more interested in the patches of thick long grass.

Ahead of them, however, water was cascading down the mountain taking the loose, previously dry earth with it and running through the pines in thick, muddy rivulets.

Noah and Emmett had a row about the best route to take in the rain, given the bleak picture ahead of them. When they didn't seem able to reach a conclusion, Logan got involved which seemed to make matters worse. She saw Noah throw his hands up in the air and Logan shake his head back, their voices lost in the wind.

Ren stayed back with Hank, who said, "Best to leave them to it."

Ren watched them bickering, Emmett shaking his head, framed by the grisly clouds in the distance, the dog moving restlessly between them ready to go.

She turned to Hank as they waited side by side. His horse today, Moby, huge and gray, was completely unaffected by the rain and stood stoic as a carthorse ready for a wagon. "Do they do this a lot?"

"Oh, yeah." Hank laughed. The rain had made his mustache form little points above his lip. "They can have some real belters. But then, I guess, what family doesn't?"

Ren tucked her nose down into Loriana's scarf, felt the

soft warmth and smelled the perfume, and wondered what it was like to have a big sprawling family, lots of opinions that had to be listened to, connections that would be there throughout their lives whatever happened.

"They've had some tough times, though, the Carter family," Hank carried on, giving a small shake of his head.

"I read about what happened to Jack," Ren said.

Hank nodded, the rain dripped from the brim of his hat. "Terrible. And then there's Ethan. Packed up and joined the SEALS and I couldn't say if he's been back since."

Ren looked ahead at where Noah, Emmett and Logan still couldn't agree. "Did he leave after Silver Sky broke up?"

Hank nodded. "If you were to ask Emmett, he'd say that band brought nothing but trouble. Nearly broke him, that's for sure—all of his boys going off around the world." He looked at Ren with his big sad eyes. "Ranching is about family."

Her own experience on a ranch was fighting for her place in the world among children who were all fighting for theirs, but she didn't say that to Hank. "Noah's there now, though, isn't he?"

"Oh, yeah. It saved Emmett when Noah came home," Hank agreed. "They might argue—" as if on cue, Noah tipped his head up to the sky in frustration at something his dad said "—but they work darn well together. It's Noah who brought that ranch back from the brink, because there was a time when none of us thought it would survive. It'd been a strong operation before those boys left and they sent money back, of course, but you gotta love something to want to work at it. And for a while there, Emmett had no love left for it."

The sky above gave a rumble of thunder and Hank looked up warily. Then he shouted up to where the Carters were still arguing. "Make up your minds! We can't hang around all day!"

They all ignored him.

Ren's horse appeared not to enjoy thunder, either, and needed calming down, but Ren wanted to hear everything she could about the Carters, drank it in with fascination because they were everything she'd never had, it was like getting a behind the scenes of a favorite TV show. "But now Logan's back for good, too?"

"Sure is," Hank said, "and with Bella, too, which is just wonderful."

"So, Emmett must be happy about that?"

Hank tipped his head, uncertain.

Ren glanced up at Emmett, watched him pulling on the reins moving into position at the front of the herd. "You think he forgives them?" she asked.

"Who knows. He'd never admit it, but they broke his heart. No doubt about it."

"What's that you're saying, Hank?" The question came with a gallop of hooves, and Noah appeared beside them. "We're moving on."

"About time," replied Hank, gathering up his reins.

Ren, who would never want it to seem like they were talking behind Noah's back, said, "Hank was just filling me in on the Carter family history."

From Noah's expression, which was barely visible

because his hat was tilted so low, it was hard to tell if he was happy about that or not. "Hank's always liked a good old gossip, haven't you, Hank?" he said, slapping the older man on the back.

Hank bristled. Water dripping from his mustache as he pursed his lips and said, "The girl's got a right to know who she's riding with, and talking to you and Emmett's like getting blood out of a stone."

Noah raised his brows, a cocky half-smile on his lips at Hank's defensiveness, but he didn't say anything more, just swung Blue around to corral the straggling cattle at the back of the herd and shouted, "Come on, let's go!"

Ruffled from having been wound up by Noah, Hank moved up to the flanks with Logan, ushering the cattle forward toward the thick bank of rolling black clouds.

Excited that they were finally on the move, Rocky stayed up at the front with Emmett.

Ren stayed on her own at the back, unfairly chastened by Noah's accusation that they'd been gossiping about his family.

She was fond of the cows at the back, they weren't always the same ones, but more often than not there was a fat black one that idled along with no impetus to hurry and drove Noah to distraction, and then a naughtier brown one with one white sock who kept veering off into the trees whenever possible and had to be brought back. Much to Noah's disdain, Ren had named her Mildred. It made her laugh, every time there was a tree in sight, off Mildred went making Noah shake his head in despair.

She settled into the rhythm of the morning, the rain

unceasing, the front of the herd shrouded in mist. Then she heard Noah say, "Hank tell you everything you wanted to know?" as he came up beside her. There was an edge to his tone, like he wanted to make sure she knew never to go there again.

It immediately put her back up. "Noah, we were just killing time while you three were bickering. But I'll tell you one thing for nothing, I'm never going to not ask questions if I want to know something and I'm *never* going to be blamed for doing so, you hear me?"

She saw his jaw tighten.

"I grew up in a place where the rule was that they spoke and we listened. We weren't allowed to ask questions, and if we did, we didn't get answers. So I go on the principle that if you want to know, you ask. Understand me?"

As she glared at him, she saw his nostrils flare and he blew out a breath as if he'd just had a telling off that he wasn't expecting. "I don't take kindly to people talking about my business."

"Noah, you don't seem to take kindly to people talking about anything. And you want to know something else?"

"Not really."

"Well, I'll tell you anyway. In my opinion, more often than not, silence is something folk hide behind." She adjusted her hat and rode defiantly on with her nose in the air. He could wallow at the back in his bad mood all he liked.

Chapter Eleven

The rain didn't ease up any, but the air got warmer, the sun trying to burn its way through the thicket of clouds made it gradually feel like they were stuck in an oven. Steam rose off their damp jackets as they were forced to shed layers, till finally Ren wore just a vest and her waterproof, and even then she was sweating.

When Emmett stopped the herd earlier than anticipated, Ren watched as Noah galloped up to see what was going on.

She moved around to hang out with Logan, who took his hat off, wiped the sweat from his forehead, and said, "Hot rain, who thought it could get any worse?"

Ren laughed as she gulped down water from her bottle.

They sat waiting, watching the rain in dark lines on the horizon. Some of the cattle drank from a giant puddle that spread across the plain, water dripping from their wet, matted coats, their legs caked with mud.

Noah came charging back on Blue saying, "Mom rang

on the satellite phone to say the road's blocked—there's landslip and there are trees down from all the water—they can't get through so—"

"Are they all okay?" Logan asked, clearly concerned about Bella.

"Yeah, they're fine," Noah replied with a frown like his brother was focusing on completely the wrong thing. "It's us who aren't going to get any supplies. No lunch, no dinner."

Logan flung his arms out wide, tipped his head back and said, "This just gets better and better!" Then his hat fell off and he had to dismount to get it, which made Noah smirk.

Ren said, "We've got food, though, right?"

"Yeah, like protein bars and stuff—" Noah shrugged "—but nothing that tastes of anything."

"You could skin us a rabbit," Logan suggested dryly.

Noah raised a condescending brow. "Haha."

Ren rolled her eyes. "Seriously, though, we could always fish."

Noah gestured her way and said, "See, a sensible suggestion."

Logan made a face like his jokey suggestion was being unfairly dismissed. "You're just taking her side 'cause she's prettier."

Noah opened his mouth, but no reply came. Instead, to what seemed like everyone's surprise, he blushed. And when he saw it, Logan's eyes sparkled gleefully.

Noah didn't hang around after that, just swung Blue around and focused on getting the herd moving again, while Logan looked at Ren and, with a low rumble of laughter, winked before riding off in the opposite direction.

She found herself glancing back, feeling a strange tingle of excitement at Noah's reaction, which was confusingly at odds with how she'd been feeling about him since he accused her of gossiping.

Time ticked by slower as the weather heated and the rain increased. The cattle trudged through what was now all soft mud beneath their feet. Star didn't like the mud or the weather and kept pulling on the reins. Ren could feel the exhaustion in her arms and back, while sweat trickled down her spine. She was ravenous. She could barely see the others up ahead.

But then Noah appeared out of the mist and came around next to her, his T-shirt rain-soaked and sticking to his chest, his arms glistening.

"Thought you might be hungry." The way he said it, it almost felt like a peace offering. And he reached into his pack and chucked her a granola bar.

"Thanks." She caught it, one hand still on the reins. She'd played a lot of baseball on the ranch as a kid and was a great catcher, but even so, there was also no way she was going to drop anything Noah threw at her. For some reason with him, everything felt like a challenge that she was determined she wasn't going to lose.

He took a granola bar out for himself and when he'd torn the wrapping off with his teeth, he said, "I'm sorry." Ren glanced over with surprise, but didn't say anything. "I'm not good at talking about anything to do with the band. I know that. And I knew what Hank was saying and I didn't like it."

Mouth full of granola, she shrugged. Then when she'd swallowed, she said, "It sounded to me like he was just telling the truth."

"Well, I'd prefer if he just kept his mouth shut."

"Sometimes you know, Noah, it's better to get things out in the open. Sunlight is the best disinfectant."

"I have no idea what that means."

"Yeah, you do," she said, like he was being deliberately obtuse. "Say things out loud and it makes them better."

"That work for you?"

She thought what a fraud she was. "Sometimes."

Noah ate his granola bar in two bites. Then he turned to look out ahead, the mist enveloping them, the grassy earth beneath the animals' hooves now carved up into thick divots of mud. "I prefer to get on with work."

"I'll bet you do."

Noah threw her a wry look.

She looked him up and down, a solid figure on the back of Blue, shoulders wide in his T-shirt, hat super low, expression always on the cusp of serious, and she grinned. "You know something? I can't imagine you singing and dancing in that band."

Noah rolled his head her way, one brow raised. "Let me get one thing straight, there was no dancing."

She smiled wider. "You don't like dancing, Noah?"

"No, I do not."

Ren gazed ahead at the black sea of wet, matted cattle. "Oh, I love to dance."

"Now why doesn't that surprise me."

She laughed, glancing back at him and found there was something about the despairing look he gave her that caused a warm feeling in her stomach. It was because, as his eyes creased at the side, she realized it wasn't only despair in his gaze but also perhaps a small flicker of endearment.

At that moment however, his cell phone rang. "I didn't think there was any signal," he said, fumbling to get it out of his pocket. "Hello. What? Sorry, no I can't hear you—" He took the phone away from his ear and looked at the screen. "She's gone. No signal."

"Who was it?"

"Willow."

"You didn't hear what she wanted?" Ren asked.

"No." Noah put the phone back in his pocket. "If it's urgent she'll call Dad on the satellite phone."

Chapter Twelve

The animals sensed it before they did.

Before Noah saw Logan up ahead yank the reins of his horse to swing around and shout words that they couldn't hear.

Before Hank's old horse, Moby, reared up and nearly toppled the old man out the saddle.

Before the sky darkened and the rain stung and the thunder cracked, echoing off the mountain and bringing with it wind like Noah had never felt before. In a second, Ren's hat had gone. She cried out in jokey alarm as she tried to catch it. "You ever had weather like this before?"

Noah was about to reply that it had never been this bad, but the wind suddenly pummeled harder through the trees and the rain lashed in a gale-force frenzy. He saw splinters of wood and broken branches sweep past them and, as his hat went as well, he shouted, "Get down!"

Up ahead, only the tone of Logan's voice carried in the wind.

And then they saw it, twisting dark and gray on the horizon, a curl of destruction heading their way, frothy clouds at its base, a column of spiraling hot wind, black against the gray sky, lightning flashing in bright bursts.

"Noah! It's heading this way!" Ren cried out.

Noah could feel his heart hammering as he looked around, tried to take in the situation, *this* had never happened to him before. On one side of them were trees, on the other, the vast undulating plains. "You need to take cover," he shouted, pointing toward the pine forest away from the path of the spiraling wind. "Get in there and get down."

Up ahead, spooked, the herd had split. Logan and Hank tried to corral the frightened cattle out of the path of the tornado and into the trees.

The cows around Noah scattered in panic as debris flung through the air, branches torn from trees nearly knocking him off-balance. "Get over there!" Noah shouted at Ren as he kicked Blue into action, trying to round up the skittish cattle, ushering them together, urging them out of the swirling black path up ahead.

But Ren didn't go. She stayed and went to round up the strays that were frantic in the mist and the rain and the lightning.

"Leave them!" he shouted again, but his voice was lost in the wind, and then he couldn't see her, the driving wind and the rain too strong.

What was she doing?

"Leave it to me!" he yelled. Branches tumbling and twisting through the air, one hitting hard against his shoulder almost unsaddling him. He couldn't see his dad or Logan but presumed they'd head to the trees, the wind tugged at the skin on his face, ripped at his jacket.

Then she came into view. "If you're doing it, I'm doing it!" she shouted back, urging the frightened cattle away from the path of the most violent wind.

All Noah could see was black destruction on the horizon, whipping up the landscape, the sky darkening with every second, the rain getting heavier and blurring his vision. But not enough that he didn't catch Ren double back when the darn pain-in-the-ass little cow that had been causing trouble since they started bolted off in the opposite direction. "Leave her!" he roared, furious. "Get to shelter!" But Ren was gone.

He wiped his face with his hands and went after her. Looking around for a flash of her red coat but seeing only wind-tumbled mist and rain, the impossibly muddy ground slipping beneath them. He couldn't see Ren anywhere. He shouted her name. Saw a huddle of stray cattle and, galloping over, ushered them together into the relative safety of the trees. But still no sight of her. Through the mist, he could see the black twisting force looming on the horizon, saw with a flicker of hope it veering away from them. "Go," he muttered, skin stinging as he watched it snaking its path over the plain. "Please." Then whipping his head around, he hollered, "Ren! Where are you?"

He could feel his heart thumping at the idea of her injured, she was his responsibility. Why the heck hadn't she listened? He was furious with her. Stupid, stubborn woman. Twigs, debris, branches hurtling in the wind catching his face, slicing into his cheek, he thought of her knocked off-balance, lying in the mud just to save that dumb-ass cow.

Heading back out into the wind, Noah shouted for her again and again. The rain blocked his vision, the wind stung his eyes. Blue pushed stoically on. Noah squinted for a glimpse of the bright red rain slicker. He rode back the way he'd come, the wind stronger and stronger. Nothing. He pulled Blue around, shielding his eyes as he scoured the area. He should never have let her come. What was he thinking? The wind got stronger, the visibility worse, his clothes pulling against his sides, Blue staggering under the force, a huge branch tumbled through the air just missing his head.

"Ren!" he shouted again, voice hoarse. The erratic swirl of the twister dragging across the landscape. "Move away, dammit," he muttered again, riding into the battering wind, searching. He felt the same engulfing powerlessness he had in the midst of Silver Sky, when it felt like his life had been snatched out of his control. When he woke up and didn't know which country he was in, on a tour that he didn't know what day it was, when they worked twenty hours a day, six or seven days a week, tiredness cracking his mind, with nothing tangible to show for it except money that he didn't want and couldn't spend even if he did. When he was out in the middle of the night looking for his younger brother Ethan, after getting a mumbled phone call and dragging him out of a dumpster, face battered, looking as vulnerable as he did when he was a little kid, and slurring, "Don't tell anyone." Or Brodie inviting half the audience back to their hotel room when all Noah wanted to do was go to bed and sleep for a hundred years but there were all these girls and the music was loud and the lights were dark and everyone seemed to want to touch him, hands grasping, and he couldn't get away.

He heard the crack of a pine tree as a branch crashed to the ground with a shudder across the earth. Blue reared back at the impact.

"Ren!" Noah hollered again, rain lashing at his face, hands raw from the reins. Then he saw it, the bright red jacket, like a beacon. Ren with her head down pushing with all her will and determination against the wind, and that pain-in-the-backside cow lassoed alongside her, and Star, ears pressed back, eyes wild, struggling against the force of the gale.

With a mix of red-hot fury and relief, Noah raced over, snatched the rope off Ren and dragged the little cow toward the trees with one hand, using Blue to urge Star forward. "What were you *thinking*!" he shouted. "You are the most—"

But the wind made it impossible to speak. The words were torn from his mouth. He couldn't hear Ren's reply, just saw her face scratched and pale. Saying anything seemed suddenly futile, the twister bearing a path in their wake, so Noah pressed his free hand against her back and together they battled against the force of the wind toward the precarious shelter of the forest, branches flying, wind pummeling like fists, until finally they were in the trees. Noah jumped off Blue, hauling Ren down before she had a chance to do it herself, letting go of the lasso so the little brown cow bolted off to its sheltering herd.

"Of all the stupid things—" he started.

Ren swept her hair from her face, holding it back with her hand. "I had to rescue Mildred!" she shouted.

Blood pumped wild in Noah's head. "You could've been killed!"

"So could you!"

The wind got louder and closer, the branches of the pines thrashing wildly above them.

"You're so frustrating," he shouted.

"So are you!"

Suddenly, there was a deafening crack and above them the tree split clean in two, the giant weight of the whole top half smashing through the other branches as it came crashing down.

Noah felt Ren grab a fist of his jacket and yank him to her and he stumbled forward, mid-insult, as the falling tree slammed to the ground, echoing around him. He threw his arm around her and pushed them both down, the branch bouncing up a fraction and thumping back with an earth-shattering boom within feet of where they'd been arguing.

Neither Ren nor Noah moved.

They stayed like on pause, wrapped together. Noah couldn't say if it was shock or fear or a feeling of pure helplessness in the face of destiny that left them braced together, while outside of the forest, the wind ripped through the open countryside, and above them, the force of the gale sucked the leaves from the trees, rattling Noah's bones.

Without thinking, he pressed his arm tighter around her as she curled into a ball, the trunk that had nearly killed them now giving them a precarious shelter. Heads together. They didn't speak. He could hear her teeth chattering, smell the rain on her jacket and the sweetness of her shampoo. Feel his own heart thumping, and his palms sweating as he tried to push down the clawing fear. He pictured his dad and Logan and Hank, imagined them struggling for cover, prayed that they were safe, felt the clenching fear inside him that something might have happened, might still happen. He thought of everything he'd said to Logan so far, all the banter and one-upmanship, what if he didn't make it through? Was that how it would end? That made him think about his brother Jack, who Noah hadn't spoken to for years before he died. Who Noah'd deliberately distanced himself from because it was too hard to disassociate Jack with how he'd treated him in the band—how, to a certain extent, he'd treated all of them, like his brothers were just stepping stones in the scramble to the top. But it was Noah, somehow, who took the brunt of it, because he was so clearly the one who was least comfortable. If things went wrong, Jack would always point the finger of blame at him, the easiest target. When Noah had heard the news that Jack had died, his first thought was *let me call him one last time*. Just let me speak to him. But there was no chance to hear his voice again, not unless he watched one of his movies, which he couldn't bring himself to do. Sometimes, Noah came into the ranch house and heard the TV suddenly shut off and he knew his mom was watching one of Jack's movies. She'd come into the kitchen red-eyed, pretending nothing had happened.

His dad had no truck with tears. Hadn't shed any, as far

as Noah knew, about Jack. The day he'd heard the news, Emmett had held his mom as she wept and done everything she needed, but then he'd walked straight out to the yard as he always did, didn't stop for a second. It was the exact textbook Emmett reaction that all Noah's siblings would've predicted. But it was only Noah who had gone for a ride a couple of days after the funeral along the Redemption River heading toward Halfmoon Lake, where the boys used to build camps and fish and stay up all night telling ghost stories. As he'd approached, he stumbled quite by accident on the sight of Emmett, head in his hands, hunched over on a rock at the water's edge, in the exact spot where he had taught the boys casting, his hands around them in as close to a hug as they would ever get. Noah would have given anything to have gone and sat with him,. but he was too uncertain of the reception he'd have gotten were he to dismount and walk over. So instead, he'd watched for a second or two longer then turned his horse around and gone quietly back the way he came.

Now, as the wind whipped violently around them, Noah squeezed his eyes shut thinking about what he'd overheard Hank say to Ren about the boys breaking his dad's heart. So many of his brothers struggled with their relationship with Emmett, but not Noah. Noah loved his dad, looked up to him, wanted him to be happy. Hated the fact he had ever deserted him and the ranch in favor of his brothers and the band. Wished, in retrospect, that he had realized what he had, what he loved, and never left.

Noah didn't want to think of the destruction if the tornado hit the forest. He thought of his family at home, his mom and Willow frantic. And Loriana would be fretting about Hank. And Bella... It was Noah who'd persuaded them all to come on the cattle drive. Logan didn't even want to be there. Him and Bella were just starting their lives together.

And what about Rocky? His heart contracted at the idea of something happening to the dog.

Noah could feel the clawing claustrophobia he'd battled in the band pressing down on him, sparks of light in his eyes, his brain whirring uncontrollably. Alert and on guard twenty-four-seven. Barely sleeping. He felt the rising nausea. Remembered the hours spent on his own, fifteen years old, locked in a hotel room bathroom, shaking, waiting for the panic to reach its peak and subside. Or when it didn't, one of his brothers hammering on the door, hauling him out, someone pushing him into a chair for hair and makeup while he'd vomit in a bucket. Jack's voice shouting, "Just get it together!" Logan trying to pacify. Brodie trying to make a joke, all while Noah's vision swam in and out of black.

He didn't think the wind could get any stronger, but it did, battering against them. He felt his lungs constrict, and just as he wondered if he might never be able to breathe again, he felt Ren reach over and clutch his hand. And the way Noah was feeling, he gripped it back, tight, almost white-knuckle, and he felt the comfort of that cool, tight grip in his. Allowed his breathing to slow and his speeding pulse to lessen, allowed the overwhelming panic to recede. He found himself able to imagine his dad and the others tucked up somewhere sheltering from the storm, he could channel the hope that the main force of the wind would be pulled away across the plain. The simple contact of Ren's palm against his give him pause, created a bridge between them that somehow lessened the fear, and he found himself focusing his every thought on the sensation of that touch, the tightness of it, the press of her fingers, the softness of the back of her hand—and in contrast to how small and fragile she looked from the outside, the solid strength of her grip. Under normal circumstances he would have been the first to pull away, but in that moment, he simply couldn't let go.

Chapter Thirteen

Noah didn't know how long they stayed there, a rain-soaked, wind-lashed huddle. But when he felt the force of the wind lessening, he looked at their joined hands and found himself more than a little unnerved, ashamed even, by the necessity of it.

He let go of her hand as subtly as he could and looked around, the wind still battering, but out of the forest he could just glimpse a thunderous gray horizon, the tornado had either lost its force and broken up or had taken a course away across the plain.

"Are you okay?" He had to shout above the noise of the wind.

Beside him, Ren looked up, her hair wild and windswept, her face scratched, her raincoat torn and eyes dazed. She nodded. "You?"

The wind shook the pine trees ominously above them.

He could see the tears on her thick black lashes.

"Yeah."

They edged out into the open forest, standing up, their hair sweeping in front of their faces, clothes sodden and crumpled by the weather, the rain still driving down. Ren looked behind her at the horses and the cattle bunched together under the pines. Noah looked, too, and saw the little brown cow with the rope still around her neck. Shaking his head he shouted, "I can't believe you went back for her."

Ren open her mouth to protest, but Noah found himself cutting her off with a seriousness that overtook any of his previous anger, "*Never* risk your life like that again."

Ren's eyes widened in surprise at the tone, Noah himself was actually surprised by the urgency of it, and instead of objecting he saw her face suddenly soften and her bottom lip tremble as she nodded.

Then before he knew it, tears were streaming down her face, her hands not quick enough to wipe them away, her cheeks blotching, her shoulders shaking.

Noah was not good with tears. He wished they were still in their protective ball, huddled together and he'd said nothing. "Please don't cry. I didn't mean to make you cry."

Ren shook her head. "You didn't." She wiped her nose with her raincoat sleeve. More tears, more trembling lips, more internal agony for Noah. "I was just so scared. I'm sorry." She pulled her cuff over her hand and tried uselessly to dry her face, the rain still hammering. "I'm sorry, I just, I went back to get her and then I was lost and I could hear you and I knew that you'd be mad but I couldn't let her go out there on her own. And then…" She paused for a shaky breath.

Noah dug around in his pocket for a tissue but found only the granola-bar wrapper. It was too wet and windy to stand out in the open and he gestured for them to go back into the relative shelter of the fallen pine tree, the large fronds like a canopy above them.

It was quieter tucked under the branch again. She said, voice shaking, "When the tree fell, Noah, I thought we were going to die." She looked up at him with her big watery blue eyes, her expression as wide open as a child's. "I've never been so scared in my whole life."

Noah knew he should probably hug her. That any normal person would hug her right now. Logan would envelop her in some huge, comforting embrace and stroke her hair and make her feel better, he'd have a tissue in his pocket or a monogrammed handkerchief. But Noah just had a scrunched-up granola-bar wrapper and his own receding fear. The memory of being huddled together mere minutes ago already felt like a dream. It had been so long since he'd had to share emotion with another human being that to touch her felt like too bold a step. "I know," he said in the end and found one of his hands reaching forward in a vague but useless attempt at comfort.

Ren wiped her face with her sleeve. "I'm okay." She took a deep breath, "Honestly. Stupid to cry." She gave him what looked like a very forced smile and then, looking around her at the destruction of the forest, the fallen branches and rivers of water, said, "What about the others?"

Noah didn't know. It would be crazy to try and search for them in this wind, the only safe option was to stay put but the idea of heading out—of escaping—sent a sudden flood of relief through him. He felt the pull of the open forest, away from the suffocating fear of their experience, the feelings, the reliance. Ahead of him was a rugged expanse of freedom, like a cool drink of water.

He looked at Ren, biting down on her lip, tear tracks still on her face, eyes red-rimmed and then, uneasy at the sight of her, at the tightening in his own chest, he stuck his head out from under the canopy and saw Blue standing head down, braced against the weather at the base of one of the great pines. He gazed almost longingly at the possibility of leaving, felt every muscle in his body urging him forward, but it was lunacy, he couldn't do it to his horse, or himself.

Instead, he hunkered down again, and, against his better judgment, took another quick glance at Ren, saw the tiny crooked-teeth half-smile of her relief—as if she could tell that he was considering going and leaving her there alone, and he felt again the chest-tightening conflict of being needed and the shame that he had contemplated going.

Ren said, "I think I just heard your phone."

Surprised out of his own pressing thoughts, Noah fumbled in his pocket to get his phone out and there was a message from Logan: *Are you safe? Is Ren with you? Me, Dad, Hank, Rocky, we're all safe.*

Noah tipped his head back against the bark, relief flowing through him like he'd never experienced before. He showed it to Ren who leaned her head forward so it rested on his arm, like she, too, had been holding it together in fear. He felt the contact like he had with their clasped hands; he wanted to pull away but at the same time didn't want to move.

He messaged Logan back that they were safe, having to stand up and brace against the storm to get a signal.

When he sat back down again it felt different. Ren had wrapped her raincoat around herself, tied back her hair that was escaping in wild tendrils from the wind. There was a feeling like this was it, they had to sit it out, together. With the worry for the others dissipating, it was just the two of them for however long it took and that brought with it a whole other set of feelings that Noah didn't want to contemplate. The urge to flee on his horse once more lodged in his throat.

But thinking suddenly of Logan's message he looked at Ren and said, "Are you hurt in any way?"

Ren looked down at herself, as if she hadn't thought about possible injuries. Then she shook her head. "No. Are you?"

In the near distance, they heard a crack and then the ground shook with another great thud of a fallen tree. It made Noah lurch suddenly forward and grasp onto Ren, grabbing her around the back, one hand behind her head. But the fall wasn't close enough to cause them any harm.

He immediately let her go. Saw something in her eyes that made him have to look away and exhale—gratitude. Same as when they'd been standing together facing down the rattlesnake. It reminded him of when they'd looked at the stars—he hadn't wanted to look at the stars with her, he'd seen the stars every night of his life, but then he found himself drawn into her wonder when she gazed up at the sky but also laughing at her complete misidentification of the constellations. He didn't want to be laughing. Same as he didn't want to be caring.

"This ever happened to you before?" she asked.

"It's been bad before," he replied, "but never like this." As if on cue the rain seemed to double in volume. "Last year it was bright sunshine," he added, still having to keep his voice raised above the noise.

He saw her teeth chattering as she spoke, "Well, I burn really easily, so this is probably better for me."

He laughed despite himself. "You always look on the bright side, huh?" he said, incredulous that she'd managed to find one in that instance.

"Try to," Ren said. "Plenty of times life's going to be bad and I'm not adding to them."

He glanced at her, one brow raised and said, "I think you can say this is bad."

That made her laugh.

Making her laugh gave him an unexpected rush of pleasure. Even if there was a slightly manic edge to it, like they were both high on their own panic.

When a gust of wind bellowed with the force of an express train, Ren shifted around so she was tight next to him, back against the trunk, arms wrapped around her knees. "Okay, it's really bad," she shouted.

As he felt her pressed against him, he felt the unaccustomed urge to lift his arm and wrap it around her, just for the closeness. Yes, it was bad.

Chapter Fourteen

Ren didn't want to be trapped sheltering under a tree with Noah in the storm. But at the same time, she couldn't in that moment think of someone she'd rather be trapped with. She didn't want to need him and yet, every time the wind felt like it was going to crush the sky on top of them or smash the whole forest down, she had never been more grateful for the solid strength of him.

When he'd countered her positive thinking with, "This is bad," it reminded her of arriving on the Texas ranch for the first time when she was seven years old. The stomach-clenching terror of being new and alone still haunted her dreams even now. Lying in her bunk bed that first night, exhausted and filled with an all-consuming foreboding that she would be trapped in that place for the rest her life, body trembling uncontrollably, a sudden scrap of hope came when the covers on her bed lifted and the girl in the bunk above hers, Liane, climbed into bed with her, freezing feet squished next to hers, and said with a knowing smile,

"It might seem bad but there are some good bits, I promise." Then told her all about what it was like as Ren listened, no less terrified, but no longer alone.

It was the same when she had reached for Noah's hand, the bellowing wind all around them, and felt him clasp hers back.

She tried not to think too much about the way his hand had felt in hers. The cool, roughness of it, the callouses on his palm, the strength, a workman's hand. She'd had it so rarely before—a tether to hold tight to when times were tough—that each time she did, it found a place in the shelves of her mind to be secretly prized and treasured.

But vulnerability was something that Ren, like her friends at the ranch, had learned to avoid. Liane, the oldest of their gang, doled out infinite wisdom that the rest of them hung off. She'd boldly say things like, "Never cry, never care," even as she wiped the tears away herself.

Right now, however, Ren felt very vulnerable. She couldn't stop her hands from shaking or her teeth chattering. She thought how safe she had felt when they had been wrapped together in the height of the storm. How time had slowed and speeded up and she had thought, I wasn't brave enough to tell my mother who I was before I died.

Another branch crashed to the ground and she jumped. Outside of the canopy she could hear the cattle lowing and the horses whinny in fear.

"Are you scared?" she asked feeling her heart thumping in her chest.

"A bit," he replied.

She looked up at him, saw his mouth tip up as if that were an understatement. "Me too," she said.

"We'll be okay," he said.

"You sure about that?"

"No."

That made her laugh. But then quickly suck in a gasp of air when something swept past, hitting the fallen branch with a loud bang and shaking their shelter.

Noah said, "You want to try one of your conversations?"

She was still trying to get her breath back and snorted with surprise. "Okay."

"Okay," he replied.

She turned to see his face. He looked like he was trying to look calmer for her benefit. "Do you want to go first or should I?"

"I think you're better at it than me."

"What do you want to do if you get out of here alive?"

"We're going to get out of here alive."

"You certain?" she asked.

"Yes." Then as if remembering the rules he said, "What do you want to do *when* you get out of here alive?"

"Deflection. I like what you did there." She smiled, body shivering with adrenaline, and though he looked down at the ground, she saw him smile. What she wanted to do was be brave enough to march right into the diner and say, "Loriana I need to talk to you." But she didn't want to tell Noah that so she said, "I've got a lot of places on my list still to see."

"Oh, yeah? Like where?"

"Everywhere!" she said, swiping her rain-soaked hair

from her face. "Name a place and I want to go there. I bet you've been to loads of places."

Water was trickling down underneath them from the mountain now, puddles forming in the previously dry earth.

"Too many," he replied.

"You didn't like to travel?" She frowned, tipping her head up so she could really get a proper look at him.

Noah's mouth was a thin unimpressed line. "I saw the world three times over and let's just say it was enough for me," he said starkly.

"But what about all the different things to see, all the sights and the sounds and the foods?"

He shook his head, his hair was slicked back from the rain, eyes obscured in the dark shade of the branch. "I've been followed through enough airports, chased down enough streets. I'm happy where I am."

She nodded, wondering what that would be like, to want to stay rooted to one place, to have found what you were looking for.

He glanced over, "What?"

"What do you mean?"

"You've gone quiet. You're never quiet."

She bit her lip to hold in a smile. The wind roared through the branches scattering pine needles all over them. She didn't want to tell him what she was thinking, so she said, "I was thinking that band sounds like it really did a number on you."

It was his turn to laugh, clearly caught unexpectedly by the comment.

He wiped his face again from the rain and said, "It wasn't the best time of my life."

From the outside, growing up, looking at the pictures in magazines or scrolling through images, she would have considered his life perfect. "What about all the people and the lifestyle and the private jets?"

He rolled his head her way, said, "I'd take a horse over a jet anytime."

She laughed. Their eyes met in the shadowy darkness. Rain-soaked faces smiling as the storm raged. "Me, too," she replied.

Chapter Fifteen

When the wind finally started to die down and the rain stopped, it was dark in the forest. They emerged from their pine-tree shelter and Noah looked around at the drenched landscape, sweeping the area with the light from his phone torch. The trees were black with rain, the floor covered in swimming-pool-sized puddles, the clouds thick as smoke above them. No stars that night. He went over and checked on the cattle and the horses, their eyes shining like marbles in the torchlight. He hoped the bulk of the herd was with Logan, Emmett, and Hank, and, he suspected, that they mainly had the stragglers from the back.

Another message came through from Logan as he was checking the horses. *Stay where you are tonight. We'll find you in the morning.*

Noah couldn't understand how just a few hours ago all he'd wanted was for everyone to be alive, now he was wincing at the idea of having to spend the night with just

Ren. Although he didn't need a text to know it was madness to ride through the forest in the pitch-black with a quarter herd of cattle.

He put his phone away and, shouting to Ren, "I'm going to look for some dry wood," he went to scour the surrounding area, relieved to be on his own for a moment. He couldn't think straight. He needed to be away from the intimacy, the fear, and the memories. But also, the unsettling new bond between them; the fact he felt better with her there.

He told himself he just had to get through the night. The weather was better, they just had to pitch their tents and sleep.

He found a pile of branches close by and dismantling it, found that the ones in the center might be dry enough to burn. Dragging the branches out, he put his boot on the widest part and snapped off the smaller twigs to make a bundle. It felt good to do something. More like himself. Simple was all he wanted in life. Simple and on his own terms.

Then he walked back into their camp to see Ren with her arms wrapped around the neck of the little cow she'd gone back for, face buried in the cow's hide, eyes closed, as if absorbing the warmth and the comfort.

"What are you doing?" he asked, refusing to succumb to the sweetness of the image.

Ren looked up, still clutching the oblivious cow who was chewing pine needles. "Hugging Mildred," she said.

He carried on forward, dumping the branches in the center of the camp, wishing he hadn't asked.

Ren took a deep breath before letting her go. "She smells nice. Like life and rain and earth."

Again, Noah refused to be sucked in. "If you say so."

"Do you want to smell her?"

"No."

She stood with her hands on her hips, a knowing half-smile on her face, one brow arched goadingly. "I bet you do, really."

He paused where he was stacking up the branches. "I assure you, I know what cattle smell like."

"You don't know what Mildred smells like."

He ignored her.

She came over crouching down opposite him as he built the fire, blowing on her hands to warm them up. "How can I help?"

"By not trying to get me to smell the cows."

She laughed out loud.

Noah clenched his jaw as he stacked the remaining branches. Desperate to watch her laugh yet at the same time desperate not to. He got up and went and got his lighter from his pack.

The temperature had dropped sharply and as he was there, he decided to swap his damp T-shirt for a dry one.

Ren started, "Do you want me to—" but paused. He turned to see what was wrong and realized from her expression that it was the surprising sight of him topless that had stopped her. She looked away and he yanked on his dry top. He was caught between a flash of arrogance and the same desperation for morning to get there quicker.

She swallowed, tried again, "Do you want me to light the fire?"

"Sure," he replied, chucking her the lighter, then tugging on a couple of dry sweaters and his jacket.

As she focused on the fire, Noah went back to the bags, rooting through them for the tents. The sooner they were pitched the sooner they could go to bed. He found one but not the other. He went over to the horses, checked that there wasn't a tent strapped to the saddle.

"Everything okay?" Ren asked, shielding the kindling from the wind as it started gently smoking.

Noah said, "My tent isn't here." He raked a hand through his hair, his mouth pursed in a thin line.

He watched Ren have to hold in a laugh. "You serious?"

Noah let his hair flop back down and looked witheringly at her. "I wouldn't say it if I wasn't."

Ren lit another patch of kindling. "I don't think that's the way you should be talking to someone whose tent you need to borrow for the night."

Noah sighed, looking around him at the damp ground, he shook his head and said, "I'll sleep outside, I'll be fine."

The fire started to catch. Ren glanced up at him. He felt like a stubborn child, she looked like the teacher trying not to laugh. "Noah, there's just been a massive storm, the ground is soaking and it's freezing cold. Of course you can't sleep outside. You can stay in my tent."

He tipped his head at the offer and said, "I'll be fine. Thank you." There was no way they were sharing a tent. He'd had enough of close proximity with Ren.

She rolled her eyes. "Fine, well, I'll sleep outside, too."

"What?" He felt himself deflate. Why couldn't she just let him suffer happily.

She stood up, folded her arms across her chest. "If you're going to sleep outside then I'm going to sleep outside."

"It's too cold for you to sleep outside," he said.

She raised her eyebrows. "Well, then it's too cold for you to sleep outside."

His jaw jutted out in defiance. "I'm used to it."

Ren tipped her head. "I've slept in a horse barn on Christmas Eve when there's frost on the ground outside."

"You have not." He made a face. "You're making that up."

Her hands on her hips, brows raised, she said, "Am I?"

He swallowed, suddenly less certain. "It doesn't get that cold in Texas at Christmas."

Ren laughed. "Wanna bet?"

He licked his lips. Folded his arms across his chest. "Have you really?"

She nodded.

He nodded more slowly, bottom lip between his teeth. "Okay."

She shrugged like it wasn't a problem and her mouth quirked up in a half-smile. "Would you like to sleep in my tent, Noah?"

There was a moment's pause. He knew he had no choice. He gave a small nod. "I would appreciate that, thank you."

"You're welcome," she replied, the smile stretching victoriously across her whole face.

Chapter Sixteen

Noah found a can of soup that he had forgotten he'd packed. They warmed it over the fire and took turns drinking it out of the can. For water, they found a narrow tributary of the Redemption that skimmed the edge of the forest behind them. It had burst its banks, so they walked cautiously to the edge to fill the can and then boiled the water over the fire before pouring it into their canteens.

They had pitched the tent and gathered more wood, but when it was too dark to do anything useful, he found himself a bit of wood and his knife and, head bowed, started carving.

Ren sat adjacent on a large tree branch that they'd pulled close to the fire. He tried not to look at her.

As it had the previous evenings, the weather only got colder. The wind gusting enough to rattle the tent.

Into the silence, Ren said, "You want a drink?"

Noah frowned at the suggestion. "What kind of drink?" He looked up from his whittling.

"It's like a pine-needle tea," she offered by way of explanation.

"Is it nice?"

"No," she said flatly, "But it's warm."

Noah was surprised that she could make him laugh so easily. He wasn't against laughter as such, just not in a way that veered off from the way he might usually laugh—at something one of his brothers said—mocking one of Brodie's ridiculous stories or winding Logan up—or a joke in the bar, or a crack made by one of the ranch hands—familiar, dry, deadpan laughter. Not something that actually made his whole body smile. It threw him off-balance. And he certainly didn't need disgusting tea in his life, but when she stood up she looked so eagerly positive about the idea that he said, "Sure, I'll have some."

"Great. You boil some water." And she went over to the fallen pine to start stripping the needles.

Noah put the wood he was carving down, resignedly folding the knife shut against his thigh and tucking it into his pocket.

"We used to drink this quite a lot when we were kids. You can't make it out of yew or Christmas trees because that's poisonous. My friend Mean Billy had to go to the hospital when we made it out of yew."

"Mean Billy?" Noah raised a brow.

"Yeah, he was mean when he arrived but he got better. He's a lawyer now. Makes big money, but we still call him Mean Billy. Makes me laugh when it comes up on my phone."

Noah shook his head, going to scoop more water into the soup can before putting it on the makeshift grill they'd made out of soaking wet wood over the fire. There was something about the ease with which she spoke that made talking seem easier, less of a giant weight thrown into the air. He realized then why even his monosyllabic dad had chatted along with her the other night.

She came over with her hands full of pine needles. "You have to crush them up." She knelt down and spreading her rain slicker on the ground, bashed the needles with a fat stick of wood, then she lifted a couple of handfuls, squeezed them tight and dropped them into the water. "Like I said, it's not that nice, especially as we don't have any honey."

Noah watched her diligently making the tea. The problem was, while he wanted to say something, he didn't know what to say. He had got so used to not talking, to keeping himself closed off—words, he had come to understand, could be weaponized. He'd seen things he'd said in the past twisted then quoted as the truth, rewordings that challenged his fidelity or stoked animosity with his brothers. He'd read hurtful comments supposedly from his friends back home that they would always deny but left him uncertain who he could trust. Their manager, Dexter, leaked information all the time for the good of album sales, so Noah found himself saying nothing. Had spent years just watching silently, voiceless. It was a hard habit to break.

His hands itched to go back to his whittling, to ignore the impulse to speak. To let her get on with the tea. But that suddenly felt like a failing on his part and Noah hated to fail. If there was one thing about him that he knew for a fact, it was that shown a problem, he conquered it. In the band, he could play any instrument asked of him simply because he saw it as a challenge to overcome. He learned to swim by just hurling himself in the river as a boy. On the ranch, he broke the toughest, stubbornest horses. He branded the meanest bulls. He fixed the roof when everyone else thought it was too high or too dangerous. And he always won at Monopoly. He did what had to be done because he refused to be beaten by anything.

But this wasn't Monopoly, and it wasn't the barn roof. It was small talk and with that, he was out of his comfort zone. As the water started to slowly simmer, all Noah could think was what would Logan do in this situation?

"You got a stick to stir it with?" she asked.

Noah handed her the branch he'd been carving, stripped of its bark.

"Ooh, fancy," she said, twirling it around like she'd been given something special.

Noah half smiled but couldn't concentrate, he was too busy thinking how Logan would take control and make easy effortless chat as he always did. Or Brodie would drop some shockingly inappropriate compliment that would have her putty in his hands.

Noah took his penknife back out and picked up another small branch.

Instead of going over to the fallen trunk on the other side of the fire, when Ren sat down, she sat next to him.

"I would sit over there," she said, pointing to her previous seat, "but it's all cold and there's darkness behind—" she waved a hand in the direction of the open, fathomless forest "—and I don't really like the dark that much." She looked at him, pale eyes hopeful. "That okay?"

"Fine," he said, although he would much prefer it if she was over there and he couldn't smell the crushed pine from her hands or the cool plastic of her jacket.

He started curling slivers of wood from the new branch while Ren stirred the tea and watched the fire, seeming to stare mesmerized at the flames as they crackled and danced in the remaining breeze.

"This is the best bit," she said. "That time before it's ready to drink, when you're just waiting, nothing to do. The anticipation's always much better than the real thing."

This was not wisecracks at the bar. This was not mocking Brodie. This was a small tightening of his muscles because she had pinpointed his exact favorite time. "I guess so."

She turned her head and smiled at him, her wide, toothy, friendly grin, easy as anything. "Especially where pine-needle tea is concerned."

There was a silence where they both looked at the fire. Noah glanced briefly across at her profile, scratched and dirty from the storm, but relaxed with calm concentration.

He breathed in through his nose. *Say something.*

Too much time passed.

He was about to go back to his whittling but instead let his hands holding the penknife and the whittled wood drop, elbows resting on his knees, and found himself saying, "Why did you have to sleep in the horse barn on Christmas Eve?"

Without turning from the fire, she smiled and said, "Noah, are you starting a conversation with me?"

He sighed, caught out. But, while he momentarily felt embarrassed by having it called out, he realized it made it all seem lighter, less important. Smiling self-deprecatingly this time, he said, "I am. But I do actually want to know why you were out in the cold at Christmas." And he realized he meant it.

Ren glanced to check his expression and seemingly satisfied by his sincerity, said, "It was a silly argument about Christmas presents." She leaned forward, stirred the bubbling tea. "We could be quite precocious when we ganged up together. There was me, my friend Liane, Billy —" she raised her eyebrows in recognition of the early chat about Mean Billy "—and a couple of the other smaller ones on one side of the table against Mrs. Watson who ran the ranch and looked after us, or supposedly looked after us, on the other side of the table. Thinking back, I mean, we were our own worst enemy, most of the time." She shook her head as she looked at Noah with a despairing smile.

"What was wrong with the Christmas presents," he asked.

She paused, bit her lip, like she'd inadvertently gone somewhere she hadn't intended to with the conversation. "There was nothing wrong with them," she said with a resigned, slightly ashamed, tilt of her mouth, "We just never really got any."

Noah frowned. "None?"

"Not really. Not like we saw other kids get at school and we couldn't understand why Father Christmas missed us out." She laughed like the reasoning was silly, and sat back, eyes on the crackling fire, hands behind her on the branch, legs stretched out in front.

They were silent for a moment, then Ren touched her face and said, "Wow, my cheeks have gotten hot talking about it. I can really remember the confusion." She touched her chest. "I can feel it here, you know, the memory."

Noah wasn't quite sure what to say. He guessed just from what he knew of her that she didn't want his sympathy. "What was it like?" he asked. "Living there."

"It was okay," she replied simply. "Could have been worse." She blew out a breath that clouded white in front of her. "I'm not very good at living by other people's rules. At not having any options. All the time I was there, it felt like I was in one of those cartoons, you know when they're running really, really fast but going nowhere, 'cause someone's got their hand pressed against your forehead?"

"Yeah," Noah replied.

"You ever felt like that?" she asked, blonde hair slipping over her eyes.

He considered the notion of being trapped by something, living with near constant frustration and fury, and he found that in lieu of pity the best he could offer was understanding. "I felt like that the whole time I was in the band."

She looked at him for a second then smiled—knowing the admittance didn't come naturally. Then she turned back to the pine-needle tea, gave it a stir and said, "We actually had quite a nice time in the horse barn. Liane swore she heard reindeer hooves on the roof."

Noah closed his eyes in despair.

She bashed him on the leg. "It's true!"

He laughed, too aware of the touch to refute it.

Chapter Seventeen

Sometimes when Noah laughed, it was just a mouth-closed, eyes-crinkling little movement of his shoulders kind of laugh. Nothing special. But it was those times that made Ren's stomach clench, made her have to turn away so she didn't look too long or allow the feeling to take hold. Not concentrating, she chucked one of the wetter branches onto the flames.

"Those are the ones we're trying to avoid," he warned as the fire started to smoke.

"Sorry."

He made a face. "You don't have to apologize, I wasn't being serious."

"Sorry," she said again, embarrassed that she'd absentmindedly misunderstood. "Not sorry. Sorry. Oh, heck." He raised a brow in confusion and she shook her head and said, "Where were we? Christmas. I think the tea's ready."

She used a wet cloth to take the pine-needle tea off the

fire, then put the can on the floor and refolded the cloth so she could pick it up properly and pour it into the caps of their water bottles, which they were using as tiny cups.

"I imagine you have some nice Christmases in that house, don't you?" she said as she concentrated on not spilling anything, "I'm a terrible pourer."

"How can you be a terrible pourer?"

As if on cue, a clump of pine needles slipped from the base of the pot making the tea overspill into a puddle on the floor. Noah said, "Ahh, I see."

Ren kept concentrating, her tongue, without realizing it, between her teeth, trying not to look at Noah and get distracted. "Your mom looks like she knows how to make Christmas good."

Noah seemed to be watching with interest as she stopped pouring a fraction too late and more tea slopped over the edge of the lid. "We did have some really great Christmases growing up," he said. "Darn. You really can't pour, can you?"

"No." Ren laughed. The pot had started burning her hands and she put it down. How could him simply casually noticing something about her make her skin shiver?

Noah picked up his water-bottle cap and took a tentative sniff. "Smells weirdly of lemons."

Ren picked hers up and smelled it, too. "Don't get your hopes up, it doesn't taste of lemons."

Noah's mouth quirked as he blew on it then took a sip. Ren watched as he swallowed then winced.

"Well?" she asked.

"It is warm," he said, as if that was the best and only compliment he could come up with.

She smiled knowingly as she sipped her own, the taste immediately taking her back to being with her friends, escaping into the woods in the night, building a fire, making tea, eating sweets that someone—usually Mean Billy—had stolen from the shop when they'd gone into town. Snatched moments of freedom. "I bet you have a big Christmas tree, don't you?"

Noah looked up from his tea, almost guiltily as he said, "To the ceiling."

Ren put her hand to her heart at the idea. "Lights outside?"

He nodded, said dryly, "Shaped like icicles."

She laughed, while inside it was like tentacles tightening around her stomach as she wondered what it would be like to have all that family. All that love. All that responsibility and annoyance and duty and dependence. It felt like a gift bigger than she could fathom. Like the pinnacle. "Boy, I bet it's amazing."

"It did used to be," he admitted, and she found herself too aware of every quirk of his features. He blew on his tea again, had another sip and put the cap down on the ground, picking up his penknife and the wood carving again.

They slipped into silence, just the sound of the wind and the shuffling of the animals.

She watched his hands. He glanced up as if he could sense it. Their eyes met for a second and when that happened, in the darkness of the forest, she suddenly found it difficult to breathe. She thought instead of something to say. She remembered what Hank had said about his dad and the boys leaving. Then she thought of the article she'd read about his brother Jack. "I was sorry about your brother Jack. That must have been really hard," she ventured, because it felt like a tiny chink in his armor had opened earlier when he'd mentioned not enjoying the band, but immediately knew it was too intimate a question.

"You been researching Silver Sky in that tent of yours?" he said, sweeping the penknife over the wood.

Ren screwed up her face, caught out by the fact she suddenly had knowledge that she didn't have before. "Maybe," she admitted.

He nodded. "Find anything else out?"

She couldn't decipher his tone, whether he was annoyed or making conversation. From past experience, she figured it might be irritation. "Not really, the signal wasn't good enough."

That made him look up, brow raised, and she thought the annoyance might have shifted to amusement at her honesty.

"Saw a photo of you, though. You looked cute." She bashed his knee with hers.

Noah looked at where their knees had touched then he sat up, flicking the penknife shut, and stretched his legs out in front of him, maybe so she couldn't touch him again, but on his lips was a vague hint of a smile. Which gave her the confidence to say, "How did it all start?"

He tucked the knife in his pocket. "We were always in a band together," he said. "The audition was because my mom was sick. In the hospital. Ethan had this idea it would cheer her up—give her something to take her mind off her treatment."

"I bet she loved that."

He ran his hand over the stubble on his jaw that had in the last three days become more of a beard, then he rested his elbows on his knees, chin on knuckles, and looking sidelong at her said, "Yeah, she did."

"But I'm guessing you didn't?"

That made Noah laugh, as if it were an understatement. "I wanted to be here, doing this. But—" he shrugged "—no one else did."

A log cracked on the fire and rolled out of the flames, spitting red embers of dust onto the ground. Noah got up and kicked it back onto the pyre then sat back down again, watching, with his collar turned up, shaggy, too-long hair fallen forward, elbows on his knees and hands clasped in front of him, as the flames leapt at the new kindling.

Ren felt instinctively the precious rarity of these insights. So she, too, focused on the fire, feeling like if they both looked ahead at the bright flickering shapes it wouldn't break the spell. "Couldn't you have stayed behind?"

His brow furrowed as he turned to look at her. "No. It didn't work like that."

"How did it work?"

"You ask a lot of questions."

"I'm interested." She shrugged, inside grasping to get the moment back. "I guess you have what I always wanted. Big family, big house, Christmas lights shaped like icicles," she added to lighten the tone.

He huffed a laugh. "You can buy the lights in town."

"It's not the same." She sipped her tea because she actually felt a lump in her throat at the idea of buying her own Christmas lights and hanging them in her flat and when she'd look at them thinking of Noah and his family gathered around their tree together exchanging presents.

He bent down and picked up his tea and said, "I couldn't have stayed because they were my brothers, and we did everything together. We understood each other. I went where they went. We were a pack. Like with you and Mean Billy and people."

It touched her that he'd remembered their names. "Yeah, I guess. But—" she bit her lip trying to explain it "—with us, it was kinda the other way around. We were *desperate* to leave the pack. To have someone come along and pick us to take home with them, or a parent to get themselves together and be able to have their kid back. That was the dream."

Noah lowered his gaze to the fire.

She looked, too, at the flames dancing and jumping in the gusts of wind. It was funny to talk about her childhood, to put in words things that she had always known but never properly considered. She'd never spoken like that to anyone. "I guess in my case, the pack was who was left behind. You know, when someone went off for a new life, we just closed ranks, quick as that—" She clicked her fingers. "We laughed about them when they were gone, you know, we were mean—Mean Billy."

Noah swung his head her way, corner of his mouth tipped up.

She smiled, feeling her cheeks stupidly redden at the

small thread of honesty. Felt stripped bare, like she was the one now handing him something precious and hoped he would take care of it. "But it was just envy. We were all wishing that we'd been whisked away by the people in the shiny BMW. Until five times out of ten they came back because either their parents had messed it up again or the new people weren't quite the right fit. It was always about fit."

Ren thought of all they'd had to do in order to impress. Be nicer. Smile more. Work harder. Help more. Talk less. Don't ruin your clothes. Don't eat so much. Don't talk back. Don't. Don't. Don't. "You forget who you are because you're trying so hard to be someone else."

Noah's eyes widened almost imperceptibly as she continued, "Probably quite similar when you're famous, I bet. Everyone wanting a piece of you."

He held her gaze then, didn't look away as he normally did, seemed to search her face, both wary and intrigued. Her breath shook on the inhale.

"Yes," he said. "That's exactly it." He bent down for his tea, as if he wasn't sure if he wanted to say more or not, but then surprised her by saying, "I think what happens is, that to give people what they want, you find you have to live outside yourself." He turned to look at his tea, said more contemplatively, "Which is never good for the mind." Then seemingly wanting to move the subject on, he took a sip and winced. "This really is bad."

The spell of the moment broke. Ren grinned. "Don't drink it."

He gulped some water to take the taste away.

She stretched her legs out, smiling, hands behind her on the gnarled trunk. Then she said, "Did you meet any interesting famous people?"

Noah screwed the lid back on his water bottle. "I hate to tell you this," he said, eyebrows drawn down apologetically, "but quite often my brothers would go out and I'd just stay in the hotel and read books on farming."

Ren snorted a laugh, couldn't help herself. "Sorry."

He looked down at the ground, shaking his head in mock shame. "I know. It's an embarrassment." He, too, sat back, mirroring her pose. "My only excuse it that I was young and homesick."

Ren looked around her at the pine trees and the fire, and behind them the tent and the shimmering eyes of the horses.

"I mean, this, it's real," he raised his hand to encompass it all, "There's the seasons and nature and land. Things you can touch, you know?"

She nodded.

"Fame, I mean, it's not real. There's nothing to grasp on to. All anyone wants," he said, "is something real."

She thought of the private investigator handing her the piece of paper with Loriana's name on it, remembered her heart pounding with a dangerous mix of excitement and hope.

She had to look away, out into the darkness of the forest. When she looked back, he was watching, hooded gaze like he could see straight into her soul. She swallowed, wanting suddenly to trust him with her secret, lessen the burden of it. But she said instead, "Why didn't you leave?"

"I did," he said. "But I figured out pretty quickly I had nowhere to go. My mom was recovering from cancer, she didn't need hordes of crying fans on the doorstep. We couldn't go anywhere without getting mobbed. And my dad was still furious with us all. He'd just shut down. Shut us out. And for me, he was who I looked up to, I guess. But like Hank said—we broke his heart." Noah raked his hair back with his hands. "I couldn't be at home. It was too much for them. Livvy had high school, I couldn't imagine going back there. Couldn't be one place, couldn't be the other." He narrowed his eyes at the fire. Ren watched his profile. "Then Logan turned up and persuaded me to come back to the band, said he'd sacked our manager, and that he'd take over, he'd make it better. We'd do it our way." He glanced over, met her gaze. "Like I said, I wanted to be with them, and I wanted to believe that what he said was true—so I went back. And it *was* better for a little bit, but then the egos got bigger and the arguments got worse. Logan really tried. He got us through it. But you only realize how not right something is till you're out of it. Till you can look back and say, boy, I was really struggling."

The frankness made her want to edge closer to him and his sad, hangdog eyes. She wanted to hear it all, never wanted the evening to end, just her and him and the fire and the stupid, disgusting pine-needle tea.

He ran his hand over his mouth, then turned his head and with a jaded smile, said, "Can't change things, though, can you?"

"No," she replied, feeling the chill in the air and pulling her rain jacket tighter around herself, "but you can't live with what-ifs either. Eats you up if you think too much about all the other paths."

There was a brief pause, then to her surprise he said, "Can I ask what happened in your past? What happened to your parents?"

"You can ask," she said, feeling an unexpected burn in her nose, behind her eyes at the no-nonsense way he'd said it. "I can't answer, because I don't know."

He blew out a breath. "That's tough. I'm sorry."

"Yeah." She shrugged. "I know all about what-ifs."

He nodded. "I bet you do."

She leaned forward, elbows on her knees, rested her chin in her cupped hands, and said, "I've come to the conclusion that there's just one path and that's the one we're on, and we gotta make the best of it."

She watched as slowly the corner of his mouth tilted in a crooked smile and his eyes softened, and suddenly she found she was struggling to breathe, as he said, like he'd known her forever, "The eternal optimist."

Chapter Eighteen

"We should probably go to bed," Noah said, tearing his gaze from the understanding in her eyes that seconds before had made him want to tell her everything that clawed inside him about the vagaries of fame, the struggle with the idea of "self" that she had somehow pinpointed, the conflict between who he was versus who people wanted him to be. The fans who wept and wrote him letters like they knew him and loved him and would take care of him, had his name tattooed indelibly on their skin. Seeing his face huge on billboards, and being so sick of the sight of his own reflection that he couldn't look in the mirror. Staring down at a carpet in a hotel room until all the patterns merged into one, wondering if there was anything left of him except who they wanted him to be.

But he couldn't say all of that. The memories were like a knot of brambles, too painful to tackle, like getting torn to shreds.

"Yes, good idea," she said, standing up so quickly she

kicked the can that had held the revolting tea and they both bent down to pick it up almost knocking heads like sitcom characters, then both letting go of the can for the other to take it. She quickly scooped it up before he could.

Noah backed away saying, "I'll go check on the horses."

She nodded, her pale skin and hair glowing almost white in the firelight. With her eggplant camo fleece on, and her red slicker undone so it hung loose around her, the blonde flyaway wisps of her hair, no makeup, she looked somehow prettier than when she'd turned up at the ranch.

He spun on his heel and strode over to where the animals stood, glad to put some distance between them.

All the talk of family, of being a pack, made him remember how close he and all his brothers had been as kids. Riding out when the sun went down, fishing in the lake, swimming when it got hot, racing to the middle and back. There was competition and hierarchy and bickering and fighting, but all of it came down to the tangible things in life. Climbing up in a saddle, branding the cattle, feeding the chickens, eating around the table, laughing and pushing each other on their way to school. It was all there, something to hold on to. But in the band there was nothing. There was adoration and glory and it changed them.

In the past, if they had a problem they could fight it out in the yard or race the horses or just disappear until the steam had dissipated and the hot heads became cool. But in the band, they were on top of each other, trapped in tour buses, hotels, dressing rooms, egos clashing. Sly asides became sudden, raging confrontations. Habits became irritations.

As he checked the horses' tethers, Noah thought of the time he'd stood beside their manager's door and heard his brother Jack saying, "It's the girlfriend that's the problem. If Noah didn't have her it'd be okay. He'd get into it."

Jack, who ducked and wheedled and found the way to the top whichever way was quickest, no matter how self-serving. Jack who suited fame. Noah who did not.

A week later, a story came out linking Noah romantically to a new young actress. He remembered pinning Jack to the wall in fury, and Logan dragging him off while Jack just grinned, hands raised in the air. "Sorry, dude."

He'd have liked to have had one last chance to fight it out with his brother. Get it all out of his system.

He found himself leaning his forehead against Blue's neck, eyes closed, breathing in the warm familiar scent. Then, when he realized what he was doing, he drew back, feeling like Ren when he'd silently mocked her for hugging the wily little cow.

He pushed his hair away from his face and blew out a breath. "Get yourself together, Noah," he admonished under his breath.

Glancing over to where she was sorting things out with the tent and the bags, he saw her suddenly as a little girl wishing for a family, waiting as the shiny cars drove up. He screwed his eyes shut, didn't want to think of her that way, sweet and vulnerable. Imagined her big smile and her bigger eyes. He found he wanted her to have happiness. He'd never felt that before—he'd wanted people to be well or safe or in love, but never looked at a person and just felt they deserved to be happy.

He shook his head, kicking a pile of dry brown pine needles at his feet as, hands thrust deep in his pockets, he walked slowly back over to the camp, determined to just crawl into that tent and go to sleep.

Then, from where she knelt rummaging through the bags, he heard her say, "My sleeping bag is soaking wet."

"What?"

Ren stood up, bringing with her a sleeping bag, the pale blue material now navy from being saturated, and dripping a puddle on the ground. "I think the weatherproofing on the bag must have perished."

Noah closed his eyes for a moment, that was all he needed. It was Willow's sleeping bag, and he couldn't actually imagine when the last time she might have used it was.

The night had got colder, so he said, "Don't worry, we'll just find everything that's dry and make—"

"—a nest," she finished for him, biting down on a smile as soon as she said it because she seemed to know him well enough now to sense his reaction to both the word and the situation.

He had to stop himself from doing a despairing head shake.

When they'd piled everything warm they owned into the tent, Ren came inside after him, her blonde hair catching in the zipper teeth of the entrance and coming loose from her ponytail. "This is so cozy!"

Noah wanted to just go to sleep. His head hurt. He didn't want to have to talk anymore. He wanted back the version of himself that happily lay in the freezing cold if he forgot his sleeping bag or didn't eat if there was no food and didn't drink forest-foraged tea if there was no hot beverage.

To make it worse, the moment she'd got into the tent he could already smell her shampoo and he didn't want to have to contemplate lying close enough that he could see the freckles over her nose or her individual lashes as she slept. But the temperature was still dropping and while earlier he'd claimed he could sleep outside, he knew it was madness.

Ren shook out the downy gray sleeping bag and spread it out over both of them. *"Voila!"* Then she beamed her crooked-teeth smile and said, "Good?"

Noah sighed, giving in to her enthusiasm, and said, "Good."

Ren then set about good-naturedly pulling on her hat and wrapping the scarf Loriana had lent her around her head, so she looked like an Egyptian mummy. Then after much kerfuffle and flumping and readjusting where he could feel her leg as it accidently kicked his, she finally lay still, but then he could sense to within an inch how close her body was.

"You're shivering," he said.

"No, I'm okay."

"Ren, I can hear your teeth chattering."

"I'll warm up."

Noah closed his eyes, resigned. "You can er—"

he paused, embarrassed. "You can lie closer, if you want. To, you know, share body heat."

She glanced over her shoulder with a little smirk.

"For survival," he clarified.

"For survival," she repeated in a mock-serious voice.

"Fine, don't, it was just a suggestion." Noah pulled his jacket further up around his jaw. "I'm fine if you want to lie there shivering."

"I was just kidding," she laughed. "Don't worry, you're a good-looking guy, Noah, but I don't find you so irresistible that I can't snuggle up to you if it stops us freezing to death. We're adults."

Noah didn't feel like an adult. Torn between an unexpected flicker of pleasure that she'd called him a good-looking guy and wanting to be as far away from her and the feelings she conjured in him as possible.

He lifted his arm and she tucked herself in close against him. Layers of clothing separated them, but she fit so perfectly and it felt so natural, that he had to try and shut it out. But it was difficult with his face mere inches from the soft silkiness of her hair, pale gold in the moonlight, and his hand tucked under her ribs so he could feel the rise and fall of her breath. He wondered if, like him, she lay there tormented by the closeness, eyes wide open.

Then she said brightly, in typical Ren fashion, "Night, Noah. Sleep well."

And he realized that she really did find him resistible.

"Night, Ren," he replied more resignedly, and burying his face into the collar of his coat, he lay staring at the nylon tent wall trying to do what he always did, which was block out everything going on inside his head.

Chapter Nineteen

"Noah! Noah, wake up! Noah, you're shouting. Noah!"

Ren had tried to rouse him softly, but now she shook him hard. He was shouting and thrashing about, and his face was damp with either sweat or tears. "Noah!" she shouted again, this time closer in his ear, at the same time as shoving him hard on the arm.

Noah sat bolt upright with a gasp. "What? What's going on? Livvy?" He looked around the tent, eyes wild with panic, breathing hard.

"Noah, you're in the tent with me, Ren," she pointed to herself trying to sound calm but in the darkness, spooked already from being ripped from sleep by his shouting and now more so by the haunted look in his eyes, she felt less certain, like the ground beneath her was less stable.

"It's okay," she soothed, stroking his back gently. It felt only minutes ago that she was lying there trying to sleep, his arm pulling her close, warmed by the heat of his body, all her senses on high alert, wide awake, she'd never felt anything like it. But now it was like a dream and this the reality. "It's all okay."

Gauging where he was, Noah rested his forehead on the heel of his hand and started taking big gulping breaths of air.

Ren, feeling the thunder of her own heartbeat, could only watch as he woke up fully. One of her hands still on his back, the other resting gently on his forearm.

Still trying to calm his breathing, Noah reached up and unzipped his leather jacket, shirking it off as if it was suffocating him, along with his sweaters, until he was just in a T-shirt. His skin was damp with sweat, his hair all over the place from yanking off the clothes.

Touching him now seemed suddenly more intimate without the layers of bulky clothing. Instead, Ren twisted around for her water bottle, unscrewing the cap as she handed it to him.

"Thanks," he said, still breathless, taking a couple of long gulps.

She waited.

He lowered the bottle, hung his head as he tried to catch his breath. She could see the sweat on his skin glistening in the moonlight shining through the tent. The wind buffeted around them, echoing in the tiny space.

As she watched him calming down, she felt her own fear begin to recede replaced by something else, something that made the air catch in her lungs as she once again became too aware of the closeness, the intensity, the long-suffering sadness in his eyes. He ran his hand through his hair.

"Wow," he breathed. "Sorry about that. I'm sorry I woke you up."

"This happen to you often?" she asked.

Noah shook his head, took another swig of water then handed the bottle back to her.

He still didn't seem to be able to catch his breath properly, so she said, "Are you sure you're all right?"

He sighed. "I don't know. It was just so real." He pushed both hands into his hair and stayed there with his arms up, elbows out. "I've never dreamed of her—" he stopped himself, letting his hands drop down in front of him.

Ren tentatively reached up to touch his shoulder in a gesture of comfort, tried to ignore her awareness of the movement. It was dark, everything seemed closer, more intimate, the space smaller.

But Noah didn't seem to notice, pushing against his eyes with his finger and thumb. "Oh, man, that was…"

"Do you want to talk about it?"

"No." Noah laughed, like he'd couldn't imagine anything he'd like to do less.

Ren said, "It's not a crime, Noah, to talk about things that have happened to you. You know that, don't you?"

He gave her a slightly disparaging look and said dryly, "I do know that, Ren, but thank you very much for reminding me." Then he lay back down, the sleeping bag half over his legs, still in just his T-shirt and jeans, and stared up at the tent ceiling.

Ren sighed and lay down, too, pulling the sleeping bag up under her arms, looking up at the pitched roof off the tent with him. Then she said, "You've never dreamed about her before?"

"No."

She rolled her head to look at him. "You think about her a lot?"

"Try not to," he said up to the ceiling. "Try not to think about any of it." He glanced over at her, and caught her expression. "Don't look at me like that."

"Like what?"

He sat up on his elbow. "Like, you know? Judging. Like I'm wrong."

Ren propped herself up on her elbow too. "I never said you were wrong."

"You think I'm wrong, though."

"Well, you *are* wrong," she shrugged matter-of-factly. "But I never *said* you were wrong."

He slumped back down, exasperated. "You're face says exactly how you feel all the time."

"Well, it's lucky then that I don't have to tell you." She feigned a sweet smile, but he deliberately wasn't looking at her.

They lay there side by side, neither of them speaking. It was cold in the tent. She could just see the cloud of his breath in the darkness. She felt herself shivering and tried to hide it.

She said softly, conciliatory, "If you shut it all out, Noah, then nothing gets through. Not even the good bits."

He didn't reply but she heard his deep, resigned inhale. Then into the silence he said, "We were on tour in Asia when I found out she was dying. I just stood up and walked out of the stadium dressing room and didn't look back." He paused. Ren felt like the beat of her heart filled the silence. "I knew in that moment that I'd never return. I'd never set foot on stage again. Which, at the time, had been all I wanted. But suddenly the price I had to pay to get what I wanted was way too high." He laughed humorlessly. Ren looked down at the fabric of the sleeping bag. "On the plane I knew I was flying home to watch her die and part of me never wanted it to land. Just pause it there in the sky. That's all I remember of the dream, just going round and round, the feeling of never getting out of that plane." He closed his eyes. She looked at his lashes fanned out on his cheeks.

She wondered if that was it, that he'd roll over now and go back to sleep. Ren didn't want to go back to sleep. She told herself it was fear, when really, she just wanted more of whatever it was that they had right then. Time away from time. Noah off-guard.

She rolled onto her side, tucked her hands underneath her cheek and said, "You got a picture of her?"

His head rolled over in surprise. "Of Livvy?"

"Yeah."

He paused, clearly not quite sure how to respond but then sat up and reached around to get his wallet out his back pocket. After rifling through various compartments, he pulled out a rumpled old photograph and handed it to Ren without saying anything. Then he stretched over to get the sweaters he'd thrown off and pulled one back on.

Ren stared at the girl in the picture so she didn't look at Noah getting dressed. There she was. Livvy. Long, glossy brown hair, dark eyes, sweet mouth. As suspected, delicate, ethereal, perfect. No older than eighteen. "She's beautiful," she said, handing it back.

Don't you dare be jealous, Ren.

"Yeah." He took the photograph from her and stared at it himself for a couple of beats then he lowered his hand to his chest. "It's funny, it's like seeing an old friend you haven't seen for years."

They lay there again in silence. Ren watching his shadowy profile as he gazed upwards, unblinking. She could hear the noises of the night outside. The shuffling of the horses. The hoot of an owl. The pine trees like maracas in the breeze.

"How did she die?"

"Lymphoma," he said. "It was real quick."

"Were you there?"

He nodded slowly, like he was only half paying attention. "At the end I was. But—" he swallowed "—she didn't tell me for quite a while so…" He frowned, glancing her way for a second.

"Why didn't she tell you?"

He laughed then, as if he knew the question was coming because she always asked too many questions, but he just shook his head and said, "She said it was because she wanted it to be normal for as long as possible."

Ren found she couldn't breathe from the look in his eyes. She wanted to reach over and touch him, lay her hand on his chest. And despite not wanting to be that type of person, she couldn't deny the flicker of envy she felt imagining what it must be like to be loved so totally by someone as unwavering as Noah Carter. "That's what I'd want," she said, "for things to be the same. As soon as the truth is out, well—" she paused, thinking about her own situation, her own fear of telling her secret "—you can't put it away again, can you?"

He gave her a sad smile at the rationale. "No," he said. Then exhaled slowly, raising the old, battered photograph and looking at it again. "I just felt like I let her down, not being there enough."

It was all too close to the bone for Ren. The sense of loss burrowed under her skin—the helpless, unforgiving pain of love that both drove and terrified her.

After a minute or two, he said, "When it was all happening, when we were away on tour, you don't think something life-changing is going on without you. I was just where I was, thinking I had it bad."

She smiled along with him in understanding, but the unfamiliar underlying desire to lean over and rest her head against his shoulder, close her eyes against his neck, hold him close, made her pull slightly away and her body clench rigid.

He swallowed and she watched the movement of his throat. "I guess I've always felt bad because I left her to go with the band, to go with my brothers."

Ren glanced at the photo. "Noah, you were just a kid. How were you to know something like that would happen."

Outside the wind blew raindrops from the leaves onto the nylon of the tent.

He angled his head slightly as he studied the picture

more intently. "Yeah. Looking at this," he said, "I can see how young we were. Easy to forget that."

"If you never talk about things, Noah," she said quietly, "you never get to understand them and let them go."

He glanced at her, then he nodded with a raise of his chin. "Thanks," he said, "for listening."

"You're welcome."

He slipped the photo back in his wallet, sitting up a touch to tuck it back into his pocket, and the movement suddenly made them closer. His head angled just above Ren's, the lines of his face highlighted in the moonlight, his eyes, as they met hers, seemed to darken, his breath seemed to still.

It felt like the tent suddenly pulsed with claustrophobic intensity. The air that had been cool with frosted breath suddenly suffocatingly hot. There was nothing but them and the sound of the wind outside whistling through the trees.

Ren didn't know what to do. Usually, she would crack a joke or change the subject, add something breezy and off-the-wall just to crack the tension, but she could think of nothing but the look in his eyes and the nearness of his mouth and the way the neck of his sweater had pulled out of shape, and she could see the dip of his throat and the tanned skin and the mouth that didn't smile often but when it did made her buzz inside. And suddenly she didn't care that she'd never kissed anyone. All she wanted was for Noah Carter to bend his head right then and give into something that she realized had been bubbling between them since they'd locked hands sheltering from the storm.

But something told her that he wouldn't. That he wouldn't take that liberty. And shouldn't. Nor should she. They'd just been talking about—he'd been *dreaming* about—his poor girlfriend who'd died so tragically young.

But still, all Ren could think about was the possibility of him kissing her or not kissing her, but her wanting him—or just having thought about possibly wanting him—to kiss her.

The wind rattled the tent, her cheeks started to burn, she was not experienced enough for this, and she found herself blurting into the tense, pulsing silence, "I didn't come to Autumn Falls because I liked the name."

And that was enough to transform the atmosphere in the tent in an instant. Noah was suddenly propped up on his hand with a frown on his face. "What do you mean?"

Ren felt the blush leave her cheeks and her panic recede. She swallowed, and sitting up said with a resigned sigh, "I hired a private detective to find out who my parents were." There it was, the big round secret, which had been sitting like a chicken sits on eggs in the middle of her head. Her private little fantasy that she'd told no one.

Noah blew out a breath in surprise. "You're kidding?"

She tucked her hair behind her ear. "No."

He raised his brows, encouraging her to go on. "And?"

Ren looked down at the diamond pattern stitched on the sleeping bag. "He found out who my mom is." This was her precious jewel. Her secret. Hers and only hers. She didn't want to say. Didn't want other opinions or thoughts sullying her jewel. "It's Loriana."

"Diner Loriana?" Noah said, as if there was another. "Hank's Loriana?"

Ren nodded.

Noah opened his mouth to say something then didn't, then said, "Wow."

Ren looked away, down at the sleeping bag, pleating the fabric with her fingers. She felt like she'd had something torn from her body and wanted immediately to snatch it back. But then when she glanced up, she saw him watching her now with what could only be described as concern. It was so unaccustomed that she thought again about what it would be like for him to reach across, put his cool, calloused palms to her cheeks, and tip her head and kiss her. Or maybe just draw her into a hug where she could rest her forehead on the soft wool of his sweater and feel his arms tighten reassuringly around her.

She could hear her foster friend Liane in her head. *Never cry, never care*. What was she thinking?

In front of her was a man who had seemingly denied every scrap of feeling for the last however long. Who thought she talked too much and said things that weren't what he wanted to hear and laughed too often and got in the way and did what she shouldn't and said what she thought. And the one thing Ren had vowed to protect more fiercely than anything else since leaving care was the precious real version of who she was.

"Please don't tell anyone," she said quickly.

"I won't," Noah replied with a small shake of his head.

There was a pause. The wind rustled the pines outside.

Noah lay back down. "I'm in shock."

She lay down, too, relieved that he didn't ask anything more. That she could gather her secret back up and put it away for safekeeping. "I do like the name of the town, though."

He gave a low chuckle.

As she stared up at the tent ceiling she felt her previous tense panic less keenly, the reality of why she was there sobering her thinking.

Beside her, Noah clasped his hands behind his head and said, "Well, you've certainly taken my mind off my dream."

Ren huffed a soft laugh. "Glad to be of service." Then, after a moment, added, "I'm sure you'll find happiness again, Noah. No doubt about it."

"I was more than happy before you appeared, Ren," he replied, voice laced with mocking amusement, "making me talk about everything!"

On instinct she bashed him on the arm in jokey rebuke then suddenly felt awkward having done it, as if he'd think she was flirting. But he said, "Hey!" like it had really hurt. And she laughed too loudly to her ears. Both of them, it felt, were like more colorful versions of themselves. Overplaying things to make it seem normal. Or perhaps it was just her.

Before anyone could say anything else, she rolled over so she couldn't see him. "Night, Noah."

She heard him say, "Ren?"

"Yeah." She stayed facing away.

"You're shivering again."

She closed her eyes. "I'll be okay."

But he moved closer, putting his arm around her and gently pulled her against him. The exquisite torture of it almost made her want to cry. She would never sleep now. Instead she lay there, eyes wide open trying to think of nothing but thinking of everything; the addictive concern in Noah's eyes, Liane's sobering disapproval, the immortalized sadness of beautiful, ethereal Livvy, and wondering what it would be like for Noah to look at her the way he looked at that photograph.

But there was nothing Ren knew better than the feeling of desperately wanting and not being able to have.

Chapter Twenty

"Wakey, wakey!"

Noah cracked one eye open to see sun streaming into the tent, along with Logan's grinning face.

Through the night he and Ren had stayed curled tight together like two cozy peas in a pod. "What time is it?" he asked, pushing himself up and as far away from her as he could subtly get. Not subtly enough, however, to avoid Logan's intrigued smirk.

"Time you two sleepy heads were up and awake!" Logan replied, his grin getting wider as he watched Ren yawn and look around her, bleary-eyed. "I can't believe you're not up. We've been waiting for you."

Then suddenly another face appeared in the tent, long, curly reddish-brown hair and a smile as wide as Logan's. Willow. "This looks cozy!"

Noah was not amused.

Ren said, "Oh, hi, Willow."

From the look on Noah's face, Logan was clearly

attempting to dial back his teasing and said, "We've got food. Willow rode out early this morning—"

"At the crack of dawn," Willow interjected.

"I thought you weren't allowed to ride," Noah said, looking anywhere but Ren. Hyperaware of the night—the nightmare, the closeness, the screaming desire to lean in and kiss her, the undisguised longing in her eyes before she blurted out her secret reason for being in Autumn Falls.

"This was an emergency," Willow replied.

"Get dressed," Logan finished, "and I'll help you round up this lot." He gestured behind him at the cattle.

Noah stood up. "We are dressed," he said and pushed past his brother and sister, knowing he was being overly prickly but unable to help it—embarrassed and off-guard, having been caught snuggled up with Ren. Running his hands through his hair, he said, "I don't know how we slept so long." Then, deliberately ignoring the suggestive look that passed between Logan and Willow, went to clean his teeth.

Ren handled it all much better and rolling up the sleeping bag said, without a hint of self-consciousness, "It was probably the pine-needle tea." Then she followed Noah to get some toothpaste.

Willow said, "Great coat, Ren!"

Ren did a little twirl in her strawberry-red slicker. "Thanks! I ripped it, though, in the storm."

"That was some storm," Willow replied, tying up her hair as she spoke. "Mom was so worried about you all. But I figured you'd be okay," she added with a little wink.

"You liar," Logan replied, "Bella said you were terrified."

Willow made a face like that was an exaggeration.

Ren said, "*I* was terrified. That tree nearly killed us." She pointed to where the giant pine had fallen the evening before.

As they all oohed and aahed, Noah concentrated on brushing his teeth, then washing his face with the water in his canteen. He was grateful for more people, for the night to be over. He could see Livvy's face, remember the taste of the terror, the empty blackness. Yet he felt an unaccustomed longing to return to just him and Ren together in the tent, her hand on his back, all calm and collected, bringing him back down to earth. Their own little world, just the two of them. He screwed his eyes shut for a second to try and clear his head.

"Dad and Hank okay?" he asked, trying to sound normal.

"Fine." Logan took a couple of strides back over to where Noah stood. "Hank's busted his back. Dad's done something to his arm, got hit by something, but he's okay. I made him a sling out of a scarf."

"You're a regular Florence Nightingale."

Logan laughed, deep and rumbling. "Tell me about it. Willow brought a proper one with her this morning."

"What about the herd?" Noah asked.

"Spooked, but they seem to be fine," Logan replied.

Noah tried not to be distracted by Ren laughing as she said something to Willow, and felt hot shame at the idea of what she might be saying. Would she recount his middle-of-the-night nightmare or the need to lie pressed close together for warmth? Now he wished all of it had never happened. That he could go back to the simplicity of her just being some girl who served him in the diner.

He blew out a tired breath.

They should just get moving.

"Shall we go, then?" he said, scooping up various belongings with brisk efficiency. It was easier just to block them all out.

"Yep." Logan started gathering up their packs while Ren and Willow squashed the tent back in the bag.

"Did you say there was breakfast?" Ren asked Willow, hopefully.

"Oh, yeah," Willow replied, "There's loads of it—muffins, coffee, eggs, sausages—Mom basically packed the whole larder. I would have brought more but Big Mac's slow enough."

Noah paused as he finished packing up their things and said, "You rode on Big Mac?"

Willow put her hands on her hips and threw him a withering glare, "You gave my horse to Ren! So yes, I'm on Big Mac."

Noah snorted a laugh, couldn't help it. The flicker of amusement brightened his morning.

Ren said, "Big Mac?"

Noah let Willow answer, found it difficult to look in her direction.

Willow shook her head. "He's actually called Macaulay but he's so old and fat everyone calls him Big Mac." She pointed to where the huge caramel horse was grazing contentedly, with his pot belly and the white beard under his chin that had made him look old since he was born.

Ren laughed, seemingly despite herself, but said, "That's kinda mean."

"He doesn't care," Noah replied, thinking that she didn't seem the least perturbed about what had happened the night before. "He's on a constant diet but he breaks out and eats everything he can find." But then was she too deliberately not looking at him? He secured the last of the bags and said, "Shall we go?"

Logan nodded. "Let's go round up these cows."

Ren said to Willow, "You take Star."

But Willow shook her head, sauntering with her pointed-toe dancer walk toward where Big Mac was docile and waiting. "Oh, no. To tell you the truth I'm more than happy on Big Mac. He's pretty comfy. It's like riding a couch."

Willow drove Noah bananas, but he had to admit she was enjoyable to have around. She was like his mom—she always added a bit of zest to proceedings. If it was left to him and his dad, they'd sit around in silence twenty-four-seven.

She was a bit like Ren, really.

Ren had come over to where he was with Blue and Star, glancing uncertainly at him as she hooked her foot into the stirrup.

"You okay?" he checked, while on reflex reached out a hand to help her up but as quickly realized she didn't need it.

"Yeah," she smiled, maybe shyly, and he felt again the

clench in his stomach at the possibility that had been there between them in that split-second their eyes met in the tent.

He said, "Thanks for last night. You know, the nightmare, I—"

She cut him off with a gentle, "You're welcome, Noah." Settling herself into the saddle.

Noah nodded, jumping onto Blue, then annoyingly catching Logan's watchful all-seeing eye as he did so.

The storm had blown in better weather. The sun peeking through the pines as they herded the cattle toward the other camp.

Noah would kill for a shower.

He was exhausted. He never usually slept more than a few hours, but that night he'd just lain with his eyes open listening to Ren's breathing and the wind battering the tent, thinking about what it would have been like to lean in and kiss her. The soft pressure of her lips. It sickened him that he'd almost lost control and allowed it to happen. He should have known better—been better. She'd never kissed anyone before, and who could be a worse person as a first kiss? He wouldn't wish himself on his worst enemy.

He wanted to be back in his trailer on his own.

His trailer, he thought wistfully. Would his mom have scrapped it by the time he got back? No, she wouldn't be that ruthless, but the clock was ticking.

As they rode in to where the others had set up camp after the storm, Emmett and Hank were waiting for them, drinking coffee. Emmett had his arm in the sling that Willow had brought with her.

"What took you so long?" Emmett called, as they all

dismounted and tied up the horses. Noah knew he would hate the weakness of an injury. Rocky sprinted over, tail wagging in excitement. "About to send out a search party."

"He was sleeping like a baby," Logan called back as they wandered into camp, reaching down to give Rocky a pat.

"Sleeping!" Emmett sat back on the rock he was sitting on, shocked. "We've already been out rounding up the stray cattle."

On the fire, a pan sizzled with sausages and there were boxes of muffins and a big pot of coffee.

Noah reached down for the coffee and Rocky came trotting over. He rolled his eyes at the dog, ready to go through another round of ribbing. As if on cue, Logan recounted to the two older men how he'd found Ren and Noah snoozing.

Running his hand over his mustache, Hank exchanged an astonished glance with Emmett and, bushy white brows raised, said, "All right for some!"

"Too much sleep seems to have put Noah in a very bad mood," Logan goaded.

At which, Emmett turned to Noah and said with feigned kindness, "Did you want us to bring you breakfast in bed, son?"

Hank snorted.

Willow grinned as she took a bite of muffin, while Logan did his best not to smile but it was there on his lips.

Noah ignored them all, focused instead on handing Ren a cup and pouring her some coffee.

As Emmett and Hank continued to amuse themselves at his expense, he looked up and, when he caught Ren's eye, she winked, pale eyes twinkling. The solidarity in her gesture made Noah pause. He felt his shoulders relax a fraction, and instead of bracing himself against everyone's continued teasing, he suddenly found himself fighting a smile. As if just by sharing a moment with Ren, having someone on his side, it became funny rather than something to be endured.

Then Willow shouted over, "Ren, you want eggs?" And the moment was gone, Ren went over to talk to Willow about breakfast.

But Noah was left feeling surprisingly lighter. Enough that he could go and sit down next to his dad and nodding toward the sling say, "So what happened—you fall off your horse?"

Which immediately wiped the smirk off Emmett's face as he narrowed his heavily hooded eyes and said, "You watch yourself." Then shaking his head muttered, "I've never fallen off a horse in my life."

Chapter Twenty-One

They set off to bright sunshine. The low hills coated with scrubby grass as far as they could see, marbled in patches of brown and green, the shadows of the pines stretching like fingers across the land. Emmett took the lead position as he had for the whole trip and always did. Hank stayed on one flank with Rocky, who delighted in keeping any wandering cattle in check. Ren and Willow hung at the back because Big Mac tended toward a very slow amble and Ren enjoyed keeping Mildred and the other loose-cannon cows moving. So Noah was forced to ride with Logan on the far side of the herd.

He'd lost his hat in the storm, which was annoying, would've pulled the brim down low and the collar of his jacket up high and happily settled into silence, but without his hat he could see Logan glancing at him every now and then, Misty, his horse, elegant beneath him.

He could hear Ren and Willow's laughter behind him and to stop thinking about almost kissing her, he thought instead about what she'd said about Loriana. He tried to decide if they looked alike, they certainly shared the same colorful fashion sense, and were both prone to doling out unfiltered opinions.

"Why do you keep looking behind you?" Logan asked.

"I don't."

"You do."

Noah glanced back to where Ren and Willow were riding and realized that he was very familiar with the sight of them, but he couldn't tell Logan any of what he was thinking. He didn't like knowing secrets. In his experience, they always led to trouble. They hadn't told their dad about auditioning for the talent show. Livvy hadn't told him that she was terminally ill. His brother Jack hadn't told them that this life had imploded until it was too late. Ethan wouldn't tell them where he was. Secrets were never a good thing.

They passed a huge puddle from the previous days' storm that a bunch of the hot cows went to stand in and cool off.

As they waited, Logan said, "Everything good with you and Ren?"

Noah nodded. He was riding on Dove again and focused on her snow-white mane, but without permission his dream from the night played out like flashes of a movie in front of his eyes. He swallowed down the shivering memory of it, remembered waking up shouting, the sweat on his skin, the fear fresh in his mind.

He looked up at his brother and found himself wanting, for the first time, to tell him what had happened.

But he never talked about Livvy. He never talked about any of it.

Then he thought about Ren telling him that his way of dealing with things was so clearly, adamantly, wrong.

Up ahead, Emmett whistled for them to continue. Rocky barked.

As they urged the cows forward out of the shallow water, he found himself saying, "I had a dream about Livvy. It was pretty intense."

Logan's eyebrows rose, clearly surprised by the admission, but didn't say anything like he knew Noah well enough not to push.

But for the first time, Noah felt like talking. Felt less engulfed by the memory. He told him the gist of it. "Woke up shouting, apparently," he said, giving Logan a sheepish look.

Logan smiled in understanding, then said, "I dream about it all, sometimes." He turned to look ahead. "Sometimes it's great, it's the early days and it's good times. But oftentimes I dream about Jack." Noah stared down at Dove's coat, focused his gaze on all the individual little hairs. "For some reason he's under water and I know he can't breathe but he's laughing," Logan continued, "and when I try and reach in and pull him out, he backs away. Sometimes I can just catch onto the edge of his shirt, but the fabric always slips through my fingers and I can never quite get hold of him before I wake up."

They exchanged glances. Noah didn't reply but he felt the horror of it shiver over him. Logan shrugged like what could any of them do.

They were riding on a muddy path now, it was dried and cracked from the heat of the morning's sun but still churned up in places. A pile of felled trees lay stacked on one side of them, but other than that, it was just grass and pines, the mountains and lagoon-blue sky.

It had been a long time since Noah and Logan had spent such endless time together.

"It was a tough time for you," Logan said.

Noah didn't respond. He found it uncomfortable when he was the subject of anything.

Behind them, he could hear the ebb and flow of Ren and Willow's laughter on the breeze.

Logan said, "It was a lot to go through."

The dream from the night before had done something to Noah's mind, made everything closer to the surface, like a crack had formed in the fabric of his memories and everything was scrabbling now to get out. He remembered the airport, the paparazzi with their cameras and endless questions—*Why was he flying home alone? Had the band split? Would they continue the tour without him?* And all he could think about was that Livvy was dying and she had been his tether to normality. What would he do without her?

He remembered his fist connecting with the cameraman. The scuffle, the shouts, the insults.

"You know, when I flew back, Dad was waiting at the airport," he told Logan.

"Really?" his brother's eyes widened in surprise.

"Yeah." Noah nodded. He remembered Emmett's grip solid on his arm, pulling him through the crowds to the waiting car. "I've never been more thankful to see him in my life," he said, still able to recall the relief. "He drove me to the hospital."

Logan smiled, sadder this time. "I didn't know that."

That little window of time had been like the circling plane. Where Noah thought that it might all just stop. Never felt more like a kid. Then he remembered pulling up to the hospital and the weight of his dad's hand as it clamped him on the shoulder, and he knew then that it was only going to get worse. Nothing had prepared him, though, for the speed that things changed. Life shrunk in an instant. Livvy in the hospital, her soft, hopeful eyes filled with courage while her body got weaker every day. Tubes and nurses and sadness everywhere he looked. Her mom, red-eyed; her dad, grave-faced. Frailty. Tests. Results. Then hospice care. And all the while she would ask him questions about Silver Sky—the tour and the bickering between the brothers, and what mischief Ethan got up to, and who Brodie had charmed. And when he said that none of that mattered right then, she looked at him and said, "But that's what keeps me going, Noah. Hearing about life."

Riding across the plains, he could suddenly feel the same burn of tears behind his eyes. Remembered the voice inside him that said he was only nineteen and it was too much, just wanting to be back with his brothers, away from the responsibility. "In the hospital, there was this moment," he said to Logan while still looking steadfastly ahead, "when I couldn't do it anymore and—" he paused at the shame of the memory "—I got up and I left."

"What happened?"

"Dad again." Noah glanced across, saw Logan's surprise

again. "Found me saddling up ready to ride anywhere I could go to get away. And he looked me in the eye and he said, 'You will go back. And you'll sit by Livvy's bed, and you'll hold her hand. You're not running away from this, Noah. You hear me?'"

Logan blew out a breath. "Sounds like Dad."

"Doesn't it?" Noah looked ahead at Emmett at the front of the herd, stared at the familiar outline of his father.

"And you went back?"

"I went back."

He told himself he would have gone back anyway, but he could never be truly certain. And he would be forever grateful to his dad for that.

He had held Livvy's hand and talked about the band and the future they'd envisaged, said it like there was still hope it might come true—the little house he'd build on the ranch, the family they'd have, their kids riding their first horses, buying their first little boots, going off to school. The life they'd mapped out. Him and Livvy. That was who they were. Childhood sweethearts. No one knew them as anything different, they were Noah and Livvy.

But Livvy was dying, and in some ways, inside, Noah was, too. Everything around him shrouded with a fear so pervasive that it'd crawled like the darkness of the forest over his skin, ever-present and unquenchable.

Up ahead, their side of the path met the Redemption River again, the water overspilling over the plain and glistening in the sunlight, three geese gliding down the middle.

As he heard Ren's laughter behind him, he thought of all

her questions the night before. He thought about her big eyes as she said, without the usual wariness that people had when they talked to him about Livvy, that she, too, would have kept her illness from him just to cling onto normality. If he was honest with himself, he'd never quite believed Livvy when she said it, always suspected that she hadn't told him in order to protect him. But now, with just those few words of validation from Ren, when he compared him and Livvy laughing on the phone while he was in Japan, him moaning about whatever was driving him bananas and her wanting to be sent pictures of the food he was eating in Bali and sniggering at his sardonic anecdotes that he always embellished to make her laugh harder, how different that was when his plane touched down and he saw she was no longer just Livvy, but sick Livvy, careful of Livvy, beware of germs—can't let her catch a cold Livvy. All his jokes had felt suddenly forced, his expression set to worry. It made him consider which version she preferred, and it wasn't hard to come up with an answer. Maybe she *had* kept it from him to protect him but equally maybe she had done it to buy herself a little more time being ordinary, carefree, fun-loving Livvy.

He wondered, staring at the glistening water of the Redemption, why that made it more painful. Because, he realized, one version made it his fault, the other made it simply a fact of life. And it was so much easier to shoulder the burden himself. To stubbornly believe just what he wanted to believe, like being reminded how young they were, that perhaps, if he considered it now, the future wouldn't necessarily have turned out how he'd imagined.

His way of coping, it seemed, was to create a myth and then set it in stone.

They rode on some more. More shrubs and bushes crowded the riverbank now—white bursts of hawthorn blossom, spikey thistles, the frilly green leaves of juniper. Wisps of cloud swept through the blue sky, their shadows carving new lines into Starlight Mountain as it watched, ever-present and, to Noah, always without judgment.

He had spent a lot of time staring at those peaks. Especially when faced with the complete absence of everything he had known and loved. But, while he might have walked away from fame, the paparazzi certainly didn't walk away from him. They were there everywhere he went taking shots of him looking haggard and vacant. Speculated about a breakdown, tailgated his truck when he left the ranch, and then that video of him stumbling out of the bar, falling flat on his face. Noah didn't care. He wanted it. He wanted them to destroy him. He'd read Logan's press statements asking them to leave Noah in peace, to let him grieve, to have some respect. But Noah was itching for the fight. The entire future he'd been dreaming of—that had got him through the craziness of the band years—was gone. Completely lost. He remembered gazing up at Starlight Mountain and realizing he had no idea who he was. Just a shell of a person. Hollowed out. And he couldn't even walk down the street without being hounded. So, he shut himself off from the world and went back to who he was at seventeen—a rancher. And he hadn't stopped since.

Logan was looking at him, brotherly concern on his face.

Noah thought how awful it was to be the subject of people's concern.

As they rode along the Redemption, Logan cleared his throat and said, with less confident authority than usual, "I'd really like to apologize, Noah. I think because you've never talked about it before, I've never got to say sorry before—for making you come back to the band. I just wish I'd told you to stay, be with Livvy on the ranch, have that time together before she got really sick. I knew you didn't want to come back. And I made you do it." He swallowed, tipped his head up to the sky then looked to Noah and said again, "I'm sorry."

Noah was horrified. "I don't want you to be sorry," he said almost without thinking. Was that what Logan had been harboring all this time? Had all of his brothers been too afraid to say anything?

He focused up ahead at the horizon wanting suddenly to be on his own. Did he blame Logan?

The apology stoked something dark inside him that lay dormant and deliberately ignored; the belief that deep down, maybe he did blame him, blamed all of them. Why couldn't they just have stayed, been happy where they were?

But he knew at the same time that he had gone willingly. If he had truly wanted to stay behind at the ranch, he'd have stayed. With the benefit of hindsight, Noah knew he wasn't someone who did things he didn't want to do. He had left the ranch because he was young and all his brothers were going and however good or bad it was on the road with Silver Sky, he wanted to be where his brothers were.

They were funny and ridiculous and stupid and when he wasn't with them, he missed them. He liked being with them more than he liked being without them. Something, again, he'd probably never acknowledged before because it meant that he had wanted to be with them more than he had wanted to be home with Livvy and starting on the path to adulthood.

He glanced across at his brother, realized in that instant how with distance came the bigger picture. Logic, reason. The complexity of feelings, he rolled his eyes to himself, that Ren was so adamant about. But there was no denying it was a relief to have a new way of looking at things. Just to say it all out loud. Like lifting a huge great boulder from where it pressed down on his chest. He swallowed and said, "It *was* a tough time. But it was always my choice to come back, Logan. Always."

Chapter Twenty-Two

It was the last night of the cattle drive. The road to reach them was still blocked from the storm damage, stopping his mom and Bella from getting through with supplies, but Willow had brought enough food to last them till they got home. It was early evening when they set up camp and, in a complete contrast to the night before, it was warm. It could even be described as balmy.

"This is what the weather *should* have been like the whole time!" Logan said as he set to work on the fire.

The Redemption ran just on the other side of the trees and Ren dug out some clean clothes from her bag and said, "I'm going to have a bath." Which made Willow laugh.

As Ren walked up the river, she realized what a relief it was to get away from everyone. She'd tried to be present when she was riding with Willow, but the whole time she hadn't been able to stop thinking about the night in the tent. Her eyes seemed drawn of their own accord to where Noah was riding ahead of them with Logan. The broadness of his shoulders, the outline of his profile when he looked across. But as she peeled off her clothes and scrubbed herself clean in the icy-cold water, she knew she would have to forget about it. Noah Carter, lost and tormented, was not a complication she could afford in her life. However heart-wrenchingly perfect it had felt, it wasn't real.

But then, as she came out from behind the cluster of rocks where she'd dressed, there he was waiting for her, pulling on a clean gray sweater, his hair slicked back from the water, his feet bare. The sight of him made her breath catch.

"Nice bath?" he asked.

"It was freezing," she replied, trying to muster her breezy enthusiasm.

They looked at each other for a moment. She felt her cheeks start to get hot, felt the air around them crackle.

She said, "You won't mention what I told you—about Loriana—will you?"

"Never."

She smiled. "Thanks."

Noah pushed his damp hair back where it fell over his face, and walking over to where she stood, said "I spoke to Logan—about having the dream about Livvy. I wouldn't have told him if it wasn't for you. So, I wanted to say thanks."

Ren tried to speak but found she couldn't get the words out, he was so near, suddenly so familiar.

In the distance they could hear the others chatting around the fire, getting food ready. Noah didn't seem in any hurry to get back. He moved so he was leaning against the rock beside her and said, "What are you going to do about Loriana? Are you going to tell her?"

Ren slid herself back on the rock, too, so she was sitting next to where he leaned, trying to act normal. "I don't know. I'm trying to build up the courage."

He frowned at the idea. "You're one of the bravest people I know."

"I am not."

"You went out in a tornado on your own to save a cow."

She laughed, "I guess I did."

"You forced me into a conversation."

"Yeah, that was brave."

His eyes creased, like he was smiling just because he was looking at her. "Seems to me you could handle anything." Then he seemed to catch himself and, turning away, said, "You'll know what to do."

She drew her legs up on the rock, wrapped her arms around them. "I hope so."

It was silent for a moment. She heard the crack and hiss of a ring-pull over in the camp; laughter because perhaps it had fizzed up everywhere.

She looked at Noah, he looked back.

She tucked her hair shyly behind her ear.

He watched the movement, seemed to think for a moment, then said, "In the tent, after the storm, I felt like—" He paused. "I could be wrong, but it felt like maybe something was going to happen."

Ren stayed silent, not daring to breathe, feeing like her heart was caught in her throat.

"Correct me if I'm wrong," he said, like he was out on a limb there.

"I will," she replied.

He bit his top lip, nodded. Then glanced away. "This is not easy for me."

She laughed. It lightened things.

He looked back. "I don't want you to be left with that." He paused, ran a hand frustratedly through his hair. "I don't know what I'm trying to say. I guess, I don't want that to have been your first kiss, you know?"

She swallowed. The noises of the camp and the river next to them faded into the background, all she could focus on was his mouth as he spoke, the little flecks of blue in his gray eyes and the lines at the side when he smiled.

"I was thinking," he closed his eyes for a second, cringed, then went on, "if you wanted someone to kiss. Just, you know, so it's not that—"

She could feel herself wanting to make a joke, to break the tension, to say something flippant and off-hand about him offering to kiss her, but she forced herself to stay quiet, to let the moment play out, listening to the thumping beat of her heart.

He looked at her, gray eyes enquiring, and almost imperceptibly she nodded.

The movement made her hair fall in front of her eyes. Noah reached up and tentatively tucked it behind her ear, then he let his hand stay, cupping her cheek, the rough, calloused palm cool against her skin. She wondered if her heart had stopped beating. He leaned forward and, ever so gently, his lips brushed hers, like a whisper. Just the sounds of the river and the forest behind them. Then she felt Noah's other hand on her back, drawing her closer, like he'd dragged her to him in the storm, close and protective, but this time when their lips met it was with an urgency, a need, the same as breathing, as living, like all the pent-up longing suddenly had a place to go. She found herself leaning forward, into the warmth of his chest, her arms raising and wrapping around his neck, his hands firm on her waist, gripping hard and tight, her whole body fizzing with a glorious intensity that made her only want to press her mouth harder against his, and her body closer.

But then suddenly, into the quiet, she heard the crunch of a footstep, and Noah immediately pulled away.

Ren felt the cold loss of the kiss. Of him.

Next second, Willow appeared through a gap in the trees and said, "You guys ready yet? Everyone's starving."

Embarrassed, Ren jumped down from the rock and said brightly, "Yeah, we were just coming!" and jogged over to join her, leaving Noah where he was, watching wordlessly as Willow looped her arm through Ren's and said, "How was the bath?"

The sun was setting and it was starting to get cooler. As they approached the campfire, Logan called over, "Ren, do you want a beer?"

Willow had brought them one each.

Ren took the proffered beer as Noah wandered back into camp. She couldn't quite look at him, looked instead at Emmett, who was holding his beer can between his thighs and opening it one handed because of the sling.

"Here's to our last night," Logan said, raising his drink,

beer frothing over the ring-pull. "We made it ... relatively unscathed."

Hank chuckled. Emmett lifted his slung arm with a wry smile. And everyone toasted in agreement. "To our last night," Noah repeated, his eyes finding Ren's.

She felt herself blush and looked away. Could think only of the kiss. She understood then that the version of her who had waited to be kissed, had waited purely for that moment.

Noah sat down on the grass, stretched behind him to reach his old leather jacket and slung it on. Ren had chosen the seat—an old bit of branch—next to Emmett and Hank and tried her hardest not to stare at him. Logan was cooking over the fire while Willow stood to the side, all long, slender limbs and graceful gestures, wearing a completely unsuitable and expensive cream jumper and doing her leg stretches while telling Logan what he was doing wrong. Rocky was stretched out as close to the fire as he could get without setting himself alight. All the tents were pitched—tonight Noah would share with Logan, thank goodness, and Willow with Ren.

"So, what's everyone most looking forward to having or doing when they get home?" Willow asked, leaning forward in a stretch.

She reminded Ren of Liane, back at the ranch. Liane had been an amazing dancer, but there was no hope of her having the time, money, or the willing adult to drive her to classes, to let it be anything more than a dream. She would sometimes do Ren's washing up if Ren would learn a dance she'd choreographed with her. That was the level of their dreams.

Once again, Ren tried to picture what it must have been like growing up in the Carter house with its wraparound veranda. Imagined having five older brothers, even if they left in her teens, fussing over their youngest sister, laughing with her, winding her up.

She wrapped her hands tighter around her beer can.

The stew bubbled gently on a makeshift wooden frame above the flames.

Logan said, "Willow, it's only been four days!"

But Hank said, "I'm looking forward to a good cup of coffee."

"You don't like my coffee?" Emmett replied with feigned indignance—or perhaps it wasn't feigned, Ren found it difficult to tell.

"Sure, it's okay," Hank replied, "but it's not as good as my wife's."

At the mention of Loriana, Ren felt the tiny flicker of nerves shimmer through her body. She looked over and saw Noah watching her, like he could sense what she was thinking. She tried to keep her expression neutral, not draw any attention, but then she saw the hint of a smile appear in his eyes and it both put her at ease and threw her completely off-balance.

Oblivious to the undercurrents, Logan said, "A shower and a warm bed," as he leaned forward to check if the stew was ready.

Emmett huffed, "I don't know when you got so soft."

"If we were meant to sleep on the floor," Logan replied,

going to get the bowls so he could serve, "they wouldn't have invented beds."

"Or goose-down Puffa jackets," Ren joked.

"Exactly!" Logan laughed.

Willow stood by Logan and handed around each bowl after he'd filled it. "I miss my book," she said.

"You've only been gone one night," Noah said, bemused, as he leaned forward to take a bowl.

"I know," she replied, going to sit crossed-legged on the ground, her bowl cupped in her hands, "but I'm at a really good bit and I forgot to bring it. Is that okay with you, *Noah*?" She threw him one of her trademark withering stares, which only made Noah roll his eyes but he was smiling. He looked genuinely happier than Ren had ever seen him, like he was suddenly allowing himself enjoyment.

Across the fire, his eyes met hers again. She remembered the press of his lips, the heat of his hand on the small of her back. Again, she felt herself blushing in the darkness.

"What about you, Dad?" Willow asked.

Emmett paused with his spoon raised to his lips. "I haven't had time to read a book for years," he stated, as if the very whim were a waste of precious time.

Willow sighed. "Not what you've read, Dad, what you're looking forward to doing when you get home?"

"Getting away from you lot!" Emmett said dryly, but there was a little smile in his eyes when he raised his coffee cup to his lips.

"What about you, Noah?" Logan asked, leaning against a tree trunk, legs stretched out in front of him.

Noah seemed to try but clearly couldn't think of

anything. "Nothing," he said, reaching forward to scratch Rocky's soft belly. "I'd stay out here another month if I could. Nowhere else I'd rather be."

Ren remembered telling him about her yearning to travel all around the world and his complete disregard for the idea. It was good to be reminded of how different they were, she realized, so she didn't succumb to the prickle of desire to be alone with him again, to talk with him more, to stand close by him while he pointed out the stars.

"And you, Ren?" Willow asked, scraping every last scrap from her bowl with her spoon.

Ren was caught off-guard thinking about Noah. "Oh, probably a big plate of pancakes and maple syrup from the diner," she covered quickly. "Loriana makes the best pancakes I've ever eaten!"

"Doesn't she just," Hank replied, clinking his beer to hers in agreement.

She felt Noah look. Felt his watchful concern. Remembered lying against him, the warmth of his body, the smell of the woodsmoke, the wind on the tent and the clouds of their breath in the freezing air. And it suddenly felt like it meant too much.

If she was honest, when she'd first met him—aside from him being all grumpy in the diner—he was good-looking enough that she would have kissed him just to jump the kissing hurdle. A couple of days ago, even on the trail, she would have done it just to get it over with.

But now, as suddenly she became too excruciatingly aware of his watchful gaze across the fire, she realized she *liked* him. She *wanted* to kiss him. And yes, kissing Noah may have gotten her over the hurdle, but it had simply created another one. Because it was all exactly what she wanted and everything she knew she couldn't have. She'd had enough heartache in her life. And any fool could tell that the stoic, long-suffering sadness in Noah's eyes would only lead to more.

Chapter Twenty-Three

"I think it's time for some music!" Hank said, unfurling himself creakily from the low branch seat to go and get his banjo.

While everyone groaned at the prospect, when he started to play they started to sing. Not Emmett—and no one would ever expect him to—but Willow, who for a family of musicians couldn't hold a tune to save her life but belted out the songs enthusiastically all the same. Ren, with her sweet warbly voice. Even Logan got involved this time, voice familiarly low and rumbling, he fought with Willow for most enthusiastic.

Noah watched, ignoring Logan and Willow's cringing display, his eyes searching out Ren across the fire, wondering what he was doing kissing her in the forest. He had wanted to give her something to say thank you for helping him, but he feared he had only complicated things that were better left simple. When the song changed,

Willow beckoned in his direction and said, "Come on, Noah, get involved!"

As she nodded at him with encouragement in her upturned eyes, despite trying not to, Noah couldn't help but remember band practices in the barn before their first audition, his little sister sitting on the rafters, swinging her legs and grinning down at them—all big, goofy teeth and even bigger curly hair, and next to her would sometimes be Bella, her hair plaited into weird creations by Willow. But other times it would be Livvy, kicking in time with Willow's legs, sharing her peanut-butter-and-jelly sandwiches and winking knowingly down at Noah whenever Jack and Logan had a row about what song to play next or who was out of tune.

He thought of Ren's words—*if you shut it all out, nothing gets through. Not even the good bits.* And he wanted to say, *It's the good bits that are the most painful.*

"Noah!" Willow pleaded, startling him out of his thoughts.

He felt all eyes on him and he hated it. Felt the unmistakable rising tattoo of his heart. His palms beginning to sweat. To bat Willow's pleas away he said, "I'm really more of an instrument guy."

In Silver Sky, he'd mostly played drums. Sometimes it was keyboard, sometimes bass guitar—whatever was needed, he pretty much learned to play it, refusing to be defeated. He'd even mastered the glockenspiel.

Hank immediately paused on the banjo and, rummaging in the front pocket of the case, pulled something out and, to Noah's horror, he threw it over to him.

Noah caught it and turned it over in his hands. A harmonica, vintage, careworn and intricately engraved.

He hadn't actually played a note on anything since he'd walked away from the tour and the band. Except once when he'd strummed a tune on the guitar for Livvy while she watched with a heartbreaking smile on her face.

Noah's hands didn't tremble as he looked down at the harmonica, but the way he felt, they should've done.

As Hank started to play again, instinct had Noah ready to place the harmonica down onto the ground with, "Sorry, never played one before."

But then he heard Ren's soft voice with its heart-wrenching catches on the high notes, and even though she wasn't looking at him, he could see in her all that tough, fend-for-yourself determination, and he remembered the feel of her arms wrapping tight around his neck as he breathed in the scent of her, and it made him feel again the pressure inside of what it meant to have someone expect something from him. And yet now as she sang, and tried to encourage his dad to at the very least sway along—and despite all her set-backs in life and the secret of her parentage that she was closely guarding—he could see across the fire that when she smiled she did it with the whole of her, nothing held back, all there on her face, completely and totally unafraid. And in response, he found himself, against his own stubborn reluctance, bringing the harmonica to his lips.

Chapter Twenty-Four

They all arrived back to a hero's welcome.

The ranch looked glorious in the sunshine, rays reflecting off the lush grass and turning the earth to burnt umber. There was the familiar red wood of the barn and behind it, Starlight Mountain, looming majestically. For Noah, the sight made his breath still and his heart calm.

Martha, Bella and Loriana were waiting for them, looking clean and fresh compared to all the riders. Like they'd all dressed up a little bit specially for the return—Martha, ready with open arms, in a long duck-egg-blue skirt and black T-shirt; Bella, next to her in a caramel cotton sundress and simple white sneakers, went straight to Logan and gave him a big hug, snuggling into his enveloping embrace. Then, when she'd whispered a loving hello, she moved on to Noah. He felt his eyes close as her arms wrapped around him, and her perfume made him think of home—always like a big sister. Even Loriana, cracking her cynical façade when she saw Hank, said, "I thought in that storm you were a goner!"

"You're not getting rid of me that easily," Hank quipped.

Loriana smiled as she cupped his jaw with her palms and kissed him on the cheek leaving a faint coral-lipstick impression that she then wiped off lovingly.

Noah looked at Ren, who glared at him like he was being too obvious.

Then everyone started talking over one another, recounting what happened—how was this, how was that? Who's hungry?

Martha came over to Noah and said, "You seem different."

"Tired?" Noah suggested, slightly wary of where this was going and hoping that no one else was in earshot. Luckily the others were all recounting stories of the storm.

"No, not tired," Martha said, as she inspected him with narrowed eyes, "Relaxed."

Noah blew out a disbelieving breath. "It's the beard."

"No." She smiled like she was happy to see the change in him. "I think your face is more relaxed, your eyes." She went to sweep his hair across his forehead, and he batted her away like a teenager.

Martha laughed.

Noah said, "My trailer still here?"

"For now," she replied.

"I bet in that storm you wished you never said yes to going!" Loriana was saying to Ren, arms folded, assessing her tired, slightly windswept and now sun-kissed appearance.

Martha moved to join them, putting her hand on Ren's arm. "Yes, you poor thing—you picked the wrong cattle drive!"

Ren, as Noah had come to expect, waved away their concern. "Not at all, it was good, I enjoyed it."

A flash of her wide blue eyes just before he kissed her came into his mind.

Martha looked skeptical but didn't argue. "Well, I'm so glad you're all safe and sound. Come inside and we'll have something to eat." She beckoned for Ren and the others to follow her.

Ren smiled awkwardly and said, "Thanks, but I should get going."

Martha shook her head and said, "Don't be silly. You've just ridden with these guys for four days—you need to eat!"

"Mom," Noah cut in. "Let Ren go home. I think she's probably had enough of us for now."

At that Martha's gaze narrowed and she glanced from Noah to Ren, seeming to pick up on something in the air. "Okay, well, if you have to go, then you go, of course. But you come back and see us anytime you want to."

They all said their goodbyes. Willow squeezing her in a big hug while Ren thanked her for the loan of her horse.

Logan gave her a big hug, the type Noah wished he had given her himself when the storm was raging, and said, "It was a pleasure riding with you."

"You, too," Ren replied.

Bella said, "Logan wasn't too grumpy about the weather?"

"Yeah, he was," Ren said. "But it was still nice riding with him."

Logan tipped his head like he appreciated the compliment.

Finally, Emmett stepped forward, and said, "If you ever want to come over and go for a ride, there's always a horse that needs exercising."

"Thank you—" she gave him an appreciative smile "—that's really kind."

"Any time. I'm serious," Emmett replied. "I'll give you the code to the gate. You'll see where everything is kept in the barn." Then he held out his hand to shake hers and said, "Thank you for helping us out, Ren. You were an asset."

Noah was astonished that even his dad was better at this than him.

Ren looked touched. She took Emmett's hand in hers. "Thank you for putting up with me. Hope I didn't talk too much."

Emmett's mouth tipped up a fraction. "Not at all."

Hank then gave her a kiss on the cheek and Loriana said, "You have a good rest before you come back to the diner, honey? Give it a couple of days."

Noah felt for Ren, saw her cheeks redden at the attention from Loriana, saw her cover it with her catch-all smile and tuck her hands in her pockets as she said, "Will do."

"I'll walk you out," Noah said.

He went to pick up Ren's bag, but she bent down for it before he could get there and threw it over her shoulder, then started making her way to her car. Rocky walked with them, trotting along beside Noah, like now that he was home and the excitement was over, he was loyal again.

"You're free!" Noah joked softly in reference to his family.

"They're lovely," she said. And he realized that he also meant that she was free of him.

When they reached her car, Ren put her bag down and dug in her pocket for her key. "Seems like months since I parked here."

"Thanks for all your help," Noah said.

She glanced across, her hair catching on her cheek at the movement and said politely, "You're welcome. It was fun."

"It was fun, sometimes." He watched her tuck the lock of hair behind her ear.

"It was *all* fun."

Noah laughed. "Okay, if you say so," he admitted reluctantly, then went around to the trunk to put her bag in.

"The trunk's stuck, you can't open it. You have to put that on the back seat," Ren said, opening the back door for him.

He didn't say anything, but of course Ren would have a car with a stuck trunk. He chucked her bag on the back seat then stood with his hands in his pockets. She turned to him mirroring his pose, her hands in her jeans pockets. She looked nice, her hair wavy, her face freckled from the sun.

He said, "Message me your bank details and I'll get your money to you."

It was all so awkwardly polite.

"I get paid?" Her eyes widened in surprise.

"Of course." He nodded toward the trunk. "You could use it to get your car fixed."

She made a face. "Noah, I spend my money on more fun things than that."

He half laughed. "Course you do."

There was a pause, and he suddenly didn't want her to go. It felt empty back at the house without her, but there was nothing left to say. They stood there, the silence stretching, until the dog got bored and ran off back to the house and Noah said, "You gonna tell Loriana?"

"Yeah."

"When?"

She swept her hair back, held it there with her hand. "Soon."

She scuffed the floor with her boot.

He looked out over the ranch, where the horses were grazing in the paddock and the chickens scratched in the dry earth.

"About the kiss…" He raked a hand through his hair, chanced an uneasy glance in her direction as he tried to formulate what he was going to say.

"I know."

He winced, trying to gauge if he'd hurt her feelings, but said, because he couldn't not, "It probably shouldn't have—"

She cut him off with a wide, open grin. "Don't worry about it, Noah, it was good, got it out the way. I've been needing that to happen for years."

He couldn't tell if she was being genuine. "You sure?"

"Of course." She leaned over and bashed him on the arm. "You've done me a favor."

"Yeah?" He felt he should say more but couldn't, torn between wanting things to just get back to normal and a feeling in his throat that he couldn't quite decipher, wondered if it was regret. "Okay, well—" he stuck out his hand to shake "—thanks for everything."

She grinned as she took his hand. "Thank *you*, Noah." Then she stepped away, a wide smile on her face like she had no qualms at all about leaving.

He watched as she climbed into the car and slipped on her shades, music blaring as soon as she turned the ignition. "See ya, Noah," she called over the noise. Then she reversed in an arc of yard dust, hand waving out the window as she drove away out the big Silver Sky Ranch gates leaving him standing there alone.

Chapter Twenty-Five

Ren tipped her head back against the headrest and sighed. She told herself it was just a release of tension, having had to keep up the act all that time after the kiss, but as she drove down Main Street she felt utterly deflated.

Once she'd let herself into her apartment, she showered off all the grime of the trip, unpacked, sewed up the rip on her raincoat, all the time trying not to think about Noah. She told herself it wasn't just Noah that she missed, it was Logan, too—and Hank, Willow, Emmett. No one was playing the banjo tonight.

But it was Noah who she really missed. Coaxing stories out of him. Seeing the way his mouth tilted up with the ghost of a smile and the feeling of jubilation at having made it happen. The way he checked if she was warm enough. The way he rode his horse.

The way he held her hand in the storm. The way at

times she had caught his eye and seen the sparkle in it that felt like it was just for her.

She sat at the breakfast bar in her tiny kitchen and pressed her fingers into her eyes. *Stop thinking about him.* She never thought about people like that.

She needed to focus on why she was there in Autumn Falls, why she'd gone on the trip; if the last three days hadn't taught her courage, then nothing would.

The next afternoon, Ren walked up to the diner just as it was closing. She had lain in bed going over and over what she was going to say to Loriana. How best to phrase it. Then she'd run through all the different possible responses, all of them playing out like a Hollywood movie; an open-armed gasp or an arm's length rejection. Her palms were sweaty, her heart beating too fast.

She glanced in the window to check she didn't look as nervous as she felt, but as Noah said, her every emotion was there visible on her face. Suddenly she wished he was there with her, just for the moral support. She paused and retied her hair in a ponytail, rummaged through her bag to find some makeup and went to put more on, but her hands were shaking. She stopped, took a breath and looked at herself in the window glass again. She thought of Noah telling her she was one of the bravest people he knew.

Then she rubbed her cheeks with her hands to give her pale face some color, and pushed the door open into the diner.

Loriana was cashing up. She'd taken her apron off and had a thin cardigan the color of grape juice on over her diner uniform, and her big brown suede purse waiting on the counter next to her. She looked tired, ready to go home. Maurice, the chef, was out the back clanging about putting things away.

Ren went and stood opposite her. Steeling herself, she said, "Loriana, can we talk?"

Loriana's head shot up, eyes wide with immediate worry. "Oh, no. Are you leaving? Is this the leaving talk?"

Ren fizzled with nerves. She shook her head. "No, I'm not leaving."

Loriana came around the counter and gestured for Ren to sit down in one of the booths. "Are you all right? You look very pale?"

Ren slipped into the red faux-leather banquette, her bag on her lap like a comforter, watching as Loriana went and turned the sign on the door to closed then came back and slid in opposite her.

Ren took in all the silver bracelets weighing down Loriana's wrists, their little charms knocking against the Formica table as she moved. They had the same taste in jewelry. She felt the little butterfly flutter in her chest again.

She looked at the scrolled name embroidered on Loriana's diner shirt, the creases in the skin at her neck, the big amethyst earrings, the hair piled up and lacquered in place with Elnett. The way her blue eyes widened to reveal the whites around her pupils when she looked worried. Ren's did that. The lines around her lips from when she used to smoke. The peach blusher on her cheeks and the blue mascara on her lashes. None of them would ever look the same after this conversation; they would belong to someone else, a different version of this same woman. Her mother.

"Loriana, I think I'm your daughter." She said it quickly like pulling off a Band-Aid. No messing. And with the words came a tightening of Ren's whole body in anticipation. Time slowed. The world seemed to pause. Loriana's face softened in surprise. Her penciled eyebrows rose.

Ren thought of the long, agonizing process of dead ends and restricted access and lost documents. No record of her original birth certificate, no one able to confirm what state she was born in because her original foster parents moved, so she was briefly adopted as a little kid in another state. She could almost taste the visceral memories of the let downs and shattered hope. She'd hit so many dead ends that she'd eventually hired a professional to see if he could do what she couldn't. She hadn't actually expected him to succeed but, when he did, Ren had never felt anything like it. The prize was so huge it almost weighed her down, consumed her every waking moment. And now it was happening, she'd said the words out loud, she felt a sudden desire to stop the moment where it was. Like Noah in his dream wanting to pause the plane in the sky to hold back time.

But instead, it was spinning like a roulette wheel. The ball going round and round.

She couldn't breathe. She couldn't believe she'd unwrapped her secret and said it out loud. She imagined

Liane and Mean Billy listening at the door. Wanting her to get what she wanted while at the same time envy making them half hope she might fail.

"I hired a private detective," she said, nerves making her fill the silence, "to find out who my mom is. And it led him to you."

She thought of all those lonely nights just praying for this. All those ghost faces of her memory, watching, waiting, breath suspended.

"Oh, honey," Loriana leaned across and took hold of Ren's hand. "I'm not your mom, I'm sorry."

Ren felt the floor slip away. From everything to nothing. There was a sudden pain in her chest like an iron fist crushing her ribs.

"It's not me, Ren." Loriana's hand was cool over hers. "Oh, goodness."

Ren could hear blood rushing in her ears.

"I should've recognized you straight away." Loriana reached over with her other hand and so both were holding Ren's across the table. "I'm sorry, sweetheart. We put my name on the certificate, but I'm not your mom."

Ren didn't understand. "Who-who put my name down?" She felt it again, that little kernel of hope. The roulette wheel took another spin.

Loriana sighed up at the ceiling. "Your mom's name was Candy. She was my stepsister."

Ren knew the moment that she heard the word *was* that she would never get to meet Candy, but all the same, she heard the tremble in her voice when she said, "Where can I find her?"

Loriana sighed and Ren got the confirmation in her eyes. "I'm sorry, Ren. She died. Not long after you were born."

It was like nothing she'd ever felt before. The ground shifting beneath her. The sharpness of features, words, smells. Her blood pulsing in her ears and her vision blurring like she might pass out. All hope slipping away. All possibility gone. Noah had said she could cope with anything, but he was wrong.

Ren knew she had to get out of there. Grabbing her bag, she said, "Okay, well, thank you for telling me—" And she slipped out the booth like she was fleeing for her life.

"Ren, honey," Loriana called after her, "wait a second."

"I've gotta go!" she called back breezily, making an effort to walk, when she wanted to run quickly out the diner before the tears that she never let herself cry spilled over onto her cheeks.

Chapter Twenty-Six

Noah was out checking on the herd, right out on the far north pasture under the shadow of Starlight Mountain when his phone rang. There was never normally reception out that far. He had half an eye on Mildred, the little cow Ren had fallen for, who had run off with his hat and was currently having a great time refusing to give it back. "Hello," he said, distracted. He couldn't lose another hat.

"Noah, it's Loriana."

"Hey, Loriana," he said, wondering why Loriana would ever call him.

"Noah, I don't know who else to call. It's about Ren—"

Noah turned Blue and was galloping back before she'd even finished her sentence.

As Loriana told him what had happened, all he could picture was Ren wrapping Loriana's big scarf around her head in the tent, just her smiling blue eyes peeking out, and the urge to protect, or rather shield her, from the almost painful sweetness of her secret tightened his chest. He felt a sympathy that he knew she would hate—because he would hate it felt for him.

"I've called and called her," Loriana was saying. "I've been to her apartment. She's not there. No one's seen her. Oh, Noah. She was so upset. She was trying to keep it together, but I could see it. I could tell."

"I'll find her, Loriana. Don't worry."

"Please do," she said, none of the usual brash confidence in her voice.

Back at the ranch, Noah whistled for Rocky and then jumped in the Jeep.

Driving along to Main Street, looking down side roads, searching faces of passersby, Noah had always thought that he didn't want that hassle again. Didn't want the emotions. Caring for someone else. Worrying about them.

But now that it was happening, he didn't stop to think, because it wasn't about him—about how he felt—it was about her. It was about Ren not being upset. About making sure that she was okay. He went to her apartment, banged on the door, while the engine of his Jeep idled outside. Of course she didn't answer. Her car was there, though. So he drove to the bus station. He scoured the back streets. The light was starting to fade when he drove out to the foothills of the mountains, called her name into the forest, sent Rocky for a quick recce then summoned him back. Nothing.

He stood under the shadow of the mountain, the apple orchard behind him, Rocky chasing bees, the sweet fragrance of the blossom filling the dusky air, hands on his hips thinking of everything Ren had said. He kept seeing her eyes, what she looked like when she was happy. He thought of her frank, weird wisdom. Her annoying questions. Felt the clutch in his chest when he thought of kissing her, the feeling of her mouth soft against his. The hurt that shadowed her face. *You don't need this, Noah.* He could feel himself rear away from the responsibility of someone else's feelings as he paced the ground, the heady scent of the blossom now overpoweringly sickly in the orchard behind him, the sound of the bees rising in a crescendo like crackling flames. He should just get back in the Jeep and leave her to it. Ren was a tough, independent cookie. She had proved herself more than capable of looking after herself and, he reminded himself, she certainly didn't need his misplaced feelings of protection.

He thought about her around the campfire, singing, joking, cajoling his dad, in the tent wrapped up like a caterpillar, laughing on her horse.

Best place to be in the world.

He closed his eyes. Of course.

Ren was asleep on the hay when he found her. Curled up in the corner of Star's stall. Noah sighed with relief then sent Loriana a message to let her know she was safe.

Unlatching the door, he gave Star a scratch. "Hey, girl." Then went and sat on the straw opposite Ren.

She was pale-faced, fast asleep, wearing bright pink leopard-print leggings and a black sweater, face all made up like she'd got ready for a special occasion. There were faint mascara tracks on her cheeks. Noah shrugged off his shirt and laid it over her. Then he sat down and leaned his head against the wooden wall, forearms on his knees, and waited.

Chapter Twenty-Seven

It was dark outside when Ren woke up. Tired and disorientated, blinking her big eyes she reminded Noah of one of the foals.

"Hey," he said, as she looked around, saw his shirt covering her and lifting it as she sat up, handing it back with an emotionless, "Thanks."

She didn't smile, didn't acknowledge the oddity of where they were, just blew out a breath and, patting her hair flat and checking it for bits of straw, sat back slumped against the wooden slated wall.

Noah didn't say anything.

Ren glanced his way. "Loriana told you?"

He nodded.

"What a fool," she muttered about herself.

"You're not a fool," he said.

She laughed humorlessly, her eyes blank. It wasn't a look on her he either recognized or expected. It made a little shiver of panic run up his spine.

She picked at the hay next to her, lifting a piece and running her nail down the center then splitting it in two and dropping the halves back on the ground.

Noah waited.

She closed her eyes and pressed her fingers into them for a second. When she opened them, she tipped her head up to the wooden beams of the barn roof. After staring for a second, she said, "It's nice in here."

He nodded. It was a beautiful barn.

She split more straw with her nail. Split and discard. Split and discard. Eyes focused intently on the job in hand.

Star stood watching them with vague interest.

As the silence grew, Noah glanced up into the horse's all-knowing brown eyes, huge like giant marbles, framed with thick Maybelline lashes, feeling like he had no idea what to do.

Star just blinked.

Aware that Ren might want privacy and that perhaps he was intruding, he was about to get up when she said, "You know, I was adopted once."

Noah stayed where he was.

"By a couple desperate for a little girl." Ren spoke without looking up, eyes fixed on the piece of straw she was holding. "They were so nice to me. They'd dress me up in little dresses and do braids in my hair. There were loads of cuddles and outings. It was like a dream." She glanced at Noah without moving her head. "Birthday cakes. Big Christmases—not that many presents—they didn't have a lot of money—but more than enough, and all the holly and ivy up the stairs and carol singing." She tied the straw in a knot.

He asked hesitantly, "What happened?"

Ren sat up, chucked the piece of straw away. "She got pregnant. It was a complete surprise—they'd really struggled to have a baby. They didn't have enough money for two children. And I had to go back. They were devastated." She lay her hands flat on the straw either side of her and rested her head dolefully against the wall. "There were these agonizing apologies. And you know what I said when she was sobbing, telling me how sorry she was? I said, 'That's okay.'" She shook her head. "I was nine years old. It wasn't okay, it was the worst time of my life."

Noah thought of himself at nine years old, riding out on the cattle drives with his dad and his brothers, skimming stones out at the lake, tucked into bed by his mom with a kiss on the forehead and a soft *I love you*, Christmas mornings in matching festive-themed pajamas opening Scalextric sets and PlayStations and boxes of brand-spanking-new cowboy boots.

"I went back to Mrs. Watson's—the foster home—with this big brave face, you know, all smiles and, 'Yeah, I'm fine, I'm glad to be back. I knew it wouldn't work out.'"

Noah watched her hands clench around bunches of straw.

"And all the other kids, they weren't stupid, they knew, but no one said anything." She paused. "It was literally the worst thing. We lived in fear of it. Finding a new family and then being rejected. And when it happened, it was as bad as we thought it was."

"I'm sorry, Ren."

She shook her head like trying to throw off the pity. "I got over it, eventually. The whole Orphan Annie, sun'll come out tomorrow kind of thing, it's a way of surviving. But, you know yourself, there's only so much you can try to make everything good."

Noah didn't like the way that sounded, like she was coming down to his level when that wasn't where she belonged. Suddenly, he didn't want to be the one who was right.

Ren sighed like she'd come to the end of the road, throwing the bunches of straw from her hands. "I've had enough now. I'm exhausted. I don't know how to make it okay." When she looked at him, every last scrap of her verve was gone.

He felt his words get stuck in his throat in his uncertainty.

She huffed frustratedly. "I shouldn't have told her. I was happy just for a bit not knowing for sure. But then I went and stupidly let myself think that maybe just this once it would all go my way. What a fool I was."

Noah looked down at the ground, part of him urging him to move and put his arm around her, the other part forcing him to stay exactly where he was. He knew somehow that she'd shake it off anyway.

Ren thought for a moment, split another piece of straw before she spoke. "My friend Liane would say, 'Possibility lives around the corner, hope gets you there.' Who knows where she heard that from, but we all thought she was the oracle." Ren paused, bit down on her lip. "What the heck happens when you don't have any hope?"

Noah blew out a slow breath, he was the worst person to answer that.

Ren dropped her head down so that she was staring at the straw. Noah sat where he was, forearms draped over his knees, trying to make sense of it, aware of how fragile she was in comparison to how strong she had been.

"I don't know, Ren," he said, tentatively, glancing up at Star and feeling the horse watching him, maybe in warning. "Maybe now you know the truth…"

She didn't look up, stayed focused instead on the piece of straw she'd picked up.

"I can't imagine how disappointing it was talking to Loriana." He swallowed, tried to do this how she did it. Star snorted. He took it as a sign to continue. "But there must be a bright side." He was out of his depth, he searched around in his head for a possible alternate view.

"Don't, Noah," she warned with a small shake of her head. "Do you know how much energy it takes to find a bright side? How many lies you have to tell yourself every day, how much you have to ignore?" When she looked at him this time, it nearly crushed his heart.

Noah closed his eyes for a second, wishing there was someone more capable there in the horse barn to do this for him. His mom or Willow.

The silence lingered, stretching on between them, he felt the longer he looked the further away from her he got. She was right, who was he to tell her to find the positive? But he had written himself off until she came along. He couldn't bear the idea of her stooping to his level, losing the bright, effervescent life force that made him roll his eyes but, he realized, he quietly admired. He ran a hand frustratedly through his hair. "Ren, you've made me look at things differently. You're like—" He paused. "This is so corny, but to me, I think you're inspiring."

She shook her head, chucked a bit of straw away and, closing her eyes, tipped her head back against the wall.

"I feel like you could survive anything," he said, the words hanging in the air, amplified by the silence.

He saw then the tears glistening on her closed lashes. He wanted to reach over and wipe them away, touch the soft blotched skin, but he didn't, because he knew he had nothing to offer her. He would never change enough. She needed better than him. The kind of love Ren deserved was too huge, too everything, required too much commitment and guarantee than he could ever give.

She wiped her eyes with the heel of her hand. "You can go now, Noah."

He sighed. Then with a nod he stood up and brushed the straw from his jeans. "I'm sorry, Ren," he said. "For what it's worth," he added without really thinking, "someone would be lucky to love you."

She glanced up and for the first time he saw true vulnerability in her huge, dinner-plate eyes. He realized that all that other stuff, all the frank honesty that she doled out day-to-day, that was the front. This was the real thing. But it was too much for him to take—like looking at the sun—it was too powerful, too all-consuming, too bone-shatteringly terrifying. So instead of holding her gaze, he looked away. Exactly as, he imagined, she knew he would.

Chapter Twenty-Eight

A couple of days later, Noah rode out with his dad. The sun was high above Starlight Mountain turning the lush pasture all around them every shade from lime to emerald-green.

"Ren okay?" Emmett asked as he hauled himself up into the saddle, arm still weak from his injury on the drive.

Noah frowned with surprise. "You heard about it?" Every night since, he'd lain in bed staring up at the ceiling of his trailer thinking about Ren curled up in the barn.

"You don't live in a town like this and not hear about something like that." Emmett adjusted himself on the back of Bandit, holding the reins in one hand while he fiddled, irritated with the sling. "We all knew her mom," he said, finally happy enough with his position to get going. "Candy Miller. She was a wild child. Good heart. Mean father. I never knew she had a baby, though."

Noah's instinct was to shut it out. He just wanted to ride. He hadn't slept well and had been up working since five. "I'm sure Loriana will tell her all about it at some point."

Emmett nodded. "I heard they were meeting later this morning."

"Yeah?"

"Apparently so."

Emmett's expression was shadowed by the brim of his hat, but Noah knew what he was hinting at.

"That's good," Noah replied. Refusing to take the bait. Just falling into Blue's rhythm, wishing he'd let his dad go out on his own, but his mom had told him to keep an eye on him because he was injured.

Clearly unhappy with Noah's reply, Emmett said more plainly, "You don't think she might need someone to go with her?"

Noah shrugged, noncommittal. "She's pretty independent."

He felt his dad's heavy gaze on him, even though he couldn't see his eyes. Noah felt exposed without his hat, he'd have to buy a new one in town.

"Something happen between you two?" Emmett asked.

"Nope." Images flashed through Noah's mind; the clasp of their hands in the storm, the kiss on the rock, the heart-crushing look in her eyes in the barn.

His dad nodded.

They rode in silence, clouds drifting casually over the sun and casting their dark shadows over the mountain.

"How was she when you saw her?" Emmett asked.

Noah half laughed. "Why the interest in Ren?"

Emmett tipped his head as he considered the question.

"I liked her. She worked hard. Shame to think that she's on her own here. That's all."

Noah closed his eyes, suddenly knew exactly where this was going. "Mom put you up to this?"

"Absolutely not," Emmett scoffed, then carried on, "It would just be good to know that someone was there for her."

"Why don't you go, then?" Noah said, knowing he'd get a hard stare for the facetiousness.

Emmett did exactly that. Tipping his head so Noah could see his narrowed eyes. "I think, Noah," he said with deliberate slowness, "that I would not be the first person she would want going with her."

Noah raised a brow. "And you think I am?"

Emmett paused, turned and looked at his son. "Well, you're not the last, that's for sure."

The implication was as clear as Halfmoon Lake on a still summer's day. With a resigned sigh, Noah tipped his head up to the sky, then, pulling on Blue's reins, he turned the horse around and said, "Okay, I'm going."

Chapter Twenty-Nine

Ren had stayed in her apartment for the last few days, woken up with a heavy sense of pointless indifference, and lain in bed for hours. Her face was puffy, her eyes sore. She looked at her pink leopard-print leggings where she'd thrown them on a chair, and even they felt foolish in their brightness.

More than once she had thought about skipping town in the night, but something made her stay. She kept thinking about Noah waiting for her in the barn. The kindness of it. Yet also the painful awareness that it would never be more than that. It all felt too much. And then Liane had called and, while Ren was older now, when she saw her name flashing on the screen, she could still taste the humiliation of walking back through the front door of the Texas ranch. Like an animal escaping and being brought back to the zoo.

"I feel like I've failed," she said to Liane. "Like everything we waited for—the dream—I feel stupid for thinking I had it."

On the other end of the call, Liane had an urgency to her voice. "You haven't failed, Ren. You hear me. You tried. It wasn't what you thought, but when is it ever? You tried—that's enough."

Ren had to swallow over a lump in her throat when she thought of Liane standing behind the counter in the motel she owned, but really just ten years old, curling up in Ren's bunk bed with her when she cried silently at night saying, "One day, it'll happen. I promise."

She squeezed her eyes shut and said, "Never cry, never care."

But rather than agreeing, Liane groaned and said, "Man, I was an idiot."

"They were words to live by!" Ren said, shocked at her response.

"No, Ren, they weren't."

It made Ren think how much they all must have cared. All of them with the same delusional wish spurring them on: That one day someone would burst through the door and say, *that's my child, that one there!* And whisk them away to happiness.

"Ren," Liane said softly, "dreams can change."

Ren was silent.

"Maybe you need to look at it another way," Liane went on. "You have me, you have Billy. Our family just looks different to other people's. Go talk to this Loriana—find out where you came from—but, Ren, it doesn't have to change where you're going."

Ren was nodding, even though Liana couldn't see her.

"Are you listening to me?"

"Yeah, I was nodding."

Liane laughed. "Maybe we're lucky, Ren. Maybe we get to build the family we want."

Ren's mind flashed to Noah sitting waiting for her as she slept.

"I know I'm lucky to have you," Liane said.

"Me too, with you."

"You go meet her, okay?"

"Okay."

Now it was the day of the meeting and Ren had butterflies in her tummy, she couldn't eat, couldn't concentrate. She'd changed her clothes twice when the doorbell rang.

She was pulling on a red sweater as she went down to answer it.

Noah Carter was waiting on the sidewalk.

The sight of him, in his threadbare T-shirt with the faded dates of some rodeo on the front, beaten up jeans and his leather flight jacket, hair tucked behind his ears, eyes warily uncertain, made her heart pause momentarily. An unexpected flicker of what felt like relief washed over her. But to cover it, because she didn't want to feel that way, didn't want to rely on him and be grateful for the support, she said, "What are you doing here?"

He shrugged a shoulder. "Thought you might want some company."

Ren had to look away down the street, anywhere but Noah's doleful gaze. "How did you know when we were meeting?"

"I asked Loriana."

She nodded. Why did he have to be so nice to her? She didn't want him to be nice to her because she knew how easy it would be to like him too much. When he'd said that someone would be lucky to love her, it was impossible not to hear the missing words: *just not me*.

"I appreciate you coming, Noah," she said, "but I think it's something I should do on my own."

He nodded. "That's no problem at all." Because he was Noah Carter, he didn't try to persuade her otherwise, and, stupidly, she wasn't sure if she was grateful or not.

She thanked him again for coming over as she walked to her car. But once inside, she turned the key in the ignition and nothing happened. The engine turned over a couple of times but didn't catch.

She saw Noah watching.

She tried the engine again. Nothing. And again.

Noah came over, leaned on the open window and said, "You should probably stop spending your money on exciting things and buy yourself a new car."

Ren rolled her eyes. "Thanks for the advice."

Noah put his hands in his pockets and stepped back, hint of a smile on his face. "You want a lift?"

"Yes, please, thank you."

He nodded and strolled back to his Jeep.

She followed, thinking about what Liane had said, thinking how lucky a person would be to have Noah in their family.

When they pulled up at Loriana's, she was standing with her hands clasped nervously in front of her, dressed more smartly than normal in a crisp white shirt and jeans, watching intently as they approached the house.

"You want me to come in with you?" Noah asked.

Ren had intended to say no but now she was here, and her courage was slipping, she nodded.

When they were inside, the first thing Ren said was, "I'm sorry I caused such a fuss—running out on you at the diner."

"Don't be silly!" Loriana scolded. "This isn't fuss, this is life!"

She directed them into the living room. The house smelled like Loriana's perfume, sweet like vanilla frosting. It was comfortably cluttered, filled with all Hank's fishing gear and lots of nicknacks, shelves crammed with porcelain animals and overspilling plants. The walls were covered in pictures, hardly a space left. It was exactly what Ren had imagined Loriana's house looked like.

Noah followed a few steps behind, kept himself in the background.

"I've made some coffee," Loriana said, seemingly as nervous as Ren felt inside and when she came back with a tray, she had to push newspapers and her reading glasses aside to clear space on the low table. She served the coffee in mismatched mugs. Ren's was blue and white striped, and there was homemade lemon cake on plates with delicate little blue flowers around the edges. Ren wrapped her hands around her mug and perched nervously on the edge of the couch. Noah sat beside her. Loriana was on the opposite couch.

There was a moment of silence. Ren wondered if everyone in the room could hear her heart beating.

She felt suddenly grateful for Noah's presence beside her.

Loriana put her mug down on the table and said, "Let me tell you about your mother, Ren."

And as she said it, Ren felt Noah's hand softly, fleetingly touch her back. It made her think that maybe, just for that hour or however long they were there, she could let him be there for her, a friend to offer support if she needed it, and then she would let it go.

Chapter Thirty

Ren listened as Loriana told her all about Candy Miller. Fifteen, daughter of Loriana's mom's boyfriend—apparently, a devil of a man.

Ren wanted to record every second so she could play it back later. Her eyes took in everything: the way Loriana's mouth moved as she spoke: "She was so much fun. If you could bottle fun and make it a person that was Candy." The tiny bit of lipstick on her front tooth that Ren could see when she smiled. "Oh, you would have loved her, Ren!" The nervous scrape of her thumbnail against her forefinger. "But her father, he was a piece of work, believe me."

Ren found she was clutching her hands together tight, and when she realized, she moved so they were tucked under her thighs, suddenly conscious of Noah watching her every movement, not wanting to give away how much every word meant.

"And I found a photo," Loriana said suddenly, as if she'd been meaning to say that first.

The couch moved as Noah sat forward, clearly surprised.

Ren's heart thumped with urgent curiosity as Loriana went and got the photograph album that she'd clearly placed on the sideboard in anticipation.

"It's from the church youth group." She came around with the album open at the right page and laid it out on the table as if brandishing treasure. "I thought I had a picture, but I wasn't sure." It was a group of teenagers ranging in age, standing against the wall of the church outside, squinting against the sun.

Loriana came around to lean down next to Ren, the bracelets on her arm clinking as she pointed to a girl in the picture. "There she is."

Ren wondered if her heart stopped in that moment. She felt Noah beside her as she stared at the face of the teenage girl with the wide grin and the acres of blonde hair and the huge eyes and the bright fluorescent-yellow T-shirt falling off her shoulder. That was her mom.

She swallowed. Stared. Felt Noah lean over and look, then glance across at her. She could smell the comforting scent of the woodsmoke still on his jacket.

Loriana picked up her coffee cup, took a sip seemingly to give Ren a moment to take it in. "She had a laugh that made you want to laugh. You know the kind? She just used to make life fun."

Ren heard Noah say, "You got that from her, Ren," and she glanced across in surprise, but he just nodded in confirmation. She closed her palm around the warmth of the comment to save it for later.

"You sure did," Loriana agreed, cradling her coffee cup in her hand. "Thing was, her dad didn't let her do anything or go anywhere. My mom learned too late what kind of man he was. But Candy already knew, and she didn't take a blind bit of notice of him." She smiled almost wistfully to herself. "She would sneak out, get up to all sorts of trouble. Hitchhike away from here, go out all night in Jackson or Sweetwater Springs, but appear at breakfast fresh as a daisy."

The whole time Loriana was talking, Ren just stared at the photograph. Looking to see herself in her mom's face.

"But I remember the time she came into my room to tell me she was pregnant. Oh, my goodness, the fear." Loriana put her hand on her heart. "She was terrified, and she didn't need to say why, believe me. If her father had found out about you, honey, he would've have killed her, no doubt about it."

Ren glanced up, saw Loriana's eyes widen with emotion at the memory. "We just tried to cover it up till we could come up with a plan. Candy wore bigger clothes. She started eating more to make it look like she was just putting on weight." She shook her head despairing. "We were very naive. But my mom and her dad had started rowing at that point so if we stayed out their way, they paid us no mind. Too busy tearing strips off one another.

"Candy went into labor very premature." As Loriana talked, Ren felt the reality that she was the baby she was talking about. This wasn't a story. It was her life. It was how she came to being. "I bundled Candy into Mom's car and I drove her to the hospital."

Ren's vision blurred a little as she kept on looking at that wide grinning face in the photograph. That was who Ren belonged to. That was who she came from.

"Because she was only sixteen at that point," Loriana carried on. "She was afraid they'd tell her dad. Or that somehow he'd find out—that someone would recognize the name or maybe tell the police because she was so young. So from the moment Candy went into hospital, we decided she should become me. Loriana Mendez. That was the name we wrote down."

Ren thought of the private investigator saying it out loud, like winning numbers on a lottery.

Loriana picked absently at the corner of her slice of lemon cake, breaking off a section then putting it down on the plate. "The hospital took care of everything from that moment on. Candy had to tell them she couldn't look after you. It was awful." Loriana's voice cracked. "Don't ever think that it wasn't. But we were just … just drowning in fear."

Ren looked up at her, saw the glisten of tears in the older woman's eyes.

"You were a tiny, beautiful, perfect little baby," Loriana added sadly. "She just couldn't keep you."

Ren closed her eyes for a second. Inside it felt like gaps in her heart were filling. She had a story. She came from somewhere. She stared once more at the smiling face in the photograph, the beautiful young girl with her big blonde hair and her big, sparkling eyes. She had a person who was her own.

Loriana went on to tell her how soon after that, Candy's

dad's relationship with Loriana's mom broke down. Candy left town, and they lost touch. Loriana found out through the church that Candy had been hit by a car crossing the road in the dark, sneaking out, Loriana liked to hope, on her way to having some fun.

Loriana talked on while Noah ate lemon cake. Ren knew the answer before she asked the question but still had to say, "Do you have any idea who my dad was?"

Loriana shook her head. "No, I'm sorry, sweetheart."

Noah winced. But this time, Ren shook her head. "It's okay. I knew it was a long shot."

She'd have a thousand more questions but couldn't think of any more right then, it was enough just to have the picture and the story. "Thank you for talking to me, Loriana."

"It was my pleasure, Ren," Loriana said as she walked her and Noah to the door. "I think Candy would have been very proud of how you turned out."

Ren laughed like the compliment was just politeness.

But Loriana shook her head. "I'm serious. And—" She paused as if uncertain about what she was about to say.

Ren glanced up.

"If it's any consolation, I'd like to see myself as your aunt." Loriana looked suddenly nervous, like she'd put herself out there but had possibly been too forward and was now teetering on the brink of rejection. "I know it's not the same as a mother, and I'm not maybe the best person for the job, but ... you're family."

Ren thought of the family she was building around her. The new dream. "That would mean a lot, I'd like that."

"I'm so glad." Loriana smiled wide and doting. "Do you want to come back again tomorrow? I think I can find more photographs, if you wanted to help me look up in the loft?"

Ren nodded, smiled. "Yes, thank you."

And when Loriana went to hug her goodbye, her bracelets indenting against Ren's back, smelling of sweet cherry perfume and hairspray, her big earring pressing against Ren's cheek, Ren closed her eyes, and knew that was what it felt like to be hugged by family.

Chapter Thirty-One

It was late afternoon by the time Noah and Ren walked over to his Jeep. She sat in the front seat, the photograph of her mom clutched in her hand.

Noah climbed in next to her and glanced across. He had found it difficult to take his eyes off her the whole time she'd been sitting on Loriana's couch. She'd listened so attentively and when she saw the photograph of her mom, a look had come on her face that was hard to describe. The kind of look you'd have gazing at something so exquisite, so treasurable, that you both want it and revere it at the same time.

"You feeling better?" he asked.

"Yeah," she said, leaning down to slip the picture into her bag. "Thanks for coming with me."

He nodded. "Thanks for letting me."

Ren looked knowingly at him. "I can't imagine you were in your element, Noah."

He shrugged, trying to hold back a half-smile. "Well, I mean, there were no tears, so I was okay."

She smiled, settling back in her seat, looking out the window as Noah cruised the Jeep away down the road.

He had found it difficult sitting beside her in the house, wanting to reach over and offer comfort while at the same time knowing not to get involved, not wanting to see her wide eyes as she listened, or her hands clench tight in her lap.

When they were halfway back she turned in her seat so she was facing him and said, "I'm sorry about how I was in the barn. I was angry and it was unfair of me to take it out on you."

Noah shook his head, keeping his eyes on the road. "It's fine. I'm sorry I couldn't be more help."

"You helped, Noah."

He glanced over but saw she was looking back out the window. He felt strangely disappointed, like she was actively distancing herself from him. But then he reminded himself that that was exactly what he wanted.

As she stared out at the houses and yards that they passed, he studied her profile surreptitiously and noticed a calmness to her face that he hadn't seen before. A serenity. And again, he found for a second that he wanted the version of her back that challenged him and his life choices, or the one needling him for answers. Or asking him if he wanted to try disgusting pine-needle tea.

And just to get her to turn her head and look his way, he found himself saying, "That little cow you saved in the storm ate my hat yesterday."

Ren snorted a laugh. "Mildred?"

"Yes, Mildred," he said, resigned by both her name and existence. "That's the second hat in a week, gone."

"Gotta love Mildred." Ren smiled clearly at the idea of her chewing her way through Noah's hat, but she didn't say anything more.

As he always did, Noah let the silence settle, but it felt less comfortable than usual, more silent, if that was possible.

When they pulled up outside her apartment, Noah said, "So what are you going to do now?"

"Carry on," she replied.

He nodded, like it was exactly the answer he expected.

She opened the car door and climbed out.

He got out, too, came around and stood opposite her on the sidewalk.

"Thanks for the lift," she said.

They looked at each other. The air seemed to get suddenly smaller, tighter, around them.

"You're welcome," he replied.

But she didn't turn to go. Neither of them moved. He wanted to, he wanted to be close enough to wrap his hand around her waist and look down at the freckles on her nose. And without thinking, he found himself stepping forward, reaching up and tracing the line of her hair, sweeping it gently away from her eyes. He saw her lashes blink. Let his thumb stroke her cheek; the soft pale skin. Saw her lips part. Dipped his head. Then before his eyes, he saw Livvy. Saw his mom in the hospital. Saw his brother dead. Saw himself gasping for breath in a dressing room in a nameless country in a nameless stadium, terrified of his own emotions.

He stopped where he was, rested his forehead against Ren's as inside he struggled to get his breath. He saw the confusion in her eyes, the hurt.

She stepped back. Then smiled. The kind that she had done when he first met her, polite and friendly. Like she knew now the things she needed in life, and it wasn't anything he could give.

Chapter Thirty-Two

A few weeks passed where Noah got up every day at five and did all the work that he always did. Then, when the sun went down, he stopped working, had dinner, and went to bed. The only thing that changed in his life was that some days he would find a reason to get coffee in the diner.

Some days it was Loriana serving and she would pause as she filled his cup to tell him things about Ren, like her coming around for dinner at hers or the stack of dusty photo albums they'd found in the corner of the attic, and he would listen and nod and, while normally he would want to be left in peace with his coffee, found himself asking the odd question back.

But each time he went to the diner, he knew it was always Ren's coffee that he went for.

When she saw him, she would smile and come up to his table in her uniform with all her necklaces and tightly tied apron and say, "White, no sugar and just pie?"

And if it was quiet, sometimes she'd slide in opposite him and have a slice herself. But Ren always had cherry or blueberry or peach, something different every time. Whereas Noah always had apple.

That day, Ren was trying out the new kiwi pie, and when she offered him a forkful, Noah shook his head, thinking it looked disgusting but was too polite to say so. Somehow, however, Ren could tell exactly what he was thinking and laughed as she took the first bite. "Noah, it's not going to kill you to try a new pie."

Noah shuddered at the idea of bright, slimy green kiwi and said, "It might, you never know."

Which made Ren roll her eyes and take an even bigger mouthful just to show him how good it was.

She was trying to chew while also laughing because she'd put too much in her mouth and Noah was shaking his head in despair, handing her a napkin, when he saw his mom and Willow walk into the diner.

He caught the exact moment they saw him sitting in there with Ren, and the conspiratorial little look that passed between them.

Immediately, all the humor when out of the situation and he found himself turning away to look out the window while Ren covered her mouth with her hand and tried to finish her pie before Martha and Willow got to the table.

His mom had quizzed him after the cattle drive about what had happened, but luckily the whole Loriana thing quickly took everyone's attention away from that. But it hadn't stopped Martha's concerned glances. Once or twice, she had cornered Noah when he came in to the ranch house, to find out what progress he'd made with where he intended to live—had he thought about maybe building a house on the land? So he stopped going up there altogether, stayed in his trailer of an evening. And when she'd knocked on the door of his trailer, he'd pretended to be asleep. His mom started feeding the chickens earlier and earlier so she could catch him as he got up to work, so he just started getting up earlier to avoid her. He found it was entirely possible to live in such close proximity with her and manage to exist almost completely alone.

Now, however, he was cornered like an animal. His mom and Willow were walking toward him. Why it had to be Willow of all people, catching him in the act of having pie with Ren. He could almost see her brain whirring.

Willow reached the table first and said, "This is cozy."

Noah narrowed his eyes at her.

She winked back.

Completely oblivious, or choosing to be, Ren said, "How are you, Willow?"

Willow grinned, all white teeth and huge hair, looking like an extra from *Fame* in her leggings and leg warmers. "I'm very well, thank you, Ren. My brother not causing you too many problems, I hope?"

Ren shook her head. "Not at all."

Noah just wanted out of there. He started to slide out of the booth. "I need to get going."

His mom put her hand on his shoulder and said, "Don't go on our account, Noah."

It took everything in him not to shake the hand off. He moved away to pick up his hat. "Don't worry, I'm not."

"We're only swinging by," his mom said, clearly not wanting to have interrupted Noah out and about in town, which was something, up to that point, he did so rarely. "I had a poster for the Spring Fling that I wanted Loriana to put up in the window."

Ren said, "I can take it." And Willow reached into her bag and pulled out one of the posters.

Ren unrolled it and said, "So what's a Spring Fling?"

Willow tipped her head, curls bouncing, "It's just a party, really, at the church hall—in the garden, if the weather's good. You wear a nice dress and drink punch and dance, if you like dancing." She glanced pointedly at her brother. "It's fun—very low key. You should come."

"I'd love to. When is it?" Ren asked, studying the poster for the date.

"Beginning of next month," Willow said.

"Darn, I'll be gone by then," Ren replied, screwing up her face with regret.

Noah stopped up short. Couldn't help himself. Felt a sudden cold sense of loss shiver through him. "What do you mean you'll be gone?" He saw his mom glance his way and tried immediately to act casual, but could feel his heart beating in panic as he pulled his hat down low.

"I'm moving on," Ren said as if the news was just casual information. "End of the month."

"That's such a shame," said his mom.

Ren shrugged like it was no big deal. "It's time."

Noah struggled to comprehend what was happening, he wanted to ask where she was going, *why* she was going, but he could feel his mom's and sister's eyes on him again, so he just nodded and said, "Okay. See you later." And walked straight out the diner.

Chapter Thirty-Three

Noah and his dad had been up since the crack of dawn moving the herd to a new pasture. It was Noah's favorite time of day; mist hovered over the lush grass while the animals appeared like apparitions, the warm scented cattle with grass on their lips, the crowing pheasant with its emerald crown, the pines waving in the gentle breeze like giants through the haze. It was a sheer delight, or should have been, were Noah not almost permanently distracted by the news of Ren leaving.

"You all right, son?" Emmett asked as they turned back toward home.

"Fine," Noah replied, pulling his hat low.

"Just seem a bit distracted at the moment." The sun was breaking through and Emmett turned the collar of his shirt up to protect his neck.

"No," Noah replied, whistling for Rocky to heel.

The dog bounded over, settling in between the pair of horses, trotting along like he was one of them.

"Is it to do with the girl?" Emmett asked, face devoid of emotion, gaze fixed firmly straight ahead.

Noah cringed. "No, Dad."

Emmett jutted his chin like he'd heard but didn't necessarily agree.

They rode on in silence for a minute or two, the sun gently rising above the mountain, casting new shadows as the morning came into being. Then Emmett said, "You know that—" he sucked in a breath, the words not coming easy "—that cattle drive, Noah." He cast a glance from under his hat, eyes like a sleeping dog's. "That was one of the best times I've had in years."

Noah frowned with surprise. "Really?" If he remembered rightly, Emmett's stony face had barely cracked the entire trip.

Emmet swept a hand around the landscape and said, "All I've ever wanted is to work with my family."

Noah nodded. The guilt was ingrained in the very fabric of his being.

"And I know that the people we have working here aren't all strangers, they're good people—work a darn sight harder than half of you lot did—but they aren't family."

As they neared the ranch, Rocky started to take the lead, eager for another breakfast.

Emmett took his hat off, wiped the sweat from his forehead and put it back. "I'm never very good at saying all this stuff, but having you, Willow, Logan, Hank—who's as good as family to me—it was…" He just nodded, didn't say the words. But after a second or so, added, "And it was nice to have Ren there, too. She was a good addition."

He gave a noncommittal nod and thankfully his dad said no more.

Once back at the barn, they made sure the horses were happy, then strolled out together into the morning sun. Noah grabbed a bottle of water and gulped down half of it as they walked in the direction of the house. Noah's trailer was on the way, and he was going to stop there and make himself some breakfast. One of the chickens was sitting on the top step.

Before Noah could shoo the chicken away, Emmett said, "Ren okay now, is she?"

Noah groaned silently, hand on the rusty banister that led up to the door. He knew his dad had more to say. "Better, I think."

Emmett scratched the back of his neck. "Tough business."

"Yeah." Noah went to take the rest of the steps. The chicken sitting in his way took no notice of him.

"And you and her?"

Noah rolled his eyes.

Emmett shrugged. "What can I say? I like the kid."

"Don't get your hopes up—" Noah turned, leaning up against the stair railing "—she's leaving at the end of the month, doesn't want to hang around here."

"Where's she going?" Emmett frowned at the news.

Noah shrugged. "I think she wants to keep traveling."

"I thought she liked it here."

"She wants to see the world."

Emmett tipped his head, brows drawn. "Girl who grew

up in care, went from pillar to post, never had any consistency, doesn't want to settle down in one place?"

Noah shook his head, mouth turned down. "No."

Emmett narrowed his heavy hooded eyes as he considered further. "Doesn't want a family around her and community and stability?"

Noah chewed the inside of his cheek.

"Prefers to go off on her own traveling around?"

Noah nodded.

It was Emmett's mouth that turned down now. "You surprise me," he said, then started to walk away across the yard.

Noah stared at his dad's retreating back. "How come you're suddenly so insightful?" he called.

Emmett turned, looked back over his shoulder. "Like I said, I like her."

Chapter Thirty-Four

A couple of evenings now, Ren had gone around to Loriana's for a drink after work and they pored through photos to find ones of Candy, or sat on Loriana and Hank's front porch and Loriana told her every story she could remember. Tonight, Hank was bowling, or "watching other people bowl because of his hip, and drinking beer," Loriana scoffed as she searched for her purse and reapplied her lipstick, "Anyways, I'm having pizza. I always have pizza on bowling nights. Wanna come?"

Ren did.

So they locked up the diner and walked down Main Street together in their matching uniforms, Loriana with her purse tucked under her arm, the sun just dipping below the mountains casting stripes along the sidewalk. They passed the theater, the doors propped open ready for the evening show, Hank's supply shop closed for the night. As they walked, Loriana said, "I'm going to miss you when you go."

Ren felt a shot of warmth at the comment. "I'm going to miss you, too."

"You'll come back and visit me?"

Ren nodded. "Of course."

They arrived at Gino's—*me and my aunt*, Ren kept reminding herself—on what was turning out to be a warm spring night. Loriana said, "We could take a table inside, but I normally just sit on the bench and eat because I like looking at the people."

"Okay!" Ren smiled. She liked the fact her aunt was someone who ate pizza on a bench rather than any formalities.

Gino's was on a sidewalk intersection, benches out front and planters of red geraniums. From where they sat, they could see down the road opposite to the church and next to it the church hall and gardens. There were posters for the Spring Fling on all the lampposts.

They balanced the giant pizza box on the bench between them and tore out piping hot slices. Ren savored not only each mouthful but each moment. This wasn't just sitting having pizza with Loriana, it was sitting having a meal with family.

Loriana said, "I envy you, you know, young and free. So much life ahead of you."

"You're not old, Loriana!"

"I know. But you, you're only just beginning."

"I feel like I began a long time ago," Ren replied, thinking of the photo of her mom that she carried in her bag.

Loriana put her pizza slice down and, wiping her hands and mouth on a napkin, said, tone more serious than it had been, "I wanted to say, Ren, that I'm sorry we didn't take more care about what happened to you."

Ren's gaze paused on the pizza box.

"The hospital promised us you'd be well looked after, and we believed them—or wanted to believe them."

There was her heartbeat again, thumping along like a drum at the words.

"I think we were mainly relieved that it might all be kept secret. But I remember us looking at you all tiny, all in white, and us just thinking you were going somewhere better—that elusive place that we thought adults knew about." She briefly touched Ren's arm, and when Ren looked at Loriana, she could see the regret there on her face.

In that moment it was like all her life appeared in front of her eyes, the ranch, the adoption, Liane, Billy, all the days and nights, the tears, the disappointment, the anger. It was all there for her to see. Along with an image of a tiny baby and two young girls sending her away. It was hard not to imagine what might have been, but who knew if it would have been better or worse. She remembered riding really fast, as fast as she could go, Liane next to her, neither of them doing what they were meant to be doing, escaping, laughing, Mean Billy shouting at them to come back, to stop because they would get in trouble. There were good times, she thought. There was a bright side.

She let her hand cover Loriana's for a second and she said, "I know. I understand."

And Loriana nodded back, a flicker of relief in her eyes, like she'd been carrying something that she could finally let go.

Chapter Thirty-Five

After the pizza, Loriana drove home and Ren walked the rest of the way back to her apartment. The sun had set, the last remaining rays painting the clouds pink like cotton candy. She felt weirdly peaceful, almost for the first time in her life, as if the puzzle pieces were slotting into place. What she had forever been missing was finally found.

Then she walked straight into Noah Carter. "Oh, goodness, I'm sorry."

He held her by the shoulders to steady her. "No, my fault."

She was so close she could smell the scent of his laundry detergent on his T-shirt and the dust and the horses, it was exactly what she wanted and everything she didn't. She stepped back out of his hold, glanced up and saw all his familiar features, his too-long brown hair falling over his forehead, eyes always hiding something. She hadn't seen him since he'd walked out the diner, had no reason to but, against her better judgment, she'd looked up unwittingly, expecting to see him, every time the door opened.

There was a pause where neither of them said anything. Then at the same time she said, "Well, I'm just on my way home." And he said, "I was just dropping something off—" Pointing behind him.

She nodded, smoothing down the front of her diner-uniform shirt for something to do.

He bit his lip, scuffed the sidewalk with his work boot, and said, "So, you're leaving."

"Yeah."

He tucked his hands in his pockets. "Where you headed?"

She shrugged, smiled a little hesitantly, feeling vulnerable in his presence. "Don't know yet. I'll decide when I get there."

He nodded slowly. "You don't feel like staying? For Loriana?" he added quickly.

Ren shook her head. "No, but it's nice to know she's there, someone to come back to and visit."

Noah looked up at her, right into her eyes and she wondered if he could see what she was thinking, that she was having to steel herself so hard against his very presence. Against the way he wore his jacket, the way his T-shirt pulled threadbare at the neck, the way he tucked his hair behind his ear and said, "I'll walk you home."

She should have said there was no need, but she didn't.

They walked on. It was cooler now. Ren got her sweater out her bag and pulled it on. Noah held her bag while she did. The gesture made it feel strangely like they were a couple.

Noah pointed out the moon, framed by the mountain it looked like a sunrise, just cresting the tallest peaks.

Ren looked and then tipped her head further back to see the stars as they walked. "Big Dipper," she said, pointing.

Noah closed his eyes and shook his head in despair. "Once again," he said, and placing his hands on her upper arms, Noah turned her around and pointed up in a completely different direction.

Ren laughed, because she had actually thought she got it right this time. Her skin tingled from where his hands had been.

After more silence, Noah said, "You can visit me."

She felt her heart tighten. Smiled at the color speckling his cheeks. "I might look you up when I'm in town."

His eyes creased with a smile.

She said, "You could come visit me if you want."

Noah laughed like it was a nice but crazy idea. "I've got the ranch."

Ren sighed a smile. The disappointment was just a tiny sting. "I know. It was worth a try."

He went to speak but didn't.

They walked on. When they came to cross the road, a car appeared too fast at the corner, Noah held his hand out instinctively to stop her crossing, didn't touch her, it was just a brief gesture, but she felt inside herself the sweetness of it, how Noah Carter it was.

They walked in silence the rest of the way to her apartment. Ren lived down West Starlight Street, just off

Main Street. She lived on the first floor, had a little balcony with room for a tiny table and one chair, above Starlight Barbershop.

When they got to her front door, there was another pause. Noah looked straight ahead down the road, scratching awkwardly at the back of his neck, as if he had something he wanted to say but couldn't.

In the window of the barbershop, there was a poster for the Spring Fling. She said, "You going to that?"

Noah looked where she was pointing and said, "No," without even thinking about it.

Of course he wasn't. She wrapped her arms around herself. "I am," she said. "Willow persuaded me to stay for it. You should come."

He made a face like he couldn't imagine anything worse. "Not my thing."

She tipped her head. "It could be, though."

He raised a brow as if it never would be.

"Maybe if you tried something, you'd surprise yourself." She looked down at the sidewalk, then up at his hooded gray eyes. "Noah, there's so much life, so much possibility out there that you're missing."

He raised a brow, said, "It's a Spring Fling, Ren."

But she didn't laugh, didn't take her eyes off him, just looked at him for the first time with what felt like pity. "You know all this business with my mom, you know what it's done? It's healed a part of me that I can now put to rest."

Noah wouldn't hold her gaze, he looked away at the scrolled lettering on the barbershop window, hands in the back pockets of his jeans.

But Ren went on anyway. "I've found what I've been searching for. The missing pieces." She took a step forward forcing him to look her way. "I understand more about who I am, what I need. I've realized that it's not about other people, it's about me. I can decide if I'm happy or sad, who I love, what I want. Life is about the future, Noah, not the past." She watched his face shutter as she said the last bit. "You've got things you need to put to rest."

Noah inhaled deeply, ran a hand through his hair. "I'm fine, Ren," he said.

"No, you're not."

"I am," he insisted.

"Why did you kiss me?"

He looked away. "Because you said you'd never been kissed."

She felt the humiliating burn of the words but stayed resolute. "That wasn't why."

He tipped his head back and looked up at the sky, clearly feeling that he was having to deliver news that he didn't want to, but which had to be done. Then he looked her straight in the eye and said more gently but with a firm finality, "I can't offer you anything. I'm selfish, Ren."

"No, you're not," she said, steadfast, because he had already broken her heart and she had nothing to lose. "You're afraid."

She saw his jaw harden, his face tense at the words.

"You're afraid of dancing, of singing, of talking, of eating different flavors of pie. Darn it, Noah. You're afraid of *living*."

Noah focused down at the sidewalk, the muscle in his clenched jaw flickering.

Ren pushed her hair back with her hands then stood with her arms crossed in front of her. "All my life, Noah, I've had to live on someone else's terms—*not in my house, young lady! We do things this way around here! We don't speak like that, wear that, say that!* You have this wonderful family who cherish you. I've seen the way your mom looks at you. And your brother. Logan was so worried about you on that cattle drive." She paused, looked up at the moon hovering beside the shadow of Starlight Mountain that loomed large in the distance. "You think you're living this life of wide-open spaces and freedom. But you're not free. You're hiding."

He looked up with a half-laugh as if she was being melodramatic. But again, Ren didn't laugh. She just stared at him, seeing for the first time the proper fear behind his eyes and knew in that moment she had lived too long searching for love to be with someone who couldn't give it.

"Good luck, Noah," she said, then she turned and, unlocking the door to her apartment, went inside without looking back.

Chapter Thirty-Six

Noah had never worked harder in his life. Sweat dripping from his brow, staining the rim of his new hat, as he whacked in fence posts, fixed feed troughs, checked and rechecked the boundary fencing, all while the cows watched curiously, chewing with their slobbery mouths as he pushed himself to the point every day that he just fell into bed and didn't have to think. Annoyingly, almost daily he had to go looking for Mildred who kept escaping into the forest. Every time he found her, innocently blinking her big black lashes at him, he thought about Ren.

At the end of the week, he returned to the ranch to see a glistening silver Aston Martin parked by the side of the house, which only meant one thing—his twin brother, Brodie, was in town.

Noah winced. He couldn't face company. He had hoped to slink away into his trailer but now he'd have to go up to the house.

At the idea, he almost jumped back on Blue and headed back out to the pasture, but he was sweat-soaked and starving, and just as he was wondering if he could in fact disappear into his own home, Brodie appeared on the veranda followed by his mom. Brodie waved as soon as he saw him. "Hey! Where've you been? Get over here?"

Noah washed his hands at the tap, splashed water on his neck and face and walked over.

"Miss me?" Brodie grinned as he got close, still the dimple-cheeked heartthrob that all the girls adored. Looking cool and relaxed, and somehow expensive, in a simple pale blue shirt and jeans. It was always made very apparent to Noah that they were not identical twins.

"Didn't notice you were gone," Noah replied deadpan.

Brodie barked a laugh. "I would hug you but..." He made a face at Noah's sweaty gray T-shirt.

"Not hugging is fine with me." Noah picked up the jug of lemonade on the tray his mom had brought out and poured himself a glass.

Brodie watched him with intrigue, like he was scrutinizing every move he made to make a judgment.

Noah glanced up, hating being watched. "What?"

Brodie shrugged, eyes still assessing. "Nothing."

Noah refused to rise to it, and downing his drink went inside to grab something to eat. Outside he heard the creak of the wicker chair as they sat down. His mom fussed around Brodie. "Are you sure you don't want something to eat?"

"Honestly, I'm fine. I ate something on the plane."

"I wish you'd tell us when you were coming."

"I didn't know till the last minute what I was doing."

Noah came out with some cheese slapped between two bits of bread. "You get dumped?"

Brodie cocked his head as he considered the statement. "I wouldn't quite call it dumped. Maybe just a 'parting of ways.'" Brodie had perfected the winning combination of his drooping puppy dog eyes and innocent dimpled grin that allowed him to get away with almost anything.

Noah smirked.

Martha sighed. "Oh, Brodie, not again!"

He waved a hand dismissively. "It's fine."

She said, "I liked Jessica."

Brodie looked puzzled. "It wasn't Jessica."

Martha sighed more deeply and said, "Why do you—"

Brodie reached quickly forward for his drink, cutting her off with, "We don't need to talk about me." Then turning to Noah, said, "What's this I hear about you spending the night with a very attractive young woman in a tent?"

Caught off-guard, Noah was too surprised to formulate a comeback, just said, "How'd you know about that?"

"Logan told me." Brodie sat back, arms over the back of the chair watching Noah's reactions.

Noah was about to turn and walk away when the sound of a car pulling up fast, spitting gravel, caught everyone's attention, and suddenly Willow was racing over, decked out in her dancer leggings and cropped T-shirt, cloud of curls flying. "Brodie!" she called delightedly.

Brodie had no problem hugging his sister. Wrapping his arms tight around her, he lifted her off the floor. "Didn't know you were here! Look at your hair, it's gone crazy!"

Willow flicked her big hair away from her face, "It's *au naturel* for the moment. I had too much straightening treatment and it started snapping off."

Martha said, "I like it curly. It suits you."

Willow made a face like she couldn't disagree more and, tying her hair up in a knot on her head, said, "I'm not here for long. I go back on tour next week." She sat down on the arm of Brodie's chair.

Brodie said, "Same thing I saw you in in London?"

Willow nodded, reaching forward to take a gulp of one of the glasses of lemonade, not caring whose it was. "And," she added, "yes, Gabriella is still in the cast so please don't come and see me again because she still wants to kill you!"

Brodie caught the surprised expression from their mom and slipped his sunglasses on guiltily.

Shaking her head disapprovingly, Martha changed the subject asking, "How long are *you* staying, Brodie?"

"Just a couple of days," he said noncommittally. Brodie infamously hated making plans.

"It's the Spring Fling on Saturday!" said Willow with more enthusiasm than Noah thought the event warranted.

Brodie held his hands wide. "Love the Spring Fling."

"Mom's playing Dobro in the band," Willow informed him proudly.

Martha waved it away like it was hardly news, but said, "You could sing if you like, Brodie?"

Brodie, who had no qualms about being on stage, said, "Yeah, if you want."

Noah recalled with a shudder a message Brodie had sent six months or so ago, when another band of their era announced a reunion tour, saying: *Maybe one day?* He had promptly deleted the message even though he knew—or hoped he knew—it was Brodie just kidding around.

"Noah's girlfriend will be there," Willow added, glancing mischievously in Noah's direction.

Noah closed his eyes with a sigh. He couldn't help, however, imagining what it would be like if Ren was there with them right then, the conspiratorial look she might give him across the table that would instantly put him at ease.

But then Emmett appeared, striding over from the direction of the barn, wiping his hands on a cloth and the atmosphere immediately changed.

Noah watched Brodie sit up straighter, was relieved with the change of focus even if it meant Brodie being in the spotlight of, what was always, his dad's disapproval. "Hi, Dad."

Emmett dried his hands and tucked the rag into his back pocket. "I thought I saw your car."

Brodie nodded. Willow studied her hands. Noah was pretty sure the absence of a hello from Emmett didn't go unnoticed by anyone.

Brodie and their dad had never had an easy relationship. Not as bad as Emmett and Jack's had been, but close enough. Emmett was a big believer in purpose and hard work which was unfortunately the exact opposite of Brodie's ethos.

Emmett didn't stop to sit with them, just said, "Well it's good to see you." And carried on into the house.

Brodie sat back with an exhale. "You said he'd changed!"

"He kind of has," Willow tried, "it just maybe takes a while to see it."

Noah studied the grain of the wood on the floorboards. He hated it when they discussed his dad with such open disregard. Made him feel like a traitor. But then he also didn't like the way he treated Brodie, and thought of all the excuses he'd made for his brother in the past.

Brodie screwed up his face. "Didn't seem like it."

Martha picked up her lemonade, the ice in the glass clinking. "I think he just worries about you."

Brodie scoffed incredulously. "I have a great life!"

Martha ignored the statement and went on, "We worry about *all* of you." She looked pointedly at Noah when she said that. "We're meant to be starting a new chapter, changing things, but so far I'm not seeing that."

Noah looked heavenwards, and Martha raised a brow in challenge. "Noah, if you don't sort something soon, I'm going to have that trailer towed with you in it." Then she turned her attention to the others. "One of my biggest regrets will always be that Jack didn't get that opportunity to change, and I refuse to let it happen again, do you understand?" She looked between them. Willow examined her split ends, Brodie looked a bit like he was fighting the urge to giggle, which he always did when he was told off. Noah stared unwavering at the gold cross necklace his mom wore so he didn't have to meet her eyes.

The silence crackled in the air for a few beats, then seemingly satisfied that the message had been understood, Martha sat back and, picking up her glass of lemonade, took a sip.

Never one to cope well with any form of tension, a second later, Brodie leaned forward, elbows on his knees, a big grin on his face and said, "Can we go back to talking about Noah's girlfriend?"

Willow giggled.

Noah closed his eyes for a second, then without saying anything, he pushed his chair back and walked away.

He heard Brodie jump off the veranda and come after him. "Sorry," he called, laughter in his voice. "Sorry," he said again when he'd caught up.

"Don't worry about it," Noah replied without turning to look at him, just walking on toward the yard.

Brodie kept pace, hands in his pockets, looking up at the sun over the mountain. "What's wrong?"

"Nothing."

"Please, Noah, really?" Brodie sighed like he knew him better than that.

"Honestly, I'm fine," Noah replied, heading in the direction of his trailer.

"Yeah, right," Brodie scoffed, slipping on his sunglasses. "Although, if it's woman trouble, you are talking to the wrong person." He laughed, seemingly at his own chaotic love life, while also, Noah didn't doubt, well aware that he was completely the right person for the subject.

As they approached the trailer, Brodie bent down and picked up a basketball that lived relatively unused on the ground by the steps and chucked it at him. "Shoot some hoops?"

Noah caught it on instinct and paused for a second as he stood there opposite his twin. Acknowledged with relief that he'd made no further attempt to persuade him into a chat.

He thought of the band days when Brodie would find him somewhere—stadium bathroom, supply room, parking lot—too terrified to go on stage, and he'd just sit down next to him and talk about his own thoughts on the world, no pressure, no questions, no complications, just there. He looked at him now and felt the reprieve of having him there, standing opposite him in his flashy clothes and red Wayfarers, familiar lopsided grin on his face, just waiting to play ball.

Noah bounced the basketball a couple of times. "Sure, why not."

They shot hoops on the same old rusted hoop that they always used to. And as they took it in turns to try and fail to score from the half-court line—which Logan had once marked out with a slab of rock that no one had ever moved—Noah found himself telling Brodie a bit about Ren. Not loads but enough.

"In my experience," Brodie said, lining up the shot, "it's always better to say goodbye properly. It's unfair to leave a person hanging." He bent his knees, released the ball. "This one's going in."

"No chance." Noah laughed at the idea.

It missed. Brodie went and got it, bounced it a couple of times, chucked it at his brother. "You owe her a goodbye at least."

Noah caught the ball as Willow appeared around the side of the trailer, hair tied haphazardly on top of her head, mischievous twinkle in her eye like she'd been listening to the whole conversation. "She's leaving after the Spring Fling, Noah," she said, leaning against the paint-peeling, wooden-slatted back wall of his trailer.

Brodie glanced over and smirked at the fact Willow had so clearly been there listening.

Noah ignored her and lined up his own half-court shot.

He knew Ren was leaving after the Spring Fling, and Brodie was right, he should say goodbye, but he wasn't someone who went to town events—he hated the attention and the crowds—but he felt in some way that he owed it to Ren. The memory of their kiss sometimes waking him up at night, the softness of her skin, the scent of strawberry shampoo and river water, the way her arms wove tight around his neck.

"If he makes that shot," Brodie said to Willow, "he's going to the Spring Fling."

Willow arched a brow. "I think it needs to be that if he *doesn't* make it he goes."

"Good point."

Noah tried to block them out and took the shot. The ball hit the backboard, circled the hoop then fell to the ground.

Brodie winced. "That was close."

Willow put her hands on her hips. "Does that mean he's going or he isn't going?"

Noah felt a wary certainty that he probably would go to the Spring Fling just to say goodbye to Ren. But he'd never tell Willow that.

"I guess you'll just have to wait and see," he said, casually bouncing the ball without looking her way, which made Willow, as he suspected it would, dash forward in frustration and try and snatch it off him. "Too slow," he said, chucking it to Brodie who immediately took up the challenge of goading their sister into trying to intercept.

It felt like old times. Looking at their faces, Noah realized the loneliness of the years they'd been gone.

Chapter Thirty-Seven

Ren packed the last of her things into her suitcase. She didn't have a lot of belongings—it made it easier to up sticks and move on to the next place—but for the first time, she found herself folding up her clothes with a sense of reluctance. The last thing to go into the case was the blue shirt with the white piping that she'd worn on the first day of the cattle drive. She almost didn't want to pick it because there was such a finality to it, tucking it into the bag and closing the zip.

She looked around her little apartment, stripped of her personality and stamp on things; the bedroom was bare, the bright quilt cover and the gauzy scarves thrown over the chair and mirror were gone, the potted plants she'd given to Thomas from the barbershop downstairs, the photographs she'd stuck on the fridge were packed. Her diner uniform had been cleaned and pressed and handed back to Loriana. Normally, there was a sense of excitement in the pit of her stomach when she'd packed up ready to leave. But that apartment had felt dangerously like a home, and leaving it was an unexpected wrench.

She went outside and stood on the balcony. Above her, the sky was dotted with rows of cartoon clouds and the sun sparkled off the windows. It was the perfect day for the Spring Fling, not too hot, a gentle breeze fluttering the leaves. She leaned against the metal railing so she could see down toward Main Street and the flurry of activity around the set-up of the event. Earlier, she'd seen Martha Carter driving the flatbed truck, the back loaded up with supplies.

Now, when she looked out, she was surprised to see Noah's Jeep and almost held her breath as he slowed at a stop sign, but then she'd realized it was Willow not Noah behind the wheel.

The disappointment was palpable.

It shouldn't have been. She hadn't seen or spoken to him since that night outside her apartment, when she'd told him everything she thought he needed to hear but knew he'd hate her for. He'd stopped coming to the diner for coffee and pie. No longer sent her messages with photos of Mildred when she'd broken out of the enclosure. And while Ren still looked every time someone passed the diner window in a black cowboy hat, or a car that looked like his Jeep drove past, she felt that she'd made her peace with the fact whatever had flickered between her and Noah had long since gone out. Theirs was a flame that wasn't meant to burn brightly.

Chapter Thirty-Eight

Noah was the only one at the ranch. His mom had gone early to help set up the Spring Fling and had roped in Brodie and Willow.

Emmett had claimed there was too much work to do for him to help, but as the day drew on—and the "absolutely necessary" tasks grew scarcer—he'd got a call from Martha asking where he was and, unable to put it off any longer, had reluctantly gone and changed his clothes and driven over.

"I'll see you there," Noah had called, having made up his mind that he would swing by, just to say goodbye to Ren before she left. He'd got changed, put on a shirt for the first time in a while, had a shave, and was all ready. But when it came to it, he found he couldn't leave.

He was sitting on the steps of his trailer, alone, all the others gone. Frozen. It was exactly like he was on tour again. Time suspended. His brain whirring a thousand miles an hour. This. That. Why. What if? He didn't want to go, he didn't want to see the people, face their stares, he didn't want to see the stage or his brother up there on it.

But at the same time, he didn't care. So why couldn't he go? Why couldn't he move?

Like Brodie said, he owed Ren a goodbye.

He forced himself to stand up from the step, but his head spun, and he had to sit back down.

He heard a car pull up in the yard. Looked up and saw his mom getting out of the old green pickup truck. She slammed the door and when she saw him sitting there, walked over. She was all dressed up for the Spring Fling in a green dress with a leather belt and new boots.

"Can you believe it," she said, lifting her sunglasses and pushing them back on her head. "I forgot my guitar."

Noah tried to pull himself together, but as she got closer, she said, "What's wrong?"

"Nothing," he said too quickly.

She paused, looked around for a second, then came and sat down on the step next to him. "Noah, I know when something's wrong. I can see it in your eyes."

He leaned forward, rested his forehead on the heel of his hand. "Honestly," he said, "I'm fine, I just need a minute."

She didn't go anywhere, just sat there next to him. He looked at her in her green dress and her fine jewelry and said, "You look nice."

"Thanks." She smiled, then looking him up and down said, "So do you."

He shook his head at the compliment.

Martha turned and looked behind her into his trailer. "I see you've made a good start at clearing things out."

Noah had to laugh. Nothing had been touched.

She put her hands behind her and leaned back. "I always imagined you building a lovely little house somewhere on the land. Maybe getting Logan to help you—or your dad. That's why I want the trailer to go, Noah, not because I want to run your life, but to improve it."

Noah looked out across the yard, felt his breathing steady as she talked.

A couple of the chickens, who loved Martha because she fed them, came over and pecked around the two of them. She caught one and picked it up onto her lap, stroking it like a cat. "You might want to move into town, or even find you want to buy your own land, start your own ranch." She gave the chicken a scratch around the collar, which it loved. "Your dad would kill me for saying it, but you don't have to stay here, don't feel that obligation."

"I don't feel an obligation," Noah said, sitting up straighter, pushing his hair back with his hands. "I just want to keep going as I am."

"Like this?" she said, with gentle skepticism, gesturing to his current predicament: pale and unsteady, forced to sit on the top step of his trailer.

Noah closed his eyes, pressing his fingers against them.

"You can have more, Noah. You and your dad are so similar, but don't forget, he has much more than just the ranch. He has me, the house, you kids. It's a rich, full life." She paused, then added wryly, "Even if he doesn't choose to see it all the time."

When Noah didn't answer, Martha lifted the chicken

she'd been stroking carefully off her lap and placed it on the floor, then said, "Take a walk with me?"

"Sure," Noah said, because he knew better than to argue with his mom.

When they got to the grass, she slipped her shoes off and holding them in her hand, led him in the direction of the paddock, circling the wooden fence when they got near, the mountains and the pine forests in the distance.

Martha said, "What are you afraid of, Noah? Because I don't think this is just about the trailer or going to the Spring Fling."

Noah didn't answer, focused instead on Blue and Big Mac who were grazing happily on the lush grass of the paddock. Behind the horses, the sun hung above the mountain and the once misty morning sky was now a clear swimming-pool blue.

Martha said, "It's okay to be wary of loving someone again."

Noah's insides clenched. He felt a prickle of fear, like he was standing on the edge of somewhere he didn't want to be. He beckoned for Blue to come over. "It was a long time ago."

Martha leaned against the fence next to him. "I don't mean that you haven't moved on." Blue ambled up and she brushed a fly from his nose. "I mean it takes a huge amount of courage to decide to put yourself through something again."

He didn't want to hear it but he couldn't not listen because it was his mom talking and when she talked they were all programmed to hear what she had to say. He felt suddenly the engulfing claustrophobia of emotion, like he had as a teenager when Martha was ill. When she'd smiled at them from her hospital bed as they told her they were auditioning for the band. Noah just wanting to flee from that room back to the safety of the barn or the land, unable almost to look at her because it was just too awful. And then, there he was again, back in the hospital, but the next time he was nineteen and wrung out, ill-equipped to cope with his dying girlfriend.

The warm air seemed to press down on him. He wondered in that moment if it he might pass out from the suffocating tightness in his chest.

"There's good things, good people, outside those gates, Noah, outside Autumn Falls." Martha stood so her shoulder touched his ever so slightly.

Noah closed his eyes. He rested his forehead against Blue's, felt the warmth of the horse's body, the sweet, earthy smell.

Then he turned his head so he was looking at his mom and said, "I just don't know if I can go through all that again."

She looked back at him with a soft smile in her eyes and said, "I know. That's what you've got to decide."

Chapter Thirty-Nine

The Spring Fling was held in the garden of the church hall. There were colorful paper lanterns and festoon lights, and bunting swathed out from a leggy larch tree in the center of the lawn like a circus tent.

There was a refreshment stand with the infamous punch, and a stage where the Autumn Falls band were playing, led by John Luke, Bella's stepfather, on guitar, Hank on banjo, Jacob, the new pastor on the keyboard. Bella's French friend, Claudette, looking all sultry in black, was the lead vocalist, huskily crooning French folk songs while tapping a tambourine.

Ren arrived on her own. She surveyed the crowd of guests and saw practically the entire Autumn Falls community. She spotted Bella and Willow standing by the punchbowl watching Martha on stage. Willow looked whimsically bohemian in a floaty floral dress while Bella was all clean lines in a cream tunic and gold sandals.

Ren tended not to wear pretty dresses if she could help it

—not since being dressed up like a doll for visits to potential families. She had on a pink short-sleeved corduroy jumpsuit with a wide leather belt and red open-toe heels. She wore the collar upturned and a million gold necklaces. She'd tied her hair up, over-long bangs swept to one side.

When Willow saw her, she waved her excitedly over. "Ren, you look incredible! Love this!" She ran her hand down the velvety sleeve of the jumpsuit.

"Thanks," she replied, but before she could repay the compliment, the man next to Willow turned and Ren was literally dazzled into taking a step back. She had never seen someone quite so attractive—scruffy blonde hair, dimples like buttons on a Chesterfield, upturned eyes heavy like they'd just woken up. He was breathtaking.

"Ren, this is Brodie."

"Hi," she almost laughed, no hope of playing it cool.

Brodie held out a hand. "Hello, yourself."

Willow kicked him. "This is *Ren*. Put that smile away."

Brodie cocked his head in fascination. "*This* is Ren!"

Ren frowned. "What does that mean?"

"Nothing," he grinned innocently, teeth as straight and white as she had ever seen.

"Ignore him." Willow waved a hand dismissively.

Brodie slipped his sunglasses on—red Wayfarers, totally incongruous with his cream chinos and pale blue linen shirt—and turned away to watch the band, still with that playful smirk on his face.

Ren found herself blushing, knowing it was something to do with Noah.

Logan and Bella came over holding glasses of punch

for everyone. "Here you go, Ren," Bella said, passing her a plastic cup of almost neon-pink liquid bobbing with fruit.

"Autumn Falls punch!" Willow said, taking a sip and wincing because it was always super sweet.

Brodie took his glass and nodding toward the stage said, "Mom asked me to sing. You want to come up, too, Logan?"

Logan made a face like not in a million years.

"Come on, bro," Brodie bashed him on the shoulder, all easy grin and boyish charm.

But Logan was steadfast, slipping his arm around Bella, and saying, "My days on stage are definitely over."

Bella looked around at the crowd. "Didn't someone say Noah was coming?" more, it seemed, to change the subject because she would know Logan hated having to say no to Brodie.

Ren felt her cheeks speckle with the reference to Noah, and her heart started thrumming like a hummingbird at the idea he was going to show up.

Willow checked her watch. "He said he might."

"Really?" Logan didn't look convinced, gesturing around at the decorations and the crowd around the barbecue and the friends and neighbors all dancing, as if pointing out reasons why not.

"I think he'll come," said Brodie, catching Ren's eye and giving her a little wink, making her face color even more and the mischievous flicker of hope inside her heart burst into a full-blown flame.

Logan, clearly having seen the expectation written all over Ren's face, said, "I'll defer to your better judgment."

Luckily, the subject changed when Willow then pointed toward the gates and said, "Hey, look, Mom's back."

They all turned to see Martha, now with her guitar case, walking through the crowds, smiling and greeting people.

But when she came up to join them, she looked suddenly more serious and, placing her hand on Logan's arm, said, "Can I have a quick word?"

Willow was on tiptoes, searching the crowd. "Did you see Noah back at the ranch?" she asked. "Is he on his way over?"

For a second, hope and disappointment teetered inside Ren like a seesaw.

But then Martha shook her head and said, "No. I don't think Noah's coming today. Sorry."

Chapter Forty

It was like Blue could sense the urgency in Noah as they galloped out across the pasture, faster and faster, the forest in the distance, sweat dripping down Noah's back as he tried to burn off some of what he was feeling.

They rode till Blue started to tire. Noah could have gone on forever.

Looking around, he realized how close they were to the lake. Immediately, the shadow of the memories made him want to turn around, but he knew that Blue would need the rest and the shade and the water so he reluctantly rode on till he saw the crystal-clear water, flat as ice, shimmering in the sunlight.

He got down and led Blue over to the lake, feeling all around him like there were ghosts in the air. At the water's edge, he yanked off his shirt so he was just in a T-shirt and splashed his face as Blue drank. Then with a sigh, he made himself turn and look around, see the spot where they used to make camp, the trees they tied a hammock between, then fought over who got to sleep in it. The stump they practiced roping on, Noah always the best, never a wasted throw. He saw the old canoe pulled up on the bank, falling apart now and covered in lichen and dirt. Thought about taking it in turns to paddle out, seeing how many of them could sit on it at a time and not capsize. He closed his eyes when he smiled without meaning to.

Then, as he started to walk, he saw on one of the tallest pines, the initials N and L carved into the trunk. He felt a shiver of cold surprise in his blood. Walked the rest of the way until he was close enough to reach out and trace the letters.

He remembered carving them with his new pocketknife. And he saw Livvy standing there laughing because it was harder to do than he'd thought it would be. And he saw himself grinning and handing her the knife and saying, "You do it!" and her doing it really well, really neat. When he thought about her laughing, he saw her at school giggling about something with her friends. He saw himself kicking a soccer ball. He saw her waiting at the bus stop for him. He saw them side by side on the swings when they were far too old for playgrounds. He saw their youth and their vitality. So, so young. He leaned his forehead against the rough bark of the tree and remembered studying the fine hairs on the back of her neck in church when she sat in front of him, mesmerized. He'd buy her a Coke and a quarter pounder with cheese but without pickles when he had any cash. Ride with her out to the mountains when she was fit and strong and her eyes shone.

Suddenly he pulled his fist back and slammed it hard

into the tree. Then he did it again. The bark splitting his skin, and again, blood pouring from his knuckles. Then he kicked and he shouted and then he rested his head against the trunk again and he realized he was crying.

But he wasn't crying for Livvy. He had mourned her life, their life. Right in that moment, it was his youth he was mourning. A time when he'd had everyone he loved around him. Precious moments he'd taken for granted. Seeing Livvy bite her lip in concentration as she dug into the bark with the knife, or his brother Jack's smile as he tipped the canoe so they all fell in. He wanted to reach back in time and gather it all close.

Noah had never again been that person who carved initials in the tree or paddled out on the lake or fought over a hammock. He had gone off with the band and come home someone different.

Someone afraid, closed, broken. Someone filled with such anger and regret, so much frustration, that all he could do was bury it deep inside himself.

He hung his head and felt his shoulders shake with the silent sobs. Covered his eyes with his bleeding hands. Couldn't have stopped even if he wanted to, overtaken by the sad futility of it all.

And then suddenly he heard the beat of horse's hooves and turned to see Logan jumping down off his beautiful dappled gray mare, Misty, concern etched on his features as he strode over. Without saying anything, he clapped Noah into a solid, brotherly hug. It was exactly the kind of hug that he knew Logan would do, firm and reassuring. And as Noah struggled to catch his breath, feeling like his guts had been ripped out from crying for the first time in years, he found himself eternally grateful for the strong, comforting presence of his older brother.

He heard Logan's voice say, "It's okay."

Noah moved back, wiping his face first with his hand then with the hem of his T-shirt.

"I know you said you don't blame us, but Noah—" Logan shook his head "—it wasn't just that we persuaded you back so you weren't there for Livvy, it was all the way through. We should have seen how much you were struggling instead of pushing you on stage in front of thousands of people when you hated it so much you were sick as a dog. We let you down. We were all just out for ourselves and you got lost in that."

"That's not true." Noah tried to get rid of the blood on the backs of his hands by rubbing them against his jeans.

He saw Logan notice and his eyes narrow slightly. Then he saw him glance at the tree and see the carved initials. He put his hand in his pocket and handed Noah a handkerchief. Monogrammed, as expected. "You think you've broken anything?"

"Don't think so." Noah wrapped the cloth around his knuckles. "You weren't out for yourself, Logan. And Ethan, Brodie and Jack—they loved it. You stayed for them just as much as I did." Noah felt wrung out, he rubbed his face with his hands trying to get himself back to normal. Then he looked out at the lake and said, "I don't blame you. I wanted to blame you, I *wanted* to blame all of you, but I don't. I can't." He could feel the pain pulsing through the back of his hand. "I went and I stayed because I liked being with you all more than I liked being without you. I didn't want to be back here on my own. I had Livvy, but we were young, and we talked about settling down but—" he looked across at Logan with a sigh "—we were kids. I wanted to be where you all were even if I hated it."

Noah could feel the press of tears again. Just thinking of himself at fifteen in the band, trying so hard to look like he was enjoying himself while feeling like he was in the wrong skin. Unable to escape, day after day, until he was just living. Numb, with only the fear of what was to come and the emptiness.

Logan looked across at him. "You okay?"

Noah nodded.

Logan said, "Probably about time it happened." Then added wryly, "And it got me out of the Spring Fling."

Noah laughed.

An eagle circled overhead and Logan watched it for a moment then went to sit on the rocks. Looking out straight ahead, with his forearms draped over his knees, hands clasped, he said, "It wasn't all bad. Sometimes I have to remind myself that there were good times."

Noah sat down next to him, watching the waves lapping at the shoreline.

Logan went on. "You remember that time Brodie's costume got caught on that trap door under the stage?"

Caught off-guard by the memory, Noah laughed unexpectedly. "Yeah! He was down there like, 'Guys, help! I'm stuck!'"

"And we were all just laughing at him."

"Ethan couldn't sing because he was laughing too hard."

Noah hadn't felt that for years—that kind of laughter that made his sides ache and his stomach hurt and left him gasping for breath.

Logan smiled fondly. "You know, I think some of my favorite bits were when we were on the tour bus or on the plane. Just hanging out, knowing there were hours ahead of us till we got there."

Noah rolled his head so he could look sidelong at his brother. "That's what Ren said on the cattle drive. About the time spent doing nothing being the best."

Logan considered it, then said, "It was less cold on the tour bus."

Noah laughed.

There was a pause then Logan added, "I know I complained about the cold, but I had one of the best—and most memorable—times in a long time on that cattle drive."

Noah wondered what it was about that drive that everyone loved so much. For him it was just another day.

But then he looked out at the glistening water and made himself recall those few days. What popped into his head weren't just the big events, but Logan grinning as he pulled on his Puffa jacket, Willow doing her stretches directing the cooking, Hank strumming his banjo, Emmett's broad back gently rolling side to side as he led the tour—and Ren on Star, laughing in her gaucho hat as she tried to keep the wayward little Mildred in check.

He stretched out his legs in front of him, maybe it was one of the best and he'd just taken it for granted. Maybe he needed to start differentiating better between good and bad—or just day-to-day and great. To realize for a while there that his life had become considerably better than average.

Definitely, his day-to-day had less spark since the drive. Since Ren wasn't there every morning when he opened his eyes.

Noah pushed his hair behind his ears and as he did, he felt the sting of the cuts on his hands. Leaning back against the rocks, he glanced at his brother and said, "It's been real lonely without you all—" Feeling his voice catch unexpectedly, he looked away.

He felt his brother's eyes on him. "I know," Logan replied, and Noah had to focus down at the water again, feeling the tightness in his chest once more. But this time, he swallowed the feeling away. Breathing in deeply and letting it go.

They sat side by side saying nothing. Time just given over to gazing out at the lake, the pines reflecting on the water and the ripples made by the fish beneath the surface.

Noah said, "I'm sorry you have those dreams about Jack."

Logan stood up with a sigh and walked to the edge of the lake. "I go to his grave sometimes," he said. "Try and focus on the good times."

The dappled sunlight through the pines danced and flickered on the ground around them.

"I'm angry with him for so many things," Logan carried on. "Mostly for the way he treated Bella." Noah was furious with him for that, too, that Jack had mistreated Bella during his time married to her was something he wasn't sure he'd ever be able to forgive him for. "But too much anger and it'll eat you up, so I make myself think of the fun we had—you know, like, being here—" Logan gestured to the lake "—or playing polo or climbing out the window at night and going into Jackson when Dad didn't know." He glanced back at Noah with a sad smile in his eyes.

Noah went to stand next to him and said, "I wish I'd spoken to him more recently. I regret the fact that we didn't really know each other." He paused. "I think how I'd like more time, but even if we'd had it, something would have had to change, and I don't think anything would have. I hate it."

Logan nodded. Then he bent down and picked up a stone and skimmed it across the water. They watched it bounce, almost to the center. "I could happily go back to the times we were here camping. Just for five minutes. Just for the laughter."

Noah skimmed his own stone, got one more bounce than Logan. Glanced over at him with a wry smile.

Logan shook his head, supposedly above it, but had another go all the same.

When there were no flat stones left, and Noah had won three out of four, they sat down again on the rocks.

Logan said, "The thing with you, Noah, is you always knew what you wanted. You may not have done what you wanted—" he gave him a regretful sidelong look "—but you've always *known* who you are. That you belonged here."

Noah thought of the joy he got riding out at sunrise, mist hanging low over the grass, the cattle up ahead, the sound of the birds and the shadow of the mountain. That was all he'd ever needed.

"I think we all were—*are*—a bit envious of that."

Noah frowned in surprise, but Logan simply nodded.

Neither of them spoke. Noah trying to process the idea of anyone being even the slightest bit envious of him in his condemned trailer working all hours. He wouldn't have imagined it in a million years.

A heron flew in low over the water and landed by the shore. They watched it stalking the reed bed.

Logan stretched his legs in front of him. "So, what are you going to do about Ren?"

Noah was only just coming to terms with what Logan had said about his brothers, he wasn't ready to talk about Ren. "What about Ren?"

"Oh, come on, Noah. We all know you like her. And she likes you which, given the kind of mood you've been in for the last few years, is nothing short of a miracle."

Noah shook his head. Thinking about Ren was like changing the subject to a jewel on the horizon that was out of his reach. "She doesn't want to stay here."

"How do you know?" Logan asked. "Have you asked her?"

"No. But—" Noah sighed "—I think she's better off without me."

Logan absently plucked at the moss growing on the rock. "Didn't look like that to me when she found out you weren't going be at the Spring Fling."

Noah swallowed, imagining the idea of someone being hopeful that he might arrive someplace. It gave him a feeling of utter, unimaginable terror and yet, at the same time, the idea lit his insides the same as having something exciting on the horizon to think about.

A fish jumped in the distance, ducks cruised the shallows, while the reflections of the clouds skated over the surface of the water. He thought how Ren would love the lake if she came here. There were so many places he could show her that she'd love. He looked out at the bright, glinting water and imagined for just a second what it would be like having Ren settle there in the town—messaging her to go for a drink, maybe her coming to ride on the ranch, maybe even one day living in the house he built on the land. Maybe he could build it right on the lakeside. He felt a flutter inside that reminded him of how she'd looked when she talked about Christmas lights. He suddenly understood the hopeful power of a dream. He pictured seeing her every day, riding with her, showing her all the places he loved and finding new ones.

It was like he'd opened a door in his mind to let possibility in and suddenly he was seeing all kinds of things. He thought of going away, to California or Hawaii or even Italy, with Ren. Did being in any of those places dim that excited feeling he got inside at the idea of her being in Autumn Falls? A little. More than a little. But if he put Ren in the picture with him on a red double-decker bus touring London, or looking up at the Eiffel Tower in Paris, it felt maybe like transplanting the good feeling of here, there.

But then there was always the other side of it. He turned his head so he was looking at Logan and said, truthfully, trustingly, "Honestly? I'm terrified."

Logan sat back on his elbows, looking out at the heron as it spread its wings wide, the tips of its feathers skimming the surface of the water as it flew away. "I guess you've got to decide if it's worth it," he said, the bird disappearing off above the trees. "Everything's a trade-off. In my experience, one day with Bella is better than every single day I spent without her." He turned his head, so he was looking his brother in eye. "Whatever happens next, I'd take that one day and if I get another, I'm a lucky man."

There was a pause as Noah listened. Then he raised a brow and said, "That gonna be your wedding speech?"

Logan barked a laugh. "Pretty good, huh? Maybe I'll ask her first."

Chapter Forty-One

Noah rode Blue through the forest, out onto Main Street and up to the church hall gardens. Logan on Misty beside him. He wasn't dressed for the Spring Fling. His T-shirt was dirty and bloody, his knuckles splitting where they'd cut, but he didn't have time to go and get changed.

He could hear the music before he rounded the corner. Pulled Blue up short when he saw his brother Brodie up on stage, sharing the mic with Bella's friend, Claudette. The sight of him with a big grin on his face, loving it, loving the attention and the fun and the crowd, made Noah's muscles tighten in retaliation, made him want to tug the reins and ride fast away, but he felt like he knew himself better now. Logan was right, he did know what he wanted, and no one could take that away anymore. He was older and wiser. He saw Brodie pick up a spare guitar, go stand by his mom, let Claudette take the chorus without him. He was a born performer.

As he and Logan watched from a distance, Noah found himself smiling, realized he could watch objectively without the creeping fear.

Logan swung himself down from the saddle and said, "You coming?"

Noah hung his head for a second, breathing in the scent of his horse and the leather of the saddle and the lake water on his T-shirt. He thought of Ren hugging that little cow. How comforting it was to have the feeling of home.

Then he jumped down, they tied the horses up in the churchyard next door and walked through the gates of the church hall gardens. The first time Noah had been to an Autumn Falls event since he was a teenager.

There was a buzzing in his head that he tried to ignore. He saw the familiar punch stand and the bunting and Hank Murphy manning the barbecue, nothing had changed.

Up on stage, he saw the moment Brodie saw him and the surprise in his eyes. Then he saw him nudge their mom to look who it was. When Martha saw him, he saw in her eyes the worry about the state of him. He looked down at himself and saw the blood smears and the dirt. But then he looked up and when he caught her worried eye, he tipped his chin up with a nod and a half-smile, and he saw her take a breath in response, her shoulders drop and her expression softening.

Noah looked over at Loriana, who was wearing her huge silver earrings and a lilac pantsuit; he saw the Sanderson twins who worked for him sometimes, and Bella with her mom and people from the hospital. He saw kids playing and dancing to the music, his father in his clean pressed shirt and his good hat, standing arms crossed under the larch tree talking with the old timers. He saw practically everyone from Autumn Falls.

But he didn't see Ren.

He walked a whole lap of the event, found himself some paper towel and a cup of water and cleaned up his hands. Realized he was starving and got some barbecue on his way past off Clay Murphy—Hank's nephew—who owned The Firestone and prided himself on his slow-smoked ribs.

As he served Noah, Clay said, "Could have sworn I saw your brother Ethan the other day."

Noah shook his head. "Don't think so. Not around here." No one had seen Ethan for years. And as much as he might want to reminisce with Clay, Noah had other things on his mind, looking around him to try and spot a flash Ren's white-blonde hair.

"That's what I thought." Clay said, basting the sizzling ribs on the coals. "I only guessed it was him because he used to ride that Desert Racer, didn't he? I saw it, a while ago now, driving down the highway. That was some bike."

Noah nodded, backing away, searching. "Must have been someone else."

Clay made a face in disagreement. "Not many of those bikes around."

Noah demolished the ribs quick as anything, wiped his hands, carried on through the crowd. People stopping all the while. "Hi, Noah!" "Good to see you, Noah." And he had to reply to them all.

But then suddenly he heard his sister's voice. Willow came up beside him, in her flowery dress with her wild red hair looking like when she was a kid, and said, "You're too late."

And he felt like the whole party stopped.

"She's gone."

Chapter Forty-Two

Noah was back on Blue before Willow had even finished berating him for being late.

He rode down Main Street to Ren's apartment, but it was all shuttered up. The blinds pulled down and little table and chairs on the balcony folded up for the next tenant. He called her but it went straight to voicemail. The barbershop. Thomas from downstairs came to the door when he saw him and said, "She took a cab, Noah, with her suitcase."

Noah's shoulders dropped in disappointment, but he just said thanks to Thomas—who told him to come and get a haircut soon—and jumping back on Blue with less energy this time, rode back to the Silver Sky Ranch.

It had never felt so far away.

He cut through the pine forest, heard the waterfall in the distance, the crash of the water, wondered if Ren had seen that yet, even veered closer just to check she wasn't there. He realized he was thinking like her—stopping the cab to see the actual Autumn Falls before she left was the kind of thing she'd do.

But she wasn't there.

She wasn't in the horse barn curled up in Star's stall, either.

He left Blue grazing happily on the lush grass of the paddock and walked back to his trailer. His hands hurt now the adrenaline had worn off. When he turned the corner, he half hoped that Ren might be sitting there waiting for him on the trailer stoop, but it was only the white chicken warming herself in the sunshine.

When he looked at the trailer now, he couldn't believe he still lived there. He thought about Willow, standing with her hands on her hips, looking at it and saying, "It's literally just a bed and a bathroom and clothes. There's not even a picture on the wall. It's like you're a teenager, Noah!"

Maybe that's where he'd got stuck all those years ago.

Now when he looked at it, he saw the peeling white paint, the moss growing around the windows, the rust, and he realized he actually wanted something more grown-up to show for himself.

He stepped over the chicken and went inside. He had a shower, changed into a clean T-shirt and jeans, slicked his wet hair back, then sitting at the fold-down veneer table, got the first-aid kit out from under the sink and bandaged up his hands.

When that was all done, he picked up his phone and called Loriana. When she answered he could hear the Spring Fling in the background.

"I don't know where she is, honey. She said she'd tell me when she was settled."

He thanked her, hung up and put the phone down on the table in front of him.

He stared at it trying to work out what to do.

There must be a practical solution.

He tried putting himself in Ren's shoes. She wasn't the most conventional of people that he knew, but all she'd ever talked about, when she was serious, was wanting a family like he had. And Logan had said that she looked upset when Noah didn't come to the Spring Fling. And his dad had said, "Girl who grew up in care ... doesn't want a family around her and community and stability?"

He sat back in his seat, there wasn't enough space to stretch his legs under the table, so he sat back up again. He thought about Logan saying, "I guess you've gotta decide if it's worth it."

He thought about her turning up to the cattle drive in her cherry-red boots and her gold necklaces. Laughing with her slightly crooked teeth and her gaucho hat on. Tucked behind him as they faced down a rattlesnake, holding his hand under the fallen pine tree, nudging his dad to make him sway to the music around the campfire. He saw it all. And he saw her standing in front of him on the sidewalk, looking up with her big blue eyes and telling him that he was afraid of living.

Was he still afraid? He asked himself.

Without thinking, he reached forward and he googled: *Liane, motel, Montauk, Long Island.*

Chapter Forty-Three

"Haven't seen her."

Noah was still getting over having been on an airplane. Brodie said he'd come with him, but Noah said it was fine. Then he'd hired a car and driven from JFK to Montauk. None of it however was quite as intimidating as facing down Ren's friend Liane.

"Have you heard from her?"

Liane crossed her arms over her chest, nails like talons, tapping. She was almost as tall as Noah, especially with her long blonde hair piled on top of her head. She was beautiful. Exquisitely so, and terrifying. Beneath thick, blunt bangs she had eyes like a sparrow hawk.

"I told you, I haven't seen her and I haven't heard from her, and even if I had, I don't think I'd tell *you*." She leaned a hip against the counter of her motel. Chin raised like she was defending her territory.

Noah nodded in understanding. "May I ask, before I

leave, if you know where I might find someone called Mean Billy?"

Liane snorted a laugh. "I do," she said, hawk-eyes narrowing. "And once again, I don't think I want to tell you."

Noah waited a beat to see if she might change her mind, then pulled his cap back on low and said, "I appreciate your time."

Once outside the motel, Noah didn't know what to do next. He felt foolish for even trying. Now he was stuck in Montauk with no plan. He walked down to the beach, sat on the sand for a bit, looking out to sea. It had been a long time since he'd seen the horizon like that; sky pale as mist meeting endless deep, dark navy. Clouds wisping through the sky. He thought then that maybe he'd missed more than he'd thought he had.

There was a world out there waiting for him. Didn't mean he had to give up on home.

Taking a deep breath of sea air, he stood up and took a walk into the center of town, past gift shops and restaurants until he came to the diner. He took a seat and looked at the menu and when the waitress came over, he ordered coffee, white, no sugar. Then he got his phone out and started the painstaking, needle-in-a-haystack search for *Billy, lawyer, grew up Texas*.

Other diners came and went. Noah drank his coffee.

The waitress took the order of the table behind him, "What can I get you?"

And that's when he heard her. "Just coffee, thanks."

His whole body froze.

"Black?"

"White."

He could hear his heart so loud in his ears he worried he wouldn't be able to hear.

"You want anything else?"

"Yeah," she said with a laugh in her voice, "I'll have a slice of pie. Raspberry."

"You want cream or ice cream with that?"

"Just pie, thanks."

Noah sat hardly able to move. He watched the waitress walk away with the order. He dare not turn for fear that his brain was playing tricks on him, but he just couldn't help himself, he looked and there she was and it was like Christmas morning as a kid.

She was sitting cool as anything, wearing all her necklaces and her hair swept to one side, shirt tied at the waist, elbows on the table, just waiting. When their eyes met, she raised a brow in challenge and Noah felt himself unable to hold in a smile. He tipped his head in acknowledgment of her and said, "Mind if I join you?"

She shrugged a shoulder. "If you want."

Noah picked up his mug from the table and his cap off the booth seat, and went around to sit opposite Ren. He could barely take his eyes off her. Like he'd been handed treasure. His brain not quite able to believe what he was seeing. "Liane said you weren't here."

"Liane lied," Ren replied, eyes unreadable. "We're very protective of each other."

"I'm glad," he said. Thinking how he'd never tell a soul where Willow was if she didn't want to be found.

The pie and the coffee came.

She pushed it into the center of the table and said, "You want to try it?"

Noah picked up the fork.

She said, "It's raspberry."

"I know." He took a bite, and it wasn't as bad as he thought it might be. "Nice," he said. "Makes a change from apple."

She raised a brow again, looked like she might be holding in a smile.

Noah said, "I'm sorry I didn't get to the Spring Fling in time."

Her eyes widened in surprise. "You went?"

"I did."

She sat back in her seat, fingers toying with her fork as she waited for what he was going to say next.

"You know what you said about me being afraid and hiding?"

She looked up at him seriously then, eyes assessing under thick black lashes. No more quirked brows and hidden smiles.

"You were right," he said, feeling the urge to glance down at the table, but he didn't, he kept looking right at her, those eyes pale as a wolf's watching wide and wary. "I was and I am but it's getting better. I promise."

He watched her looking at him, examining his face, his expression, wondering whether she could believe it.

"I did have things to lay to rest."

She nodded.

"But I think I'm ready now," he said, "for the future, not the past."

"Yeah?" she asked softly, a little hesitant.

"Yeah." He leaned forward, elbows on the table, not wanting to take his eyes off her for a second. "I found what I've been looking for."

Chapter Forty-Four

And there was Noah. Gray-marl T-shirt, jeans, boots. Hair washed, no hat, two days of stubble, knuckles on his hands all cut up.

Ren couldn't speak, her heart felt lodged in her throat. But she couldn't stop her lips pulling into a smile. "You came all this way to tell me that?"

Noah nodded. Then he said, almost like the words wouldn't stay in his mouth a moment longer. "I'd go anywhere you wanted me to go, as long as you were there, too."

Ren felt her bottom lip tremble.

Noah looked at her with unwavering sincerity in his hooded gray eyes.

"You would?"

He nodded, "Yes."

She felt every muscle in her face pulling into a smile. "Really?"

"Really."

"For me?"

"For you." He paused, then added, "But also for me."

She feared for a second that she might cry.

"I'm gonna build a house in Autumn Falls. There's a lake right on the far side of the ranch, it's really beautiful there. I think you'd like it a lot."

Ren nodded, couldn't quite allow herself to get her hopes up but her fingers were trembling when she pushed her hair out of her eyes.

"I was hoping maybe one day you might want to live in it with me. We don't have to. It's just an idea."

She bit her lip to hold in the smile bubbling up inside her. "Living together? That's some forward thinking, Noah."

Noah took a forkful of raspberry pie, washed it down with some iced water then said, very seriously, "It might take me a while, Ren, but I'm the kind of person who when I know what it is I want, I know."

He looked so sure, so absolutely certain, that she wanted to take her heart and hand it to him there and then for safekeeping.

"I'm a pretty all or nothing guy," he added.

"So I'm realizing," she laughed.

Then he paused and said more consideringly, "I just want to be with you." Then he smiled, his doleful eyes creasing.

Her heart lurched. "We might not be compatible."

Noah tipped his head as he thought for a moment, Ren bit down on a smile, then he pushed himself up, leaned across the table, and with his lips a whisper away from hers, said, "Maybe we should find out."

Ren found herself giggling. "Maybe we should."

And Noah cupped her face with his rough, cool hands and kissed her full square on the lips. The second proper kiss she'd had in her life. Even better, she realized, shivering with excitement and happiness and hope, than the first.

Noah's lips grinned against hers and then he pulled back, resting his forehead against hers for a second, he said, "Well?"

She pretended to give it some thought. "I think we're compatible."

He sat back down. "I thought we might be."

"Did you now?"

"I did," he said with a wink, scooping up another forkful of pie, and she felt a burst of joy explode inside her.

Then with a smile on his face, he stood up and came around her side of the table and she scooted along so he could sit down next to her. He lifted his arm and she tucked herself into his side, her head resting against the hollow of his neck, his fingers toying with the bracelets on her wrist while she felt him bend his head and kiss the top of her hair.

She closed her eyes and breathed the moment in, while Noah said, "That Liane's pretty terrifying, isn't she?"

Ren looked up at him and laughed. "You wait till you meet Mean Billy."

She would have stayed there in that booth forever, but after the pie was finished and the waitress had asked them if they wanted anything else, Noah said, "Do you want to go to the beach?" And she thought how she'd never thought Noah would ask her that ever, she still couldn't quite believe he was there, had come all that way just for her.

They left the diner and walked in the direction of the beach. The sky above was hazy with clouds and seagulls drifted on the warm air. Ren reached down tentatively to wind her fingers through Noah's. All the while still wary that he might pull away. But instead, he squeezed her hand tight and brought it up to his chest like he never wanted to let her go.

As they walked, the sea breeze whipping her hair in front of her eyes, Ren said, "Noah?"

"Yeah?"

She looked up at him and said, "If I ask you a question will you promise you'll always answer it?"

He stopped walking and turned to face her. "You can ask me anything you like and I will do my best to answer."

She nodded, absorbing what he was saying. "You promise?"

"I promise."

Smiling as wide as she'd ever smiled, Ren reached up on tiptoe and, hands on his shoulders, kissed his rough cheek. He had chosen her. For the first time in her life, someone had said, I choose you.

"I just want to be with you, too," she whispered.

Noah looked down at her, then up and around for something. Next thing, hands laced tight, he led her around the back of the beach bar they were standing in front of like they were teenagers. Ren giggled when he stopped, her back against the wood-clad wall, him standing a breath away. She looked up into the dark intensity of his eyes, felt her breath hitch, and tucked her hands behind her, feeling suddenly nervous, shy. Noah braced himself against the wall, hands either side of her head, then he bent down and let his lips brush ever so gently against hers. She felt a shiver rush up her spine. Then he did it again, harder this time, more urgent, all the sounds of the town and the beach and the waves disappeared. She felt her body draw toward his, her head tip back, her breath gasp when he pulled away, half smiling, eyes glinting. She bit her bottom lip, shy again but smiling now. His hands moved from the wall to her waist and no messing this time, he pulled her in toward him, fingers splayed on her back, thumb stroking her ribs, and dipped his head. And when their lips met, she let her arms snake around his neck, pulling him tighter, closer, but couldn't get close enough. She never wanted to let him go. Their warm bodies pressed together, her fingers curled into his hair, her other hand on his cheek, the hard press of his mouth against hers, so perfect, so exactly what she was waiting all those years for, that she almost forgot to breathe. This was it, this was the kiss, and she could have stayed in that moment a lifetime.

It was Noah who pulled away first, leaving her momentarily bereft, afraid that he might say they should carry on walking to the beach. But he didn't say anything, didn't loosen his hold even a fraction, just gazed down at her.

"Why are you looking at me like that?"

"Just taking you in," he said. "Thinking how lucky I am and what a fool I nearly was."

"Yeah?"

He nodded, the corner of his mouth tilting up. "Yeah."

Her arms looped around his neck, she said, "What are we going to do now?"

He glanced right and left but settled back on her and said, "I'm having a pretty good time doing exactly what I'm doing."

She grinned, went up on tiptoes and, drawing his head down to hers, kissed him long and slow, like they had all the time in the world, the waves hitting the sand in the distance, the cry of the gulls above them. Then she rested her cheek against the soft fabric of his T-shirt, her arms still wound around his neck, and stayed there listening to the beat of his heart, her body pressed close against the hard plains of his chest, her fingers in his hair, his arms casually possessive around her waist.

"Anywhere you want to go?" he asked.

She bit her lip thinking for a second, then she pulled away just enough to be able to look up at him and say, "Well, I know a nice little apartment above a barbershop. It's not cheap but it's got a view of the mountain, if you lean right off the balcony."

She watched the smile spread over his face and added, "Problem is, it's right over the other side of the country."

His eyes sparkled as he said, "You want a lift?"

Standing up on tiptoes again, she smiled against his lips and said, "I would like that very much."

Bonus Chapter
BRODIE CARTER

Brodie only flew back to Autumn Falls because Noah'd asked him to, wanted him to meet Ren properly. He was meant to be playing golf with friends in Monterey, but he'd canceled because he'd never heard his twin sound so happy in his life.

Pulling up in the Silver Sky Ranch driveway, Brodie had itchy feet before he'd even stepped out the car. He'd been back too recently for there to be any novelty to the occasion.

He was doing it for Noah, he kept telling himself. As he walked toward the house, slipping his sunglasses on to hide his hungover eyes, he tried to avoid looking out at the mountain that always reminded him of his dad, dark and immobile, judging his every move.

Jumping the veranda steps, Brodie paused at the side door to the kitchen as he saw what looked to be quite the family scene.

They were all peering over blueprints on the table. Emmett, Noah, Logan and Ren. Brodie knew that work was beginning on Noah's new house, and they all seemed to be on board.

He heard Ren say, "You know anything about building a house, Logan?"

Logan shook his head. "Not a thing."

She grinned, all overlapping teeth and scrunched-up nose, like a little mouse. "Me either."

Brodie felt himself smile. He liked her, the no-nonsense frankness that his family could do with a dose of.

"I think you need a veranda," Ren said, going to sit in one of the kitchen table chairs and tapping the plans that Emmett, who was at the head of the table, had spread in front of him. Noah had pulled up a chair next to her, but Brodie could tell he was struggling to concentrate, he watched his brother's eyes as they kept straying toward Ren—her hands when she picked up her coffee, her mouth when she drank it. That made him smirk, the idea that Noah was anything less than one hundred percent focused on the work he was doing.

Logan went to sit at the other end of the table, Bella next to him, while Martha was busy at the kitchen counter. Rocky slept under the table.

Brodie wondered why he wasn't going inside, making his presence known. Wondered why he was just watching like a stranger from the doorway.

Ren said, "I love a veranda."

Noah tapped the plans. "Okay, let's add that." Then to Logan, "Put wood for the veranda on the list."

Logan picked up his pencil and said, "Wraparound?"

Noah looked at Ren who nodded. "Definitely wraparound."

Brodie watched his mom smiling indulgently—secretly—at the exchange. This was her dream, he realized, this was what made her happy.

He took his sunglasses off, they felt suddenly stupid and frivolous, and looked away from the tenderness of the expression down at the kitchen floor, wooden floorboards that were totally familiar yet seemed like they were from a different life.

Noah pointed to the plans again and said, "We need to raise the height of the living room."

His dad looked up in surprise. "Why?"

"For a Christmas tree," he said matter-of-factly.

Emmett shook his head in veto. "You can't raise the ceiling for a tree, it's ridiculous."

Brodie found himself bracing against the familiar disregard of his dad's tone.

Logan drank his coffee. "Noah," he said with an incredulous smirk, "when have you *ever* cared about the height of a Christmas tree?"

"He doesn't," said Ren. And Brodie watched as she slid her hand across the gap between hers and Noah's on the table, hooked their little fingers together and said, "But I do."

And that seemed to shut them all up. Logan drank his coffee, silenced. Emmett got his ruler and eraser out and started altering the plans. Even Brodie felt ashamed of his detached cynicism, wondered if just for a fraction of a second he was jealous.

But then his mouth stretched into an incredulous smile at the very idea.

He liked Christmas skiing in St. Moritz.

Without another moment's hesitation, Brodie pushed the door open and swaggered into the kitchen, and, never one to miss an opportunity to side with a woman, said, "I don't think a ceiling can be too high when it comes to Christmas trees."

"Brodie!" his mom dropped her spatula in the pan and came over to give him a hug.

Over her shoulder, he caught his dad's eye, saw his lips purse before he turned his attention back to the plans.

Who cares, Brodie thought. He lived a darn near perfect life and he wasn't going to have his dad judge him for it.

Noah's face, on the other hand, lit up when he saw him, there was genuine happiness in his eyes that reminded Brodie of when they were kids.

They went through all the hellos. When he hugged Ren, Brodie whispered, "I knew he'd see sense eventually."

"You want pancakes, Brodie?" his mom asked, fussing around him.

He'd already had eggs Benedict and champagne on the plane, but he wouldn't refuse his mom anything. "Of course."

"So," he said, idly wandering over to the table, ignoring the fact his dad had barely glanced his way. "You're building a house?"

Noah said, "You want to help?"

Brodie laughed and said, "No way," almost to spite his dad. As expected, it made Emmett shake his head in disapproval and Brodie felt a sense of satisfaction at having got a reaction.

Sitting down, he put his feet up on the chair opposite. His mom immediately bashed them down before sliding a plate of pancakes onto the table in front of him. "There you go, honey."

"Well, isn't this the dream?" Brodie said with a grin, looking down at the plate of fluffy white pancakes and syrup. But it wasn't the dream at all. He was very happy for Noah and Ren, but small-town family life? No, that wasn't for Brodie. More than a weekend here and he felt his skin start to itch.

The dream for him was the moment he got to drive out those gates with the top down on his car, heading out to freedom, not a single responsibility or care in the world.

FALLEN IN LOVE WITH THE CARTER BROTHERS?
DON'T MISS OUT ON WHAT HAPPENS NEXT...

The Carter brothers were once inseparable – five boys, a band, and a bond that seemed unbreakable. But it's been ten years since the band broke up and even longer since they left the family ranch and the wide-open skies of Autumn Falls. Fame, secrets and time have left cracks that no one wants to face...

Meet Brodie in Redemption River!

DID YOU MISS *AUTUMN FALLS*?

READ ON FOR AN EXTRACT...

For Bella, the Carters were her first friends and her first heartbreak. Especially Logan Carter, the boy she loved in the quiet moments between music and long summers spent in the apple orchard.

Now tragedy pulls them all back to Autumn Falls. The brothers are fractured, the past impossible to escape, and the spark between Bella and Logan burns as dangerously as ever.

AVAILABLE IN PAPERBACK, EBOOK AND AUDIO

Prologue

"Tell me you won't miss this."

Bella and Logan stood side by side at the edge of the waterfall, the sun glistening off the endless cascades of water, the pool beneath them inky blue in the early evening light.

"I won't miss it," Bella replied.

Logan rolled his eyes. He knew her well enough to know when she was lying. "Yes, you will."

She took a step closer to the edge, thought back to the first time she'd stood there, toes curled over the rock, Logan beckoning from the crystal-clear pool below. It had taken all her courage to dive, the sound of the waterfall rushing in her ears, but it had felt as close to flying as she ever could have imagined before she'd plunged into the icy mountain water. When she came up laughing, Logan's eyes glinted like he'd shown her treasure.

"Okay, I admit, I'll miss it."

She watched his mouth tilt up in victory before adding, "Not as much as you're going to miss me, though."

"I'm not going to miss you!" He made a face like the idea was ridiculous, his dark brows drawn together in a frown.

"Yes, you are!" She laughed and went to bash him on the chest for trying to deny it, but on reflex he caught her hand with his—too much time spent sparring with his brothers.

The touch was so unexpected that it seemed to catch them both off-guard. She looked up and saw Logan's laughing blue gaze become suddenly serious. Felt her heart tighten in her chest as something passed between them that had always been otherwise ignored, contained, unspoken. She watched his throat as he swallowed, as his hand held hers a fraction too long and a look came over his face that she'd never seen before. *Don't do it, Bella,* a voice said in her head. *You're going. You're out of here. Look away.*

So, she forced herself to look away, anywhere. And her eye caught on the signet ring glinting in the sunlight on his finger.

"What is *that*?" she asked, incredulous.

Logan winced and immediately dropped her hand. The moment thankfully diverted, back to friends, her thrumming heart the only giveaway the look had ever happened.

"My dad gave it to me," he said, slipping the ring off and passing it to her. "It's been in the family for years. Handed down from father to eldest son for generations. You know, 'Here, the ranch is yours now.' Or will be."

"But you don't want it, do you?" She frowned, studying

the insignia of the Silver Sky ranch engraved on the surface before passing it back.

"Yes." He put the ring back on, looked at it. "No." He paused. "I don't know." He tipped his head up toward trees above them. She knew his expressions so well, the sharpness of his jaw, the depth of his sigh.

The waterfall roared behind them, the sun flickering through the pine trees danced on their skin.

She could say, "It's not too late to come to New York with me," but she knew that he never would.

The wind rustled the trees above them scattering pine needles. One must have landed in her hair because he reached forward and untangled it gently, chucking it absently to the ground as he kept his eyes on hers. "I will really miss you."

When he said it, she felt the aching pull to do what she would never do and reach up and trace the side of his face with her hand. And maybe he would wrap his arms around her and she could stay there forever.

But she could never stay. Just as much as he could never leave.

Their paths led in different directions.

Fearing he might step closer, that his hand might reach over to touch her and then she'd never leave, with all her willpower she backed away, one step, then two. Then when she knew her feet were close enough to the edge, she turned and she dived, flying down, down into the deep, dark pool of the waterfall. Slicing through the glassy surface, the shock of the cold leaving her breathless.

When she came up for air, she looked to see Logan

standing at the lip of the rock, watching, the sun behind him so she couldn't see the expression on his face, her heart thumping with a mixture of relief and something dangerously close to regret.

Chapter One

Logan reclined back in his chair and checked his watch.

The interviewer could sense he was losing him. "Last question." He glanced down at his notes and back up with a mischievous glint in his eye. "Carter Media's one of the major independent contenders in the global music industry, there are always rumors of offers on the table. What are the chances of you selling up?"

Logan raised a brow at the stupidity of the question. "Zero."

"Haha. Seriously. You're one of six siblings. You've been incredibly successful first in the boy band, Silver Sky, now as head of Carter Media. Do you ever think about slowing down? Starting your own family? For the listeners, Logan has just shaken his head."

"I'm pretty happy as I am, thanks." Logan remained impassive while internally rolling his eyes.

"So, life's good?"

He angled his head, wry smile on his lips. "Life's great."

The interviewer knew that was the best he was going to get. "Good to hear it," he said. "Any final words of advice for fellow entrepreneurs?"

Logan didn't need to think about it. "Work harder and smarter than everyone else…"

Before he could add any more final words of wisdom, there was a quick rap on the door and Marianne, Logan's PA, said, "Sorry to interrupt. Logan—it's urgent."

Logan frowned.

Sensing something was seriously amiss from the look on Marianne's face, the interviewer gathered up his papers and said, "Thanks for talking to me, Logan." They had a quick distracted handshake. "Always a pleasure."

Marianne stood restlessly in the doorway, ushering him out.

When the door closed and she started walking toward him, Logan said, "What's going on?"

"It's your brother," she said.

"Which one?" Logan asked, immediately alert. *What had happened now? What disaster needed clearing up?*

"It's Jack, Logan. He was in an accident—car crash. He's dead."

Jack, Logan, he's dead.

Jack, Logan…

He kept replaying it as he sat on the plane to Autumn Falls. The way Marianne's lip had pulled in a subtle gesture of sympathy, the buzzing silence in his head.

It was hard to comprehend that he was flying home for his brother's funeral. It still felt so unreal.

He glanced back to the newspaper in his hand, the aircraft bouncing through turbulence, his heart tightening at the sight of Jack's face lighting up the front cover, the infamous dimple in his cheek, the lazily laughing eyes. Everyone knew, if you wanted a good time, you went to Jack.

Logan steeled himself to turn the page to where the pictures continued, the most recent showed Jack on the red carpet at an awards ceremony, taken just weeks ago. He was the big Hollywood star, now. Or had been.

Logan had to squeeze his eyes shut for a moment at the idea that he'd never see Jack again. It was like every few minutes his brain still had to catch up with the reality. He felt the sudden claustrophobic tightness of the plane, the lack of escape, the sound of his heart in his ears. But he pushed it down, unscrewed the cap of his water and took a cooling sip.

On the opposite page were photos of Logan and his brothers. All of them young, on stage in Silver Sky, Jack with his arm punching the air, grinning wide. Images that Logan had barely glanced at in years. Toothy, youthful faces full of hope and promise and excitement, guitars around their necks, sweat on their brows, eyes shining bright, it was like looking at wax figures, paused in time, wondering who they all could have been had they taken a different path.

Of course, the article had matched the pictures of them as boys with who they were now. There was Noah getting into his SUV in Autumn Falls looking furious at the camera intrusion; Brodie at the airport, hand raised in open greeting—relaxed and confident when it came to the press.

Logan's jaw clenched to see shots of his baby sister, Willow, coming out of the Cornelia Street Ballet studios, head cocked defensively, he imagined her confronting the faceless lenses with a, "Really? You think this is helping? My brother's just *died*!"

There were no recent pictures of Ethan, of course—it seemed even the press couldn't find him—just an old shot of him out on maneuvers in desert camo gear, looking blank-eyed and ruthless.

And then there was Logan himself, striding stony-faced past reporters outside his New York office. Memories of having the camera shoved in his face had made him surge with an anger, he was surprised to discover, he could barely suppress. Transporting him instantly back to his time in the band and the suffocating relentlessness of the paparazzi—camped outside every hotel they stayed at, confining them to their rooms, the grasping hands snatching at their clothes, running after them in the street, nails scratching their skin. The tapped phones. The undercover journalists masquerading as room-service waiters. The honeytrap kiss-and-tell stories. The lies conjured up by their manager on slow news days, stories that sowed the first seeds of mistrust between them and had his mom crying on the phone and his dad retreating further into resentment.

Then at the bottom of the page was the photo Logan had been avoiding. There was Bella outside the front door of her apartment, cap pulled low, face hidden. The lights of the hounding camera flashes reflected in her sunglasses. He'd be lying if the photos of her didn't make him uneasy. She looked terrified. She may not be his favorite person in the world, but seeing her there in black and white he felt some, perhaps misplaced, duty to protect her through this mess. At the same time, he remembered Jack sobbing on the phone, "She's left me, Logan. She's gone!" and reminded himself that Bella was more than capable of looking after herself.

Acknowledgments

First and foremost, my thanks always go to the One More Chapter team, with special mentions to Charlotte for her editorial brilliance, Sofia for being Team Noah from the start, and Kara for being so on it with everything. Also huge thanks to my agent, Rebecca Ritchie.

I've always loved a story with a cattle drive, from *Lonesome Dove* to *City Slickers*! And when I started this series, I knew that Noah's book would start with one. So I'm really grateful to all the cowboys out there who take their GoPros with them at the crack of dawn to round up cattle and film their adventures, their mishaps, their lunch breaks, and their general chat—or lack thereof—as they ride their way home, then put it on YouTube. I've enjoyed hours of those journeys. Thank you.

Also, thanks to my friend, Mariah, for saying there had to be only one tent. And big thanks to my parents for always insisting on a Christmas tree that touched the ceiling.

Finally, thank *you* for reading Noah's story. I'm more than a tiny bit in love with him, and I hope you are too.

The author and One More Chapter would like to thank everyone who contributed to the publication of this story…

Analytics
Imogen Wolstencroft

Audio
Fionnuala Barrett
Ciara Briggs

Contracts
Laura Amos
Inigo Vyvyan

Design
Lucy Bennett
Fiona Greenway
Liane Payne
Dean Russell

Digital Sales
Laura Daley
Lydia Grainge
Hannah Lismore

eCommerce
Laura Carpenter
Madeline ODonovan
Charlotte Stevens
Christina Storey
Jo Surman
Rachel Ward

Editorial
Janet Marie Adkins
Rosie Best
Kara Daniel
Charlotte Ledger
Jennie Rothwell
Sofia Salazar Studer
Emily Thomas
Helen Williams

Harper360
Emily Gerbner
Ariana Juarez
Jean Marie Kelly
emma sullivan
Sophia Wilhelm

International Sales
Peter Borcsok
Ruth Burrow
Bethan Moore
Colleen Simpson

Inventory
Sarah Callaghan
Kirsty Norman

Marketing & Publicity
Chloe Cummings
Grace Edwards
Katie Sadler

Operations
Melissa Okusanya
Hannah Stamp

Production
Denis Manson
Simon Moore
Francesca Tuzzeo

Rights
Ashton Mucha
Alisah Saghir
Zoe Shine
Aisling Smyth
Lucy Vanderbilt

Trade Marketing
Ben Hurd
Eleanor Slater

The HarperCollins Distribution Team

The HarperCollins Finance & Royalties Team

The HarperCollins Legal Team

The HarperCollins Technology Team

UK Sales
Isabel Coburn
Jay Cochrane
Sabina Lewis
Holly Martin
Harriet Williams
Leah Woods

And every other essential link in the chain from delivery drivers to booksellers to librarians and beyond!

ONE MORE CHAPTER

One More Chapter is an award-winning global division of HarperCollins.

Subscribe to our newsletter to get our latest eBook deals and stay up to date with all our new releases!

signup.harpercollins.co.uk/join/signup-omc

Meet the team at
www.onemorechapter.com

Follow us!

@onemorechapterhc

Do you write unputdownable fiction? We love to hear from new voices. Find out how to submit your novel at
www.onemorechapter.com/submissions